Rocky Mountain High-Jinx

A Small Town Romantic Comedy

Lisa Wells

Up All Night Publishing

ROCKY
MOUNTAIN
High-Jinx
ROMANTIC COMEDY
LISA WELLS

Rocky
Mountain
High
#1

For those of you who have not yet found your own true love, dare to dream bigger than your wildest imagination, because within our thoughts exists magic. Rocky Mountain High-Jinx is dedicated to agent Ann Rose with The Prospect Agency. She was my original cheerleader for this book. Without her enthusiasm, I would have never written this book.

1

Luna Parker had a special ability. She knew when someone was gaping at her bare ass while she balanced in tree pose.

Or to be fair, maybe the slight aroma of manly cologne mixed with a hint of cannabis was what had set off her clairvoyance.

Luckily, this mixture of smells had tickled her nose on another vital moment in her life. One tattooed with flaming-red ink on her memory bank. She knew the identity of her gaper. A conundrum of a man who was currently on her top ten list of individuals she'd like to punch in the nose.

Which meant her nudity wouldn't scar him for life. Nor would it trigger a police investigation. *Thank the naked-loving gods for that.* She'd had more than her quota of interactions with the law of late.

Without turning to verify his identity, she asked, "May I help you?" At one time, she'd known his name. But, upon discovering he was the proprietor of Rocky Mountain High, her brain had deleted the information and had replaced it with the moniker Mr. Pot Guy. And thus far, she'd failed to find an opening to say, "Hey, by the way, what's your real name again?"

And also thus far, none of her neighbors had mentioned him by first name. Nor by his last name. In fact, they made it a point not to mention anyone to Luna, as that would mean they talked to the newest resident of Rocky Mountain Springs.

No one answered, but Ms. Houdini, her black-and-white spotted Nigerian Dwarf goat, trotted over and collapsed in front of her. "Hey girl, where have you been?" Fingers crossed the answer wasn't with Mr. Pot Guy. Her weed-loving goat loved to seek him out and sniff his pockets.

Ms. Houdini bleated and rolled over on her back for tummy rubs. Luna maintained tree pose while warm gooiness filled her chest, pushing away her desires to punch anyone. She'd not been allowed a pet growing up. Never been given the chance to be an animal's human. So having not one but three goats as part of her first ever entrepreneurial endeavor, Luna's Goat Yoga, touched her soul with mountain sunshine. "You missed gossip hour," she said to Ms. Houdini.

Her visitor laughed and cleared his throat as if the laugh hadn't meant for Luna's ears. "May we talk?" His tone was crisper than this morning's burnt kale chips.

Even if she hadn't recognized his scent or voice, she would have known the laugh. A month ago, she'd done him a favor by buying this land at auction so he couldn't. He'd all but burst his funny bone when she'd told him that her purchase of the land had saved him seven years of bad luck for every tree that he had planned on murdering via bulldozer. Like he didn't believe that bad luck was a thing.

It was totally a thing.

She lowered her leg to the ground and turned to face him.

Nailed it. Her gawker was the local would-be-tree-murderer.

"Fancy seeing you here on *my* property." She picked up the lemon-lime-colored kimono pooled beside her mat and wrapped it around her body. The silky material felt like a lover's hand as it settled over her skin. Not that she'd experienced that since moving to Colorado.

By the redness, which showed up despite his summer-tanned cheeks, she'd say he hadn't seen any action in a while either, otherwise her naked body wouldn't have him all hot and bothered. Which surprised her because with his Clark Kent blue eyes he wasn't, well, hard on the eyes.

"I didn't mean to intrude." He pivoted as if to leave.

"Wait." Friend or foe, she didn't want him to go...yet. Her day thus far hadn't gone great, what with the family drama. She could really use a distraction.

He glanced over his shoulder, but instead of focusing on her, he frowned at Ms. Houdini.

"Did you need something?" Luna asked.

He sharply turned and perfectly squared his body with Luna's. By the pinched look on his face, she had the distinct impression what he had to say would not be neighborly.

Her slight hope he'd come to apologize for turning the town against her had briefly caused her walls to crumble. They quickly rebuilt themselves.

"Just bringing your goat back to you," Mr. Pot Guy said.

Luna inhaled and exhaled, all while reminding herself of her goal to win him over. It wasn't like she wanted to spend her energy on thoughts of punching a guy's nose. "What a delightfully nice gesture."

"Again," Mr. Pot Guy added in a clipped tone.

"Again, what?" Luna asked.

"I looked out after your goat...again." He took off his drab, black-framed glasses and cleaned them on the hem of his not-drab Superman T-shirt.

He'd been wearing the same shirt at the auction a month ago, just twenty feet away from where they were standing now. That's what had initially drawn her to sit next to the stranger. She'd thought they could talk superheroes and maybe, just maybe, she'd sweet talk him out of his shirt so she could add it to her collection of superhero tees. She was very good at sweet talk when the mood struck.

Instead, Mr. Pot Guy had rudely ignored her. So she'd repositioned her chair, placing her back to him because, you know, two can play the ignore-the-other game. Unfortunately, in the process of executing her childish counter move, the leg of her chair had landed on his vintage flip-phone nestled in the grass.

And of course she'd broken the thing. Crunch.

Her immediate heartfelt apology hadn't done a damn thing to dissolve his horrified glare. He'd simply yanked the mangled phone out from under her chair—nearly toppling her in the process—and stalked over to a couple standing by a tree. A tree she'd paid zero attention to until he had proceeded to lean against it like a wounded geek god.

And holy Batman, how could she have not noticed it immediately?

It wasn't just any tree. It was a Thundercloud Plum Tree. A tree whose flowers in the spring could be harvested and used in the most delightful recipes. A tree that had caused her dream of the previous night to crystalize. She hadn't been directed to this auction to bid on a cast iron skillet but to purchase the property.

With the flowers from that tree, she could add an additional source of revenue to her Goat Yoga income. Something she'd greatly needed since she'd been stripped of her trust fund and had only the dwindling proceeds from an insurance claim on which to live.

Luckily, she'd outbid the grump on the house and its land. Unluckily, from everything she'd been able to learn since that auction, losing out on the property had been a hairy big deal to Mr. Pot Guy, thus giving him a reason to not like her.

She raised her eyebrows at Mr. Pot Guy, who had the whole broody stance going on. "Then thank you...again." Forgetting her goal of winning him over, she did air quotes around *again.*

His eyes narrowed, and he pushed his glasses back up his nose. He really did have hints of the whole Clark-Kent-Superman-incognito thing going on. And while she had an unaccountable love of superhero movies, smarty-pants were not her type. Which was just as well because she was currently focusing on her own journey of self-growth.

She glanced down at Ms. Houdini. "Darling, how many times do I have to tell you not to take yourself for a walk? It's a big bad world out there."

Mr. Pot Guy huffed. "Then you admit you knew she was missing?"

"What, are we in court?" She might have snapped her response a little more vehemently than necessary, but he'd hit a soft spot.

"I'll take that as a yes. And yet, instead of searching for her, you were out here…" He waved his hands around, and she noticed his right ear reddening.

"I'm waiting," she taunted when he didn't finish.

His ear got brighter. "Posing in the nude." He used a bland, vanilla tone, but she wasn't fooled. It shouted implied disdain. Hell, the 1.0 version of Luna Parker, a prickly version of herself she was trying to kick to the ledge of Colorado's highest mountain peak, was the queen of implied disdain.

Are you kidding me? Mr. Pot Guy had an issue with her lack of clothing while doing yoga in her own freaking backyard.

Instead of responding with a much-deserved insult, she shook off her irritation, because in order for Luna 2.0 to be a success, she had to keep her eyes on the now, not the past. And at the moment, her cranky neighbor was very much her now.

She inhaled deeply and exhaled slowly. "Au naturel is my preferred way to stretch." Truth was, her work-out clothes were dirty, and her washing machine had died a melodramatic death. Who knew all soap wasn't created equal? Bubble bath should clearly come with a not-for-washing-machines warning label.

"Of course it is," he muttered. "I suggest inside your house would be a better choice for such debauchery. What would you have done if the whole town had come around the corner of your house instead of just me?"

Debauchery? Was he for real? "You mean after I passed out from the shock of any locals coming to see little ol' me?" She reached up and let her hair out of its ponytail, allowing it to cascade over her shoulders in red curls. Curls that adored the lack of humidity in the mountains of Colorado.

"Why would that cause you shock?"

Because you whined about my winning the bid. Or that was her working theory. And as theories went, it held its own. Why else wouldn't they like her? The new her was very likeable. "Never mind. Your criticism of my wicked ways is noted."

His jaw tightened. "It's the fact you did yoga, nude or otherwise, while fully aware your goat was missing—that's the current point that bothers me. It is highly irresponsible not to have them fenced in."

If she had a skinny mocha latte for every time she'd done something deemed highly irresponsible as of late... "Aren't you a doll for trying to teach me responsibility? As it turns out, it's not a lesson I need to learn. You see, there was no reason for me to look for Ms. Houdini when I knew of her whereabouts, and she knew of mine. She always finds her way back."

Carefree earth-loving Luna 2.0 didn't believe in fences. And that was not a characteristic the old Luna had attached to the new Luna all willy-nilly. There were reasons. Good fucking reasons.

Mr. Pot Guy fisted and unfisted his hands. "That's not how pet ownership works. It—"

She sighed. "Would you like to come inside for some lemonade?" If he expected her to listen while he droned out a lecture, she would need refreshments. "I freshly squeezed it this morning." It seemed Mr. Pot Guy liked to follow rules. Probably a math or science major in college. Those who thought Art History majors were Fifth Avenue snowflakes.

She grabbed her Chacos and padded toward the back door. The sound of rumbling phrases like, "No, I would not..." and "I've better things..." paused her steps. She turned in time to witness Mr. Pot Guy disappear around the corner of her house in a full-on angry stride.

"It's quite rude of you to leave without so much as a goodbye," she shouted.

Hell. The guy had her yelling. Luna 2.0 didn't yell. She'd worked hard and made huge sacrifices to win her state of Zen. If she lost it now over a guy, then the leaving behind of her shoe collection would be all for naught.

Not okay at all.

 2

Mitch Johnson stood on the sidewalk and locked his shop after a long day of trying to not recall his encounter with his neighbor this morning.

As if the world mocked his desire, he caught sight of Ms. Houdini out of his peripheral vision.

"Shit." He stuffed the key in his pocket, huffed out a breath, turned, and watched as she trotted like a trollop down the middle of the cobbled-stone street, daring anyone to say a word.

The goat came to a stop in front of him. She wore a straw hat with a fluttery pink ribbon tied under her chin.

"What are you doing here?" he asked.

The goat bleated and licked at Mitch's pockets.

"If I've told you once, I've told you a dozen times, I'm not sharing my pot with you." She was always in search for remnants of the stock Mitch sold.

He hooked a finger in her collar, preparing to return her to her owner for the second time in one day. The sound of a female voice in the distance halted his actions. Mitch glanced down the street.

"Ms. Houdini, you get right back over here this very minute." Bad Luck Luna rounded a corner and walked toward him with two more goats on leashes. She wore a wide-brimmed floppy hat, sleeveless sunny yellow dress, white lacy gloves, and strappy sandals.

As if he'd just smoked a damn Sativa containing a record amount of THC, his heart kicked up its beating pattern. "Fuck." He had no idea what he was supposed to say to his neighbor that he'd recently seen naked. He'd really been hoping to steer clear of Bad Luck Luna...forever.

Deciding to avoid conversing with Bad Luck Luna, he gave her a brisk nod before turning and walking away. He had plans tonight that had nothing to do with his neighbor and everything to do with a drink and good friends that he could bounce some ideas off for his next course of action.

Two minutes later, Mitch arrived at Moody Blues Tavern. Before ducking inside, he paused to check if his neighbor had followed him and was relieved to discover she hadn't.

He quickly read the establishment's sidewalk sign. Its content often led to rowdy conversations by the bar's patrons. It had done so ever since the owner, Song Li, had started experimenting with what she referred to as "mindful sign therapy." Something she'd taken up as a hobby after her husband left her for another woman.

Today's sign: *Don't be a dick.*

Mitch frowned. Hell, he'd been a dick not once but twice today. Then again, that woman—on a whim—had destroyed his carefully laid plans to buy the old Murphy place. All because of a damn innocent comment said between friends that she'd overheard and taken as truth.

His desire to own his home wasn't just rooted in making a good investment. It was rooted in trauma from his childhood. Trauma he'd worked hard to get past, but some things just weren't fixable. At least, not for him.

Mitch shook away the image and stepped inside. A rowdy chorus of "You're late!" from his friends, Amahle and Johnny, assaulted his ears.

The couple were the first friends he'd made when he'd moved to Colorado. Not because he'd wowed them with his personality. Quite the opposite.

They'd been his first customers at Rocky Mountain High. Amahle had listened to his sales pitch and then immediately laughed at him and told him he would be out of business within the week if he didn't liven that shit up, cut about twenty minutes off the history lesson, and learn to smile like he meant it instead of like he was having a vasectomy.

Luckily, she'd proceeded to draft a mock-up of what he should say when new customers walked through his door. Not because she was particularly sweet, but because they'd waited for a long time for the town to get a dispensary, and she didn't want it going belly up...*ever.*

As he strode to his friends' table, several of the natives hollered their hellos, and he waved.

"You know what this means?" Johnny bellowed even though Mitch no longer stood clear across the room. A sure sign he was lit.

"I'm paying for all of this evening's libations?" Mitch took a seat next to Amahle. She was a former Miss Black America contestant who was far too everything to have settled for the likes of Johnny—a guy with more tattoos than brain cells. Then again, he was also the kind of guy who would bury a body for you and go to prison before he'd snitch.

Tina, the waitress, stopped at their table. "Did I hear right? You're buying all evening?"

"Until the ugly lights come back on at closing," Johnny answered for him. "His rule, not ours."

Tina glanced at Mitch and raised her eyebrows.

"I didn't use the moronic phrase 'ugly lights,'" Mitch said. "But rules are rules." He gave Tina his debit card to start a tab.

"The only reason to make rules is so you can break them," Tina said.

Asinine philosophy. Sounded like something Bad Luck Luna would say. The two of them would probably become best friends. Which would be awful, because then his neighbor would start hanging out in this bar. *His* bar. Then again, he might not be living in this town much longer thanks to the blasted woman.

"Hell," Tina continued, "my last rule was to give up women, and that lasted less than a week."

"I don't understand why you would create a decree with the intention of breaking it." Because he was still thinking of Luna, his words came out harsher than he intended.

Tina leaned toward him and whispered, "Because breaking them is a whole lot of fun."

Her statement contained no logic. Breaking rules caused chaos. He hated chaos. And he was about to explain to her why she was wrong when Amahle kicked him under the table.

He scowled and pulled his leg back. Kicking him meant, *don't say what you're thinking of saying.* "I'll have a High Life IPA."

"Make that a pitcher and keep them coming," Johnny ordered.

"Dude," Amahle said to Mitch after Tina left, "you know what this means, right?" She wore no makeup. So different from Mitch's ex-fiancée, who had never left the house without spending at least an hour putting on her face. The same woman who'd vowed vengeance upon him the last time they'd been in the same room. Not just any room—the wedding chapel where she'd run out on him. The woman who'd been the last renter of the Ol' Murphy place.

"Didn't we just establish what it means?" Mitch slipped off his cardigan and arranged it over the back of his chair. Amahle referred to it as his "educated pot-seller lab coat." The title didn't bother him because he was proud to be a college graduate. Getting that diploma hadn't been a given. More like a long shot.

"Besides that," Amahle said.

"That my bank account is about to take another hit from you lushes?" Mitch asked.

"Besides that." Amahle rubbed her hands together like she was about to plot a world takeover.

"There is nothing else."

"You have to sign up for a dating app."

He grimaced. Hell. He'd forgotten about that. Last Wednesday night, after one too many shots and Mitch getting melancholy over not having a woman in his life, he'd declared the next time he arrived late, he'd sign up for cyber dating—because maybe, just maybe, the right woman existed. "Drunken deals don't hold up in court. I should know, I just spent the last hour talking to a group of lawyers." A big part of his customer base included groups of professionals in town for conferences. Once their conferences ended, they usually dropped in full of curiosity about a product that wasn't, for the most part, legal in their states. Combine them with the college students, and he had a booming business.

Amahle grinned. A sweet, uncomplicated grin. A superpower she deployed to sway men to say yes without realizing what they were saying yes to until it was too late.

Or at least, that's how Johnny explained it.

Amahle folded her hands on the table in a prim posture of superiority. "Good thing we're not taking this to court."

Johnny leaned back in his chair and laced his hands behind his shaved head. "Fuckhead, give up now. There'll be a lot less carnage."

Amahle gave her husband the stink eye and then offered Mitch her full attention. "It's time for you to get back in the double raft."

Stalling, Mitch glanced at his watch. Only ten minutes had passed, but it seemed like a year. He threw out a Hail Mary. "Why do women get the prerogative to change their mind, but men don't?"

Amahle lowered her hands to her lap. "Do you think I've been mentoring you on the intricacies of finding a *good* woman just for kicks and grins?"

"I've always assumed it's because you're a sucker for punishment." Mitch glanced around to see if anyone was listening. He'd prefer the whole town not know of his personal business. "Otherwise, you would've never married that guy." He pointed at Johnny.

"What the hell, man?" Johnny exclaimed, sounding like a surfer dude instead of a mountain man. "Don't throw me under the garbage truck. I've been loaning you my woman's brain for a year."

Amahle cleared her throat and, like obedient school children, both men quieted. "Besides wanting to have another female around to talk to, not just you two clowns, I did it because I don't want to see you get hurt by another woman who disguises her authentic self from you."

He did not want to talk about that.

As if realizing she'd taken the conversation too far, Amahle quickly added, "Besides, this is your fault. All you had to do was show up on time. I think, secretly, you wanted me to force the issue, and you purposefully arrived late."

Could that be true? Of course not. "That's not what happened."

"Let me guess, you were in the middle of the latest comic book?" Amahle teased.

It was a logical guess. He did have a habit of getting caught up in books, but also in superhero movies and deep thoughts. And when any of those things happened, he simply forgot to show up where he was supposed to be. Work, the bar, supposedly his wedding ceremony.

By creating a New Year's resolution that anytime he was late meeting his friends, drinks were on him, he'd hoped to break the habit by the end of January.

Now it was June, and he was still buying drinks.

"Don't look so glum about getting on a dating app." Johnny cracked his tattooed knuckles. "Just think of all the kinky-ass sex in your near future." His words were quickly followed by a grunt of pain.

Mitch grimaced in sympathy. Johnny's woman sure knew how to connect her cowboy boots with a man's tender shins.

Amahle gave Johnny a serene smile. "News flash. Just because a woman is on a dating app doesn't mean she wants to have kinky-ass sex."

A commotion on the wooden stage caused the room to grow quiet as everyone watched the band settle into their spots.

The lead singer stepped to the mic. According to the flyer, he and his band were a hot commodity in Louisiana. "Good evening." His thick Cajun accent forced Mitch to listen closely to understand him. "I have to say, I'm loving Colorado. I got some smooth-ass buds this afternoon from a little place called Rocky Mountain High."

Several people in the audience whistled and made noises.

"Best damn shit in the state," Johnny shouted. "The owner's sitting right here."

Mitch grunted. *Shut the fuck up.* He hated the limelight. Which, according to Amahle, was probably why he'd showed up late to his own wedding. Either that, or he hadn't been in love with the bride. One of these days, he should tell her and Johnny what had really gone down.

"Dude," the musician said, "take a fucking bow."

Mitch stood. Applause ensued, and he quickly sat. "Asshole," he said to Johnny.

"If that's the worst thing that's happened to you today," Johnny said, "you've got nothing to moan about."

Mitch took a sip of his beer. "The worst thing that happened to me today was having to take Ms. Houdini back to her owner."

"And?" Johnny asked.

Mitch didn't respond.

"And..." Amahle prompted, elbowing Mitch. "We want to know what happened. Did you promise her not to destroy any trees and ask her to sell to you at a profit?"

He rubbed his ribs. "Nothing happened, and she's not interested in selling." If he mentioned her state of undress to high Johnny, the guy's head would spin. "She's...different."

"We all knew that the moment she sent out formal invitations to her Under the Stars sleepover." Johnny held up a fist to Mitch. Another sure sign he'd already indulged plenty.

Mitch bumped his fist. "I haven't RSVP'd yet. You guys?"

"Hell, yeah," Johnny said. "With a big fat suck my giant"—a grunt swooshed out of him—"we're busy," he finished.

"To be fair," Amahle said, "he failed to consult with me before declining."

Johnny raised his fist again.

"It might've been fun," Amahle continued, ignoring her husband's juvenile antics. "Not that I would've gone, considering she's the enemy for thwarting your plans."

"She's not my enemy. She's just not my favorite person." How could she be when her actions meant his future was now in limbo? As long as he lived in a rented home, he'd continue to wake up in a sweat from a reoccurring dream where he and Mom had to grab as much as they could and scramble out the window because the big bad property owner was coming to evict them and take them to jail. Winning the old Murphy Place at auction at a reasonable price had been Mitch's perfect plan to put the nightmare to bed forever. But with it gone and nothing else available, he was now looking at other options.

All of this because Luna had crushed his phone, and he hadn't been able to call the bank quickly enough for permission to raise his bid above the agreed amount before the gavel had come down. "You guys feel free to love her."

"Excellent!" Amahle said. "I followed Luna's Goat Yoga account on Instagram, and she's a hoot."

"You followed her and never mentioned it?" Mitch asked.

Amahle gave him an unapologetic shrug. "Haven't you ever heard the saying, keep your friends close and your enemies closer?"

He nodded. Small towns were nothing if not loyal to their pot guy. No one wanted to see him leave—not because they loved him so much as because they loved their cannabis. There was no guarantee they'd get a new dispensary in town. Licenses to sell were highly sought after and hard to come by. "Again, she's not the enemy."

"What would one even wear to an epic Under the Stars Sleepover?" Johnny grumbled. "Do you arrive in your pajamas? Or change when you get there?"

"I don't sleep in pajamas." Pajamas were an unnecessary luxury when you grew up poor. "Would lack of sleeping garments be a rational reason to RSVP *no*?"

"I think you should go," Amahle said. "It's possible she might be so wowed by your personality that she'll up and decide to sell the property to you."

"I don't see that happening," Mitch said.

"If nothing else," Amahle said, eyeballing him with squinty eyes, "you can practice your rusty flirting game on her. You know...in prep for the dating app you're going to sign up for."

The door to the establishment squeaked open and a brisk breeze swept through the place.

"Whoa," Johnny said. "Look what the cat dragged in."

Mitch glanced toward the door. Bad Luck Luna.

Luna made eye contact with him before he could look away. She smiled, waved, and started toward their table.

"Damn," he muttered as he watched her approach. She'd changed out of her goat-walking clothes. *Who walks their goats?* Now she wore a white T-shirt with the words *Let Go and Let Mother Earth* emblazoned on the front in bright orange and a long floral print skirt. She had rings on every finger and lots and lots of bracelets.

Amahle patted him on the arm. "I've got a good feeling about my plan for you to woo her into selling you the property."

"Why would she do that? She's started a business."

"Yeah, but if her business doesn't make it because no one in town supports it, and she has to up and sell, you'll be her first choice if she's sweet on you."

He blinked. "You are evil."

"Not evil, just a mother hen protecting her pot-selling chicken," Amahle said. "Now, play nice."

3

"Fancy meeting you here." She used her best care-free tone. One meant to convey Mr. Rude Guy had not hurt her feelings when he had rudely hurried off before she could say hi in person while out walking her goats. Just as he had when she'd invited him in for lemonade.

"Why is that fancy?" he asked.

Was he serious? Or was he messing with her? Probably the first, because the latter would require a sense of humor. "It's just a saying." It was too bad he was here. With him grumping around, she'd have no chance of changing the town's cranky locals' thoughts about her.

The only woman at the table surprised Luna by smiling and holding out her hand. "I'm Amahle. You'll have to excuse Mitch. He tends to awkwardly flounder around beautiful women."

"That explains so much." Now she had a name to put to Mr. Rude Guy's face. *Mitch!*

Mitch sat there looking stupefied while Amahle introduced the fierce-looking guy next to her who looked like he'd done serious jail time, as her lover, Johnny.

The subject in question smiled a crooked smile that instantly diminished his thug persona from real-time thug to juvie-time thug. "I'm also her significant other." Love filled his voice. "It's nice to officially meet the newest resident of Rocky Mountain Springs. I've heard a crap-ton about you since the auction."

"Nothing good, I'm sure, if it came from the poor loser," Luna replied, glancing at Mitch.

Mitch blinked.

"It was from me," Amahle said. "And all good. I follow you on Instagram. I love all your pictures of Ms. Houdini, Ms. Tinker, and Mr. JJ. I'm excited for your evening yoga classes to finally start."

"Me too. I was beginning to think my licenses and permits to operate from my home would never get approved." There'd been so many delays, she couldn't help but feel they were intentional.

"I'm sure we've taken up enough of your time," Mitch said abruptly. "Have a good evening."

Luna glanced at him and placed a hand over her chest. "Be still, my heart. What you lack in charm you make up for in...nothing."

Amahle laughed. "Are you meeting someone?"

"I had a date," Luna answered. "Emphasis on *had*. I don't know what I was thinking signing up for a dating app." Of course, she *did* know what she'd been thinking, but she had no plans to share those thoughts with anyone other than her diary, Ms. Rosie Nosey.

"Isn't this a fun coincidence?" Amahle reminded Luna of an acquaintance back home. A woman often referred to as the social glue in the group Luna had run in. "We were just talking to Mitch about his plans to join a dating app."

Luna studied him. The guy didn't have the whole app vibe going on. Besides, with those eyes, why did he need an app? Then again, he lacked charm. "I hope you're more reliable than the men I've attracted so far."

"Please, don't let us keep you," Mitch said, then grunted and winced.

"Mitch, darling, that was abrupt." Amahle glanced at Luna. "He's not usually purposefully rude."

"You're saying I not only bring out his awkward social skills, but I also bring out his uptight side?" Damn. That hadn't been a nice thing to say. Positive words fostered positive Karma. Luna 1.0 had never worried about Karma because in the circles she'd traveled, money trumped Karma. But Luna 2.0 had a healthy respect for the lady of fortune, and she also simply wanted to be nice for the sake of niceness alone.

"Hell no, uptight's not on you," Amahle responded. "This guy is tighter than spandex on an elephant."

Luna glanced at Mitch. If she wasn't mistaken, he wanted to be anywhere but at this table. "To be fair, he can't be that tightly wound. He saw me naked today and didn't immediately run away."

Amahle spewed beer. "He...what?"

"Fuckhead!" Johnny exclaimed, slamming his hands on the table. "Why didn't you lead with that?"

"It was no big deal," Mitch said gruffly, his right ear turning red.

This elicited peals of laughter from his friends.

Luna fluttered her lashes at him and twirled a curl around her finger. "You are the first guy to ever declare my body in the buff as no big deal." It had been a while since she'd been around a man who wasn't smooth as silk pajamas with a woman.

She sort of liked his ragged edges. A guy who couldn't spew pretty words at the drop of a hat probably couldn't spew lies either. He'd probably make a decent friend in this town.

His brows jerked together. "I didn't... That's not what I meant."

"I'm listening."

The music changed. "I love this song," Amahle said.

Luna was pretty sure Amahle was trying to change the subject for Mitch's sake. Luna let him go. "Me too. It's a great dancing song."

Amahle gave her a look of approval. "Let's all get out there and shake our asses." She hopped up, grabbed Johnny's hand, and tugged him to the dance floor.

Luna glanced at Mitch. "You can dance...can't you?"

"I can dance." He stood and walked out on the dance floor.

Shocked, she followed. She'd been prepared for a cold shoulder.

Once her hand was in his, he smoothly pulled her into him and settled his right hand on the small of her back, causing her to shiver.

His fingers spread, and he tugged her a little closer. He leaned down and placed his lips close to her ear. "Are you cold?"

If she said no, he might guess what had caused her shiver. If she said yes, she'd be lying. "If anyone would've asked," she murmured instead, "I would've sworn you were the type who didn't like to dance."

"You would've been correct."

She settled her left hand on his bicep, which was not in any way wimpy, and stared at his Adam's apple.

He spun her out and back in, causing her to laugh. The guy had moves.

"Why don't you like to dance? You're excellent at it." Much, much, much better at it than being friendly.

"Do you not believe it's possible to be first-rate at something you don't like?"

"My gut says no." She couldn't think of one thing she was first-rate at that she didn't like.

"Your gut's wrong," he said. "I'm proof."

She relaxed. "I don't think twirling a girl once on a dance floor proves your theory. More data is required."

For the rest of the song, they danced in silence.

Halfway through the next one, he said, "I have other data."

She waited for him to share details.

He didn't.

"For instance?" she prompted.

"Kissing." Again, he twirled her out and back into his arms. "I've been told it's my superpower, but it's not my favorite part of sex."

She stumbled and stepped on his toes. "Very funny. For a moment there, you had me going." He had been joking...right? He had to be.

"Why would I jest?" He sounded slightly in pain.

She stopped dancing and tilted her face upward. He met her gaze. No hint of duplicity showed in his beautiful eyes. "Who can verify what you're saying?"

His right ear turned red. Just the right one. "No one I plan to introduce you to." He stepped out of their embrace, sharply pivoted, and strode off the dance floor.

Luna had to hustle to catch up. What had she said wrong?

As soon as they reached their table of friends, Luna caught up with Mitch.

"I beg your pardon," Luna exclaimed. "Asking who can verify your claim to possessing a superpower isn't ridiculous."

"You have a superpower?" Mitch's friend Johnny struggled to sit up straight.

"You don't?" Mitch asked.

Johnny frowned. "I'll tell you mine if you tell me yours."

Mitch shrugged. "Kissing."

"Mine too." Johnny slouched back into his chair.

"If you're going to brag about being a great kisser," Amahle said to Mitch, "Luna is justified in asking you to offer up someone who can back your claim."

"Or just kiss her and prove it," Johnny said.

"I am not going to kiss someone who is not my type just to prove something to anyone," Mitch snapped.

"So, you're saying you're not a fan of independent women who question your half-baked claims?" Luna asked.

"Props for speaking your mind," Johnny said, giving her a nod.

"Tread lightly on the insults," Amahle said softly to Luna. "While I've got mad respect for a woman who's not afraid to stand up for herself, I'm also a fierce friend. Mitch is a lot of things—half-baked isn't one of them."

"Understood." Damn Mitch for once again getting under her skin and bringing out Luna 1.0.

Amahle handed Luna a beer. "What's the guy's name who stood you up tonight?"

"Not worth mentioning," Luna said.

"I believe if you tell someone you're going to do something, you follow through," Mitch declared. "It's not a hard rule to keep."

"Real stickler on that kind of thing, are you?" In Luna's old world, you always kept your options open. Which meant committing to nothing.

And you judged the newcomers.

And...her old world really wasn't all that great of a place, which was why she now lived in the small town of Rocky Mountain Springs. Well, one of the whys.

Johnny tried to prop his elbows on the table and missed. "What exactly does one do at a sleepover party?" he asked as he tried again to land his elbows.

"You'll have to excuse Johnny. He's not the best at following the conversation when he's high," Amahle said.

"Not a problem." Luna welcomed the change. She waited until Johnny righted himself to reply. "It greatly depends on the crowd. We might sit around and chat or go swimming or even watch *Justice League* on a large outside screen." Great parties were all about having the right mix of people, and then a never-ending string of conversation starters ready to get people thinking and talking. At least that's how it had worked in her social circles. In her old circles, she never had to wonder if people would come. They might not RSVP early, but they'd show up. Here, she wasn't sure. Did people have to like you before they would attend your party in this town? If that was the case, she was doomed.

"You should promise Mitch you'll show *Justice League*," Johnny said. "That shit makes him hard."

Luna glanced at Mitch. If she could get him to come, others would follow. "Is that true?" When she'd reinvented herself, she'd embraced her guilty pleasure of watching movies with comic heroes. Luna 2.0 didn't worry about appearing too cool for fools. Luna 2.0 worried about being authentic while undoing some traits that were more a result of the excessive environment in which she'd been raised than they were her true nature. Or at least she hoped that was the case.

"It's not a crime to like superhero movies," Mitch said. "You do know *Justice League* is superheroes and not some courtroom romcom, right?"

"Bite me."

His gaze burned through her. "I'm to believe you're showing *Justice League* at your preposterous party?"

What was so preposterous about throwing a party to get to know your neighbors? "If you commit to attending, I am." Look at her rock the whole commitment thing.

"I don't need to attend your party to see a movie I can stream anytime."

"How about this offer...if you come early to help me set up, in return, I'll help you sign up for the Get Hitched dating app." It would give them something in common. Swapping future dating app horror stories could be the foundation upon which they built a neighborly friendship. His back yard ran along the side yard of her property.

"Fuckhead," Johnny shouted, "you should totally go. I've never heard a woman say it's okay to come first."

Luna chuckled. She had a feeling things would never be boring if she were to hang out with this crew on a regular basis. She would have to try harder to mend the fences between her and Mitch.

4

Mitch did not arrive at Luna's Under the Stars sleepover early. Trading favors with Bad Luck Luna would result in her getting all up in his dating life business, and that wasn't happening. Ever! With any good fortune, Amahle would give him a break and drop the whole sign-up-for-a-dating-app thing.

At exactly one minute before the party was due to begin, he took the uneven steps that led to her wrap-around porch and knocked on her fire-engine-red front door. The last time he'd knocked on that door, it had been a crisp white and it had been his ex-fiancée who had lived there.

The rhythmic tinkling of chimes hanging along the rafters distracted him from those thoughts. He rather liked the off-key sound. They reminded him of his favorite bookstore as a child. That had been the summer he'd turned eight, if he remembered correctly. A place that had offered him warmth during those numerous times when his mother had told him to get lost so she could entertain a male friend.

Unfortunately, by fall he and Mom had moved, and never again had he discovered a friendly bookstore within walking distance of where they lived. Especially not the winter they'd lived in a car in a junkyard. He squeezed his eyes shut and forced away the memory of how that living situation had ended. It had been worse than eviction.

Opening his eyes, he knocked again. He was about to turn and retreat when the door swung open revealing a smiling Luna. "Mitch, welcome," she said warmly.

His gaze quickly went from her face to her pajamas. The vision that met his eyes caused them to malfunction. There were so many bright colors in her silky tie-dyed pajamas he felt the need to shade his jacked-up eyes with one hand and caress the material with the other. When neither hand was given permission to roam, his mouth took over. "You look like a rainbow drenched in melted gummy bears."

She momentarily studied him and then shrugged. "I choose to take that as a compliment." She punctuated her comment with air kisses on either side of his cheeks.

Air kisses! Fuck. He'd read her wrong. She'd obviously not grown up on a hippie compound like he'd assumed but instead in an environment where don't-mess-up-my-lipstick kisses and designer labels reigned. Amahle would be disappointed to know that after a year of mentoring him on how to read women, he still sucked at it.

"Let me take that." Luna took his sleeping bag and plopped it on the hardwood floors of her foyer. "I'm so happy you came."

Mitch scowled. "I told you I would be here." He shrugged off his backpack and dropped it beside the sleeping bag. "Did you think I lied?"

A look of bemusement crinkled her nose, shifting its asymmetrical smattering of freckles, which weirdly resulted in his stomach dipping toward his toes. Were there more freckles tonight than there had been last night? "It crossed my mind you might change yours."

"Promise keeping is a hard rule for me." If she didn't expect others to keep their word, did that mean she didn't keep her own promises?

Of course, all his rules were hard rules. Rules he'd adopted as a result of his upbringing. They'd given him hope as a child for a better future.

"I like that in a guy."

He didn't know how to respond, so he changed the subject. "I brought edibles for the party. I hope that's okay."

"Thank you." Luna took the brownies. "Your mom raised you right."

Her comment caught him in the soft underbelly. There were a lot of things Mom had taught him. To bring something to a party wasn't one of them. "The last time I went to an event, I showed up with a cheese and cracker tray, and everyone booed." Johnny and Amahle being the loudest of that night's hecklers. He really should get new friends.

Luna laughed. "If you didn't bring loaded brownies, it would be like a new momma showing up without her baby."

Her laugh reminded him of the chimes over the door at that long-ago bookstore. A fraction off-key but soothing.

"I'll just put these on a platter." She pivoted and strode away, her free arm swinging, her steps graceful, her hips whispering *follow me...follow me...* He tripped in his hurry to obey.

His footsteps faltered in the once-familiar kitchen.

Luna had done away with the winter-white walls and painted them a warm, sunny summer yellow. The windows were bare. On a round table, a colorful set of plates was displayed. One with a chip big enough he could see it from where he stood.

Which was the real Luna? The air kisser or the compound dweller?

He frowned. He'd sworn off dating the locals. His ex-fiancée had been a local. Well, localish. She'd moved to Colorado to attend university. From the moment they'd gone on their first date, everyone in town had gotten involved. He'd received so much advice he'd had to threaten to raise all his prices at the shop if they didn't back off. There just wasn't enough room to breathe in a relationship that existed under the microscope of a small town.

"Am I the first to arrive?"

"You are." Luna mumbled something, and he thought he heard the word last.

"What was that?"

She transferred the brownies to a platter and padded barefoot to the refrigerator. "What can I get you? Beer? Bourbon?" She turned and scrutinized him like he was a bug under a magnifier. "A virgin Bahama Mama?"

"Water." He didn't like to mix alcohol with weed consumption, and at Amahle's insistence, he'd already had one brownie an hour earlier. She claimed the real him came out to play after a brownie, and that was the *him* Luna needed to get to know.

Luna took a faded blue metal tumbler from the cabinet. The kind you stumble across at the estate auction of a centenarian. She filled it with water from a scratched and dented silver metal pitcher and stuck a straw in it.

"Thank you." He fingered the straw. Paper. Impressive. "As president of our local chapter of Volunteer Outdoor Colorado, I appreciate your doing your part to save the environment."

Her lips twitched.

"Did I say something amusing?"

Her lips stopped twitching.

Was he the joke? Was being the president of VOC equivalent to being the president of Math League in high school?

"What's on their current project list?" she asked in a serious tone.

He considered changing the subject but didn't. He was who he was. "Our next project is the semi-yearly maintenance of the Temptation Trail."

"Want some help?" She wiggled her eyebrows in a suggestive manner. "I've been told I'm really good at temptation."

"I have no doubt you are." He tugged at his ear. A habit he had when he felt off balance. "If you're also good at hard work, I can let you know the time and place." Amahle had taught him you could tell a lot about a woman based solely on her willingness to get her hands dirty.

Bad Luck Luna leaned a hip against the counter. "Thanks. It'll be a great way to make connections with the locals."

It wasn't exactly an altruistic answer. "And a great way to keep your new state healthy."

A wrinkle appeared between her eyes. "Duh."

She cared about his cause. They finally had something in common.

"Are you ready for a brownie?" She reached for one and glanced at him from over her shoulder. "Warning, no is not an option."

"It's not?"

She turned and held out a brownie for him to take. "It's not, because after the day I've had, I could really, really use a brownie, and I don't like to consume alone."

"I try to never stand in the way of a woman's happiness."

She handed him the brownie, picked out another for herself, and proceeded to devour it in one bite.

They weren't bite-sized brownies.

He did the same with his and washed it down with a drink of water.

Silence ensued. The kind of silence that invites intimacy.

Intimacy was the last thing he wanted with Bad Luck Luna. "Do you have a list of topics to cover tonight?"

She gave him a funny look. It started as an amused smirk and melted into a confused stare. "Topics?"

He'd seen that look more times than he cared to admit. "Never mind." His mother used to tell everyone that his brain didn't work normally and to ignore him when he spoke. "It was a stupid question." Mom had also told others that he had a demon inside of him that caused the fierce panic attacks that sent him spiraling into a guttural shell of himself. He now knew neither were true.

"I've always found asking the right question to be highly overrated. In fact, asking the wrong one has so many more possibilities."

Her answer caused something in his chest to shift. He shifted it right back to where it belonged. "You should know I have no interest in a relationship. I'm here simply because you're my neighbor."

She chose another brownie, popped the whole thing in her mouth, closed her eyes, and made intriguing noises as she chewed and swallowed. Orgasmic noises. "Smart guy. Someone taught you to run from fire instead of into it. I hope it was a parent and not an ex."

"It was an ex," he said honestly. "But I learned my lesson."

"I'm so sorry."

What was she sorry about? She hadn't broken his heart. "You know, I've never met anyone like you."

She laughed. "I've never met another like you, so I do believe that makes us a great pair."

He startled. "I have no interest in being a pair." He'd said those words so often since the demise of his last relationship the knee-jerk response rolled automatically off his tongue. Mostly, he had said it to Amahle and Johnny, who were nothing if not enthusiastic in their attempts to fix him up on blind dates.

Luna's nose did that funny twisty thing again. The thing that moved her freckles. "I'll keep that in mind."

"Who else is coming to this sleepover party?" he asked.

She sighed. "You're the only one who RSVP'd with a yes."

Fuck. "It's early yet. Maybe they'll come late." No way could he spend an entire night with this woman without someone around as a buffer. For whatever reason, she unsettled him. Made him feel like a schoolboy trying to flirt for the first time. Flying solo, he would continue to spew nonsense. Or worse, intimate facts.

Luna gave him a counterfeit smile. "I sent out fifty invitations, ten people RSVP'd they couldn't make it. and I never heard from the rest. Other than you, and you were coerced."

He should probably make up a lie and say something comforting about himself once throwing a party that no one attended, but he had a hard rule about lying. "Don't take it personally. Your invite screamed peculiar." He would discreetly text Amahle and Johnny and tell them they had to come. And bring friends. Those two had more friends than Colorado had boulders.

"Did not." She yanked her bracelets off one slender wrist and put them on the other. "It whispered fun."

He chuckled. "To you, maybe. But to the rest of us, it reeked of weird vibes."

She popped up on a barstool before giving him her full attention. "Weird how?"

"You freaked the town out with your blanket invite to an Under the Stars sleepover." He walked to the counter, chose a brownie, and ate it. Too late, he remembered he should probably pace himself.

"I thought it sounded like a lot of fun and a great way to meet the residents of Rocky Mountain Springs when their cranky-meters were hopefully switched to off."

"Next time, host a bonfire that consists of a start and end time."

"I didn't want people to consume and drive. It's called being a responsible host."

Her thoughtfulness was refreshing. "You probably should have mentioned that in your invitation."

"I'm used to having a party planner take care of the details."

Her response sobered him. "Then you come from money?"

She glanced away. "I have—*had*—a friend who planned parties for a living."

"Why had and not have?"

"I moved here."

The loneliness in her voice tugged at him. He'd been where she was. "Have you made any new friends?"

She shook her head.

That was his fault for being pissed at having lost the bid at the auction and blowing off steam by floating the infantile idea of moving to another town and taking his dispensary business with him. He should have kept that thought to himself until it was more fully developed. No one had taken the news well, and everyone had immediately gotten all up in his business by freezing out Luna in the hopes she'd run, and he'd stay.

The least he could do was offer an olive branch. "Before I leave tonight, would you help me sign up for that dating app you mentioned the other night at Moody Blues?"

She hopped off the barstool. "I'd love to. It'll be fun knowing someone else who is going through a ton of first dates. We can have weekly check-ins and compare notes."

He tugged at the collar of his T-shirt. The room had gotten awfully warm. "It's hot in here. Maybe you should open a window."

She checked him out and then plopped her hands on her colorful hips. "You're wearing too many clothes. Follow me." She crooked a finger at him.

He followed, and she stopped at an open door that led to a room dominated by a massive unmade bed with a light pink comforter and a ton of haphazardly placed fluffy pillows. A dresser drawer stood open, and a pile of clothes sat unfolded in a laundry basket. Most of them appeared to be pink. The sight made his head feel light and his fingers twitch to straighten things up.

She pointed to a sky-blue coatrack in the corner. The same color as his counter at work. His mother would swear it was a sign. "You can strip down and hang your clothes on that."

"Are you trying to seduce me?"

She folded her arms across her chest. "There is no try in seduction. You either do or you don't."

He was hot. His head felt light. "Did you even invite anyone else to this party?" He stuck his hand in his pocket to retrieve his keys. They weren't there. "Did you steal my keys?" What did he even know about Bad Luck Luna? Nothing. She could be a serial killer.

"What are you babbling about? Are you feeling okay?" She pulled her pajama pockets inside out. "See. No keys."

"You could have hidden them."

"Are you always so super paranoid?"

"Who are you calling para—" He snapped his mouth shut. Paranoia could occur if one consumed too many edibles too quickly in one setting. But he'd only had two. Plus the one he'd had an hour before coming. Early enough for it to take the edge off by the time he'd arrived. Two plus one didn't induce paranoia. Not in him. His tolerance was high.

Unless...had he grabbed the wrong batch of brownies?

Had he fucking grabbed the triple-whammy batch he'd made special order for a bachelor party? The fast-acting batch? He must have. "I have a confession."

"Oooh, me, too." She put one finger to her lips and leaned toward him and whispered, "Shhh. Don't tell anyone."

Were his ears stoned, or had she skipped the actual secret? "Tell anyone what?"

A grin split her face and lit up her eyes. "I'm not me."

5

una was considering sending a search party for Mitch when he finally appeared in her kitchen wearing a pair of pin-striped pajamas. Baby powder blue. *Be still my clit.* She'd never considered herself the sort to be attracted to a geek, but she suddenly couldn't help but wonder if she had been missing out on something by not.

"Why are you staring?" he demanded.

She leaned against the counter and forced her gaze up. "I told you my secret. It's time for you to tell me yours." She had no idea what had possessed her to blurt hers, but it was imperative she learn his so that they both had a reason not to spread the other's.

Mitch leaned against the door frame and thrummed the fingers of his left hand against his thigh. "The brownies I brought contain triple the normal amount of cannabis."

As secrets go, it was super lame. She grinned. "That would explain the fact I can't feel my cheeks." She pinched her cheeks to make sure she still couldn't feel them. Nope. Numb little fuckers.

He mimicked her and pinched his cheeks. "Me neither."

She laughed, and after a moment where he looked totally confused, he joined in.

Once they started, neither seemed able to stop. It was as if they'd just heard the punchline to the funniest joke of the century.

Unable to continued standing, she slid to the floor and sat cross-legged. When was the last time she'd laughed? Really laughed? Probably when the police had showed up at the university to arrest her. That was until she'd realized they weren't joking.

Finally, Mitch choked out, "If you're not you, who are you? The new Mrs. Claus?" He wrapped his arms around his waist and grabbed his sides as if holding in a gut-busting, belly laugh.

She frowned. "The new Mrs. Claus? When did Santa divorce the old Mrs. Claus?" How had she missed the news? Had it happened when she'd been on a social media hiatus? "How can you laugh at something so sad?" She wiped a tear off her cheek. And then another, and another. Why was she crying? "Do you think there's any hope they'll reconcile?"

The old her wouldn't cry at the news. The old her would have made a joke. Hell, the old her hadn't even cried when she had gotten arrested. To do so would have caused her mascara to run, and no way would she take a bad mugshot.

Mitch strolled toward her in the determined fashion of a man with a plan.

She gulped. Not because he worried her, but because...well...she wasn't sure why.

He squatted until they were at eye level and then he wiped away the tears on her cheeks. "Look at you with a case of the stoner-tears." He lost his balance and sat with a thud.

She sniffed. "Why don't you have stoner tears?"

"I'm a boy. We're not allowed to cry."

"Never?"

He scooted around so they sat shoulder to shoulder and leaned against the base of the counter. "Didn't your mom teach you that about boys?"

She laid her head on Mitch's shoulder. "I bet you're nothing but a big teddy bear when you're not being grumpy, aren't you?" The kind of guy who tended to get hurt by girls like her. The old her anyway. And let's face it, she was still a whole lot more the old her than she was the new her.

Hell, Luna 2.0 hadn't even gotten her walking legs yet. Until she knew she had what it took to stay on this path of being a person who cared about others more than herself, she didn't deserve love.

It was one thing to want to be a better person, another to actually execute the changes it took to make it happen.

"I am not grumpy." He rested his cheek on top of her head.

"You didn't want to come to my party. You don't like me. No one in this town likes me. Why?"

"I don't dislike you. I mean, you have a great ass and everything."

She scooted away from him and turned so she could see his eyes. "I don't dislike you either. I think you have a nice...a nice set of teeth." She'd been going to say nice ass as well but forced herself to say something Luna 2.0-ish. Something that would not lead him on into believing they could ever be more than friends.

He stood. "I should go."

"You can't go yet."

He frowned. "Why not?"

"Well..." Good question. One she was pretty sure she had a good answer for. "I don't know. I think maybe it has something to do with your keys." Was that it? Or was it because her feelings would be hurt?

"I don't need no keys to do the walk of pot." He spoke loudly.

She giggled. "Is that like the walk of shame?"

He awkwardly waved a finger in her direction. "It's the safer choice."

She managed to stand. She'd screwed up every-thing...again. "Was it because I said I like your teeth? They really are quite nice. Very white."

His gaze slid to her lips or maybe her toes. It was hard to tell because her focus was definitely out of whack.

While he remained stoically silent, she spent the time giving him a closer look. With his dark hair and blue eyes, it truly was quite possible Mitch could be Super-man.

Superman posing as a pot seller instead of a reporter. She chuckled. *Holy Batman. My neighbor is Superman.*

Superman tilted his head so far to the right she thought he might fall. He didn't, but he did stumble.

She giggled.

"That's not why I have to go," he said.

"Oh." She held out her hand. "Before you go home, give me your phone."

"Why?"

"I promised to help you sign up for the Get Hitched Dating App. I can't very well let you leave before I get it done."

She watched as he did the head tilt thing to the left. And again, he stumbled.

"Okay." He pulled out his phone, the one she'd bought for him after destroying his flip phone and handed it to her.

She narrowed her eyes, realizing that her grumpy neighbor totally looked like Superman. "I'm going to be Superman's dating coach." A thought hit her brain groggy with the aftereffects of his special brownies. "I'm going to need to know if your superpower really is kissing."

Superman blinked and dragged a hand down his jaw. "Why?"

She giggled and tapped him on the nose. "Because if it is, we need to upsell you on your kissing ability when we answer your app questionnaire."

"Why did you go and buy this place?" he said grumpily.

She was beginning to get used to how he changed the subject when the subject they were on wasn't tame. "Because the tree in the backyard—her name's Mildred—has the secret ingredient to a secret recipe I recently inherited. But I can't tell you the secret. Now, about that kiss? It's okay if you say no. I mean, it's not like I really believe that's your superpower. But on the off chance it is, mention of it could get you a lot of dates."

He leaned his head back so that her finger wasn't touching his nose. "I have to go home."

She lowered her hands to her sides. "Now?" Was the thought of kissing her so awful?

"Forty-five minutes ago would have been better." He turned toward the front door.

Oh God. He was really leaving. "Wait. I have a question, and you have to promise not to laugh."

He paused midstride and turned to face her. "How do I know if I can make that promise if I don't know the question?"

"Will you help me make friends with the locals?"

He didn't laugh. Quite the opposite. He flinched. "It's not that they don't like you. It's just that you're a thorn in my side, and I'm their special brownies guy, and, come to find out, people don't like people who abuse their special brownies guy."

"What a bunch of boobs."

He glanced at her boobs and then into her eyes. He opened his mouth like he planned to reply. Shook his head no. And then turned and left. Not even stopping to pick up his belongings in her house.

"So, is that a maybe?" she hollered.

6

Mitch poured charcoal in his Webber Grill and lit it, then stood on his deck and glanced past the rows and rows of beautiful cannabis plants growing in containers in his field, focusing instead on the sun which dangled languidly above a distant tree.

Not just any tree. Mildred. The tree that, according to stoned Luna, was why she'd bought her new home. That and his comment about a parking lot. Which had been a total insider's joke between him and his friends. One she could have at least asked for clarification on before going after the property.

How could someone just starting a goat yoga business afford to purchase a home? Unless she'd had help. Had she gotten a loan from her parents? Were they well off? It would explain her air kisses last night when he'd arrived for her party.

What exactly were her stories? Everyone had two. A story they shared and a story they kept close to their heart. Hell, he damn sure did. So, he couldn't fault her if she did.

Regardless of her story, she'd gotten in the way of him achieving his mission in life and now he had to pivot. Not away from the mission, but away from the path he had thought would take him there.

He wanted to be mad—stay mad—at Luna for forcing him to look at new avenues for home ownership. But after last night, he couldn't seem to conjure up those feelings of hostility. Not that he wanted to be best friends, but it simply wasn't possible to stay aloof toward someone you've gotten high with. He chuckled. His friends really were boobs.

Amahle's plan for him to woo Luna out of her property was asinine. And even if it was solid, he wouldn't play those types of games with another. It was too bad the mayor continued to refuse to sell Mitch the home he lived in and the building where Mitch had his dispensary. He'd tried several times, but the guy didn't like to let go of property he owned. For now, Mitch would keep trying to change his mind. But if after a year the answer was still no, hard decisions would have to be made.

The fragrant aroma of hot coals drew his attention away from his musings. Grilling relaxed him. It was even more calming when he had friends over. He'd thought about inviting Amahle and Johnny for drinks and dinner. Even Luna, as a neighborly gesture. But tonight, he hadn't been in the mood for company. He'd been in the mood to ponder. A man can't ponder surrounded by people.

He couldn't help but wonder what Luna was doing on a Saturday evening. Did she have a date? What kind of guy would match up with her? A yogi? A zookeeper? A stoner like Johnny?

Then again, she might be home and practicing naked yoga at sunset. He smiled. She did indeed have a great ass.

He banished the last thought to the junk compost pile in his brain, but when it got there, his cock blocked its plummet into the smelly purgatory and urged him to reconsider. The damn appendage had nagged him all day to take her up on her request for a kiss to prove his claim.

A classic high idea. Under no circumstances did his kissing ability need to be mentioned in his profile in the dating app.

Luna had said something else that had been classic, but he couldn't remember what. He'd been trying to recall it all day.

He scrubbed a hand down the stubble on his jaw. It was a good thing he'd left before she'd talked stoned Mitch into things better left alone. Not only was she not his type—she was also his neighbor.

Besides, he needed to stay focused on building his business. There wasn't time for a distraction in his life.

In an attempt to regain his peace, he deeply inhaled the sweet aroma of his crop, exhaled slowly, and studied the colors of tonight's sunset. Sunsets were his go-to natural high. Or at least they were when they weren't reminding him of Luna. With their brilliant shades of oranges and yellows, he had always viewed them as magnificent masterpieces meant to be discussed and enjoyed with the opposite sex.

Unfortunately, the infamous *altar*-cation between him and Brandy, his ex-fiancée, had left him uninspired to put his heart out there again. Instead, he'd been working hard and heavy to expand his business. While he'd flippantly told Amahle and Johnny he planned on building a parking lot on the land Luna now owned, he'd been joking. What man wouldn't joke about bulldozing his former fiancée's home when accused of wanting to own it for warm-fuzzy dick reasons?

The heat coming off the coals drew his attention from his reverie and back to the task at hand. Grill time.

Luna had dropped off his belongings this morning. If she had knocked, he hadn't heard her. She'd also left him detailed instructions for the dating app. Instructions that required nine pink sticky notes.

He'd discovered her hit-and-run visit when he'd stepped outside with his morning cup of coffee and found a huge blueberry muffin. On the surface, it had resembled a concoction a millionaire's chef might have created.

Unfortunately, it had tasted like an unsupervised toddler had cooked it.

Which just added proof to his theory that expensive pretty things weren't always as appealing on the inside.

Hell, if he took the dating-app plunge, maybe he'd get lucky and find a smart, sensible, standard woman looking for a smart, sensible man with a brain just shy of normal. A woman who could also cook. Which left Luna out because there was no way she was sensible or standard or a good cook. If nothing else, the app could help him find a plus one for an upcoming work-related event.

He glanced at the invitation sticking out of his shirt pocket. It had arrived in today's mail. The Colorado Cannabis Ball. He'd skipped the event last year. He should probably go this year. It was a great way to make contacts and talk to others in the business.

He dug out his phone and called Amahle. As soon as she answered, he said, "I need a date for the Cannabis Ball."

"Hello to you, too," Amahle said. "How did last night go? Did you have fun?"

"I was home by eleven. It's black tie."

"AM?"

"PM." He should have waited to call Amahle until he had devised canned answers regarding last night.

"It didn't start until ten. What did you do in that amount of time to cause her to send you packing?"

"It doesn't matter." No way in hell was he telling Amahle he'd gotten Luna high and she'd wanted him to kiss her.

"Oh, but I think it does matter."

He glanced toward Luna's place. "Can you give me the accountant's name and number you tried to fix me up with last fall?"

"Johnny, Mitch wants the accountant's name and number so he can ask her to attend the weed shindig with him," Amahle yelled.

Johnny's muffled voice vibrated in Mitch's ear, but nothing was distinct.

"I'm sorry. Johnny said if you can't remember her name, you don't deserve her number."

Since when did Johnny have scruples? "Her name wasn't important until now."

"I agree with Johnny. If you didn't commit her name to that freakish elephant brain of yours, she's not the right person for you to take to the shindig. You need to go with someone who will charm you and, at the same time, charm your cohorts."

Amahle liked to make fun of his brain power, but it had been his freakish brain that had helped him ace the GED and earn a full ride college scholarship despite his lack of a high school diploma. Mom had *homeschooled* him more than she'd ever enrolled him in actual schools. "Then why don't you attend with me? You have a great knack for small talk." According to Amahle, he had a habit of swooping into what she called boring tirades.

She sighed. The same sigh that was usually accompanied with a kick to his shins if he was within striking distance. "My answer is no, and before you ask why, it's because I'm married, and I'm busy."

"I haven't given you the date."

"I can't be your crutch forever. It's time to fly, little bird. Why don't you ask Luna?"

He started to say no, but Luna was a lot like Amahle in her ability to make small talk. Perhaps she wouldn't be an awful choice. And he'd remembered her name from the moment she introduced herself. "I don't know."

"Because you have so many options?"

"If I ask Luna, it'll feel like I'm using her."

"Then don't use her. Find out what she wants and trade services."

"That's not an immoral idea." Then again, he could just man up, fill out the dating app, and hope to get a date between now and then. "See you around." He hung up before Amahle responded.

If he had to choose between taking a stranger to the ball or taking Luna, he'd choose his weird goat-walking, outdoor nudist yoga sexy neighbor next door, who he was 100% not interested in.

What could go wrong?

 7

Luna stood in the open doorway off Mitch's deck that gave her a clear view of his kitchen, holding her nose to block off the offensive smell of grilled meat as she watched him pour sautéed mushrooms over a steak. As of yet, he was unaware of being scrutinized.

"Sorry to bother you," she said in a nasally tone. "I was hoping I could borrow a stick of butter." Which was true. She did want to borrow butter—a request which implied she had none at home. Not as true. But the request gave her a reason to stop by and see him.

He set a cast iron skillet on a potholder—the very pan he'd outbid her on at the auction. She was sure he'd done so out of spite—and turned to study her. When their gazes finally connected, his pupils looked a tad dilated.

She glanced down at her overalls. Damn. She'd forgotten to put a shirt on over her sports bra. The guy was going to think her a serial tease.

"So, it's butter you're after. Not a kiss?"

She released her nose. "I know how to take no for an answer." How pathetic to stand in a guy's doorway, lying to him out of utter loneliness.

"Why were you holding your nose?"

"I'm a vegetarian. To me, the stench of meat grilling is the same as the stench of trash day in August in Manhattan following a month-long sanitation worker's strike." Sort of true. She didn't like the smell but of course had learned to live with it.

A burst of unexpected laughter left his lips, and she jumped in surprise. "How did a vegetarian from Manhattan end up in Colorado? Isn't there some type of law against that?"

She hadn't meant to tell anyone in Rocky Mountain Springs where she'd last lived. The less they knew about her, the smaller the opportunity they'd uncover her darker secrets. Like Luna 2.0's true identity. This was what happened when you lied about why you stopped in to see someone. Your brain was so busy keeping the lie believable it didn't guard against other things coming out of your mouth. She shrugged. "The law says a Manhattan vegetarian can't marry a Coloradan carnivore. But it doesn't make it illegal for me to live here."

"I see." His lips twitched as if he got her humor and didn't find it dull.

Which caused her insides to tap out a little happy dance.

"Let me get you that butter," he said. "Salted or non?"

"Salted."

He walked to the refrigerator, tugged a paper out of his pocket, frowned at it, and stuck it there with a magnet in the shape of a cannabis plant.

What about the paper had caused him to frown? It looked to be some type of invite. Was there to be a big party in town and she wasn't on the guest list and that bothered him? The thought kicked her in the soft part of her pride.

He retrieved a stick of butter and handed it to her. "Is the smell so bad I can't talk you into staying and having a glass of wine while I eat?"

For a Manhattan second, she froze. Had she heard right? An invite to stay from the guy who'd ditched her on multiple occasions? Smelly or not, the answer was easy. Of course, she'd deliver the response without all the emotional sauce. She did have her pride. "It would be rude of me to borrow butter and then not stay when invited."

"Red or white?" He strolled to another corner of the room and glanced back at her.

"Red." She took the opportunity to zip over to his refrigerator, swipe the invitation, and quickly peruse it. Her intent was to stick it back on the door before he even noticed.

He turned toward her, saw the invitation in her hand, and again frowned. Obviously not a big fan of snoops.

An apology for being nosy would be insincere, so she didn't offer one. It was an invitation to some sort of ball for those in the weed trade. "Are you going?"

"If I can get an appropriate date."

She put the invitation back where she'd found it and took a glass of wine from him. "Speaking of dates, have you filled out the Get Hitched app yet? Were my instructions clear enough?"

"I got as far as downloading the app." He picked up his dinner plate and stuck it in the oven. "Shall we sit out on the deck? I can eat later."

She nodded and led the way. She took a seat in an old-fashioned yellow iron chair, expecting him to plop down in the matching one next to it. He didn't. Instead, he sat as far from her as he could. "Then you haven't answered the questionnaire portion?" she asked.

"Not yet. By the way, thank you for returning my items and the muffin."

She grinned and waited for him to follow the thank you up with a brag about the muffin. She'd refrained from trying one herself. As much as she'd been baking lately, if she tried one of everything, she'd outgrow all her clothes and purchasing new ones would be a frivolous use of her dwindling funds. But she had no doubt it would be tasty because she'd found the recipe on Pinterest and it was her understanding they didn't allow substandard recipes to be pinned.

He didn't do a follow-up brag.

"You're welcome," she said a half-beat later than she should have. Did he not like her cooking? Damn. She should have done a taste test. "I left a basket of them for the mayor on his front porch. I'm hoping to get on his good side."

Mitch's jaw tightened ever so slightly. "That was nice of you, but I wouldn't get my hopes up. He doesn't trust newbies. It takes him a while to warm up to anyone."

She shrugged. "That's his loss. I'm a delight when you get to know me. Give me your phone, and I'll help you fill out the questions."

"I'm capable of tapping in my own answers."

"Yes, but will you? If you're wanting a plus-one for your industry event, time is of the essence."

"Why do you say *event* like it's a dirty word?"

Because she'd been to plenty in her lifetime. They were always boring unless someone came along to liven the shit up. Which was what the old version of herself had loved to do. Mother had called it a character flaw she needed to erase. Luna 2.0 planned to fully embrace that side of herself at all parties in the future. "Look at how I'm dressed. Of course I'm going to find something one has to get gussied up for tedious." *Gussied* had been a word Nanny Nonna loved to use when she was alive. As a result, Luna tried to sprinkle it into her own conversations. She missed her old nanny. They'd stayed in contact even after Luna no longer required a glorified babysitter. Now that Nonna was dead, they stayed in contact via Luna's dreams, but it just wasn't the same.

Much to Luna's delight, Mitch pulled his phone out of his shirt pocket, unlocked it, and handed it to her. "Here. Knock yourself out."

She took his phone. "First things first, I know why I'm on a dating app—I'm new and don't know anyone—but why do you need a dating app?" She pulled up Get Hitched and read through the questions while he sat quietly. "I would think you had a whole string of women waiting to be asked out by you."

"After my engagement ended badly, I decided to take time off and regroup," he said. "According to my former fiancée, I'm not good at relationships."

Having one of those herself, she knew by experience it wasn't something one liked to talk about, so she resisted an urge to inquire into the gritty details. "And is she right?"

For a very long time, Luna had blamed her parents for her own failed engagement. *Long* being a relative term. Two months. She'd broken off the engagement right before disappearing. If it hadn't been for her parents pushing for her to get betrothed to Darren as a way of salvaging her reputation after the felony incident—an incident they had caused—she would have never agreed to marry him in the first place. And crushed him in the second place.

But Luna 2.0 had come to the conclusion her parents couldn't make her do anything she didn't want to do. Therefore, it wasn't their fault. She'd willingly said yes to Darren's proposal in hopes of taking a shortcut to getting her reputation back. A completely selfish act that hadn't even worked. If anything, it had made things worse. Thus, the change of name when she'd moved to Colorado. It was hard to start over if your demons followed you. She gave Mitch an encouraging smile who'd yet to respond. "Are you bad at relationships?" she prompted.

"Let's just say, she wasn't entirely wrong. Amahle's been helping me smooth out some of my rougher boyfriend edges."

Weird on so many levels. "I would think Johnny would prefer you got someone other than his wife to teach you dating stuff." Funny. They both felt a need to fix themselves.

"You're probably right. But I do give him a massive discount at my shop as a way of saying thank you."

"Why not simply show up to the ball stag? Instead of rushing to find a date?"

"The last time I went, I was there with my fiancée. She was well received by my cohorts because they viewed her as way out-of-my-league, and they all wanted to know my secret. As you can imagine, there will be questions and awkward responses from me as to what I did to screw it up."

"And did you screw it up?" Luna was familiar with the out-of-your-league conversation men had when someone was dating someone hot. She used to like the idea of a guy viewing her as out of his league, but hearing Mitch say it made her sad. Any woman would be lucky to have him as their fiancé. Probably.

He shrugged. "Officially, yes. Unofficially, no."

Luna 1.0 told her to pry the hell out of that statement. Luna 2.0 told her to read his body language and be respectful. "Why go at all?"

"Because networking in this industry is important. We have stringent rules and regulations that aren't the same as they are for everyone else. And not just at the state level but also the local level. Hell, locally, they go so far as to say licenses can be revoked if one's character becomes tarnished."

"You're kidding!" She couldn't even wrap her brain around how they'd regulate such.

"I wish. I must maintain a reputation without repute. If I screw that up, the consequences will be far greater than a slap on the wrist or a fine."

She took a sip of her wine. "Why is the industry so hardnosed?"

"Weed is illegal in many states which makes the regulating of it in legal states wonky. And when things get wonky, politicians go into cover-my-ass mode. I could tell you the exact details of it, but a beautiful woman like you would find them boring."

The comment hit a nerve. "I'll have you know, jackass, I'm quite capable of carrying on a real conversation without getting bored."

His right ear turned red. "I called you beautiful. Take the compliment."

She reminded herself Luna 2.0 didn't label people with expletives. "I'm sorry I called you a jackass." Time to get back to the dating app. "What three words describe your perfect mate?"

He stretched his legs out in front of him. "Let's see. Low maintenance. High visibility. Patient."

"Low maintenance?"

He tugged at his ear. "My ex came from money. A lot of money. Experience tells me those kinds of women are high maintenance. I don't want that or need that in my life. I relate better to women who get excited when a man brings her a flower he found growing on the side of the road. Not a bouquet of imported roses from an exclusive boutique in Italy."

"Got it." Now might be a good time to mention she came from money. That her parents were well known in Manhattan socialite circles. How would he react? Would he see that as further reason to not want to even be friends? Then again, she wasn't her parents. She wasn't even Luna 1.0 anymore. Luna 2.0 shopped the Dollar Spot at Target and liked wildflowers. She had nothing to mention.

"Turn-offs?" she asked, after typing in his answers.

"Brashness. Rudeness. High heels."

Well...hell. She loved her high heels. It had gutted her to leave them behind. But she'd done so as a test of her resolve to be a new person. Now that she'd gotten use to her Chacos and Birkenstocks, she was beginning to love them almost as much as her Brother Vellies. The sandals were crazy comfortable, if not sexy. Luckily, Luna 2.0 wasn't worried about being sensational. Just real. "Superpowers?"

He set his wine glass down. "It does not ask about superpowers."

She fluttered her lashes. Her real lashes. Long gone were her fake ones that she used to have reapplied every two weeks. Once upon a time, she'd had a lash lady, a nail lady, and a hair lady. Now, she had none of those ladies in her life. "It does." She turned the phone around to show him and held it at an angle where he couldn't actually read it. "See."

"I don't have any superpowers."

"I thought kissing was your superpower?" She really should drop it, but why? Ever since he'd mentioned it on the dance floor, she hadn't been able to stop thinking about it.

"It is, but I don't want you to put that on the application."

"Why? Women will go bonkers wanting to date someone with smooching as a superpower. I mean, I'm not even attracted to you in that way, but I would one-click to get the chance to kiss you and find out if you're all that and a Gucci Bag."

"You're not attracted to me in what way?"

"As a lover?"

He sat back in his chair and scratched his head. "Not that I want anything more than friend-zone status, but I'm curious as to why you've placed me there."

"My gut tells me that under your prickly outer shell lives a nice, chill guy. I like guys who don't need to grow thorns around their hearts because their hearts are legit black and won't be bruised if I love them and leave them. Which...is my norm." Granted, she was trying to change but some character traits were harder to rid yourself of than others.

His brows furrowed. "Interesting. Tell me, if I do something so scandalously nice as to offer to help you make friends with the locals, would that firmly place me in the friend zone with you?"

A teeny-tiny part of her was insulted he appeared to love the idea of never being anything more than her friend. Of course, that teeny-tiny part was completely irrational. "It would indeed. A guy with a dead heart would never offer something quite so nice. Are you offering a friendship?"

He stood and walked to the railing where he looked out over his crops. "The thought is growing on me. After all, for better or worse, we are neighbors."

She tried not to smile and give away just how happy the thought of having a friend in this town made her. "Shall we get back to the questionnaire? You do have a date to find, and I need to get back to my goats. It's their dinner time."

"Why not?" He drained his wine. "I'll need someone who isn't afraid to interrupt me when I fall down a boring conversation rabbit hole."

"Excuse me?"

"I tend to go off on tangents. Amahle kicks me when I do that. It would be nice to date a woman who's not afraid to push in and change the subject when I'm waxing poetic over mind-numbing shit. That's why I listed patience as a quality I'm looking for in a woman."

So that's why he would occasionally grunt for no reason. It was because of a well-placed kick, not a tic. "I find you utterly okay as is, but if that's what you want in a woman, we'll find a way to mention that on your questionnaire. But again, I personally find your conversational abilities...intriguing."

His jaw tensed. "So did my fiancée until she didn't."

"She sounds like a real drag." And she sounded way too much like Luna 1.0, who had indeed been anything but a breath of fresh air. "Does she live around here?" Was she a local? Had they met?

"She's no longer local, and I don't wish to discuss her any further." Mitch turned and gave her his full attention. "Let's circle back to the idea of us being friends."

Luna did her best not to fidget as his gaze bored into hers. "If you're only offering because you feel sorry for me, I'm not interested in being friends. I'm in the market for authentic bonds." She was glad he didn't want to talk about his ex, because that would have meant she should mention hers, and she wasn't ready to go there.

He studied her. "I'm not easily guilted into doing something I don't want to do. If I offer to be your friend, you can trust the offer is authentic."

"Authentic real friends or authentic fake friends?" She twirled strands of her hair as she nervously awaited his response. Back in the day, she'd had a dozen or more authentic fake friends. As in they played the part when they were around each other, and then gossiped about each other when they were apart.

He stabbed his fingers through his thick, black hair, leaving it topsy-turvy on top. "I'm too old to get tangled up in fake anything. Real is all I can offer."

She beamed at him. "In that case, I'm all on board with the idea of us pursuing a friendship. If for no other reason, as you said, than because we are neighbors."

He stood. "You should know—if you ever lie to me, our friendship will end. That's a hard rule for me."

She stood and held out his butter to him. "In that case, you should know I didn't really need to borrow butter. I came over because I was lonely. And there will be times I won't lie to you, but I might omit things."

He frowned. "Why would you omit things?"

"Because I feel we are all entitled to our secrets and are under no obligation to share them until we are ready."

For a hot second, she thought he might pull back his offer. Like maybe her terms were beyond unacceptable. Like maybe in normal friendships, people always told each other the truth. They'd never dream of allowing you to show up to a party wearing two shoes that didn't match. Or have knowledge your guy was cheating on you and fail to mention it when you say you think he might be.

But that's not what happened. Instead, Mitch nodded sharply. "I can live with those terms."

And just like that, Luna suddenly wanted to know his secrets. The ones that made her terms reasonable. Because she'd bet her last package of 24K Gold eye mask that it was a secret that had him agreeing.

8

Monday morning, Luna twirled drunken-ballerina style in the rays of sunshine streaming through her kitchen window. Excitement, an emotion she hadn't experienced in a very long time, did a matching pirouette inside her belly. Things were looking up. In the past forty-eight hours, not only had she made a friend in Mitch, she'd also booked her first goat yoga event.

An out-of-state bachelorette party for seven had retained Luna's Goat Yoga for one afternoon of their festivities. According to their assistant, the bride-to-be had discovered Luna via her Instagram account.

Luna came to a dizzying stop and then shuffled through the papers on the counter in search of her planner. If there was one thing she'd learned in college, it was to add all due dates to the handy device, because her brain weirdly rebelled at having to remember dates, times, or the middle names of her former boyfriends. Not that middle names really mattered, unless you're trying on new names for yourself, but it was, nevertheless, a weird brain defect.

I should buy a new planner just for my business engagements.

A girl could never have too many planners. Especially when prone, as of late, to losing them. Having grown up with a housekeeper who picked up after her, Luna 2.0 had discovered it somewhat of a challenge to learn how to keep track of her own things. And how to do laundry. And how to cook her own meals. But she was making progress. She now knew how to create a basic budget. And it felt good. Really good.

Not finding her third planner in a month, she wrote the date on a sticky note—she'd discovered a pad of them in the Dollar Spot at Target—put a cute sticker of a girl in downward dog pose on it, and then stuck the note to her refrigerator.

Her phone rang. For a whole second, she simply stared at it in awe. It had to be another booking. She was doing this. Really doing it. Luna 2.0 was making her own way in the world. A way that didn't include her parents' money. *Or anything she'd learned in college.* But that couldn't be helped.

Some would say her new course was nothing more than her cutting off her nose to spite her face, but she had her reasons for traveling this path.

The phone shrilled a second time and she quickly answered. "Luna's Goat Yoga. How may I help you?"

"It's time you gave up this utter nonsense of living in Colorado and teaching goat yoga." Mother managed to make the words *goat* and *yoga* sound like curse words.

"Hello to you, too." Luna refused to let Mother ruin her perfectly superb day.

"And come home," Mother said, as if Luna hadn't yet spoken.

Two could play the ignore-what-the-other-just-said game. "I take it you and Father are doing well. You survived your guilt-trip trip to Colorado? Did you buy some good weed from Mitch at Rocky Mountain High?" She'd meant to ask him at her under-the-stars sleepover if a group of stuffy lawyers had descended upon his shop. She'd sent them there in the hopes of garnering some good will with him.

That had been before he'd said he'd be her friend.

"You say his name like he's a somebody. He's not. The man is nothing more than a glorified drug dealer."

Mother had an unattractive habit of looking down her enhanced nose at the working-class stiffs of the world. This included anyone not bringing in at least six figures a month. "He's my friend," Luna snapped. "I'd appreciate it if you refrained from saying negative things about him."

A tiny gasp came through the phone. "Do you not realize what you just said?"

"I said I have a friend."

"He's a drug dealer."

"Next subject."

"But—"

"I'm serious." Luna had learned long ago it was a waste of time to try and argue with Mother that the worth of a person did not rest in his bank account balance. Or stock market portfolio. Or family tree. Luna regretted that she had been, for a short time of her life, similar in her thought process. It had taken being arrested and sitting in a jail cell until getting out on bail to clear her brain.

Mother sighed loudly. "Fine. I'm much more interested in your coming to your senses and returning home."

Luna blew out a silent scream. "This is my home. I like it. And I like teaching yoga. And I like the new me." Which was mostly true. Sometimes, though, the new her scared the crap out of her when she glanced in the mirror and saw a face that hadn't had a proper facial in ages.

"Love, what is there possibly to like about the new you?"

The question cut through Luna. She bit her lip to keep tears at bay. Ruining perfectly good mascara over Mother's thoughtless comment would be a waste of hard-earned money. In the grand scheme of things, Mother's opinion of Luna 2.0 didn't matter. "The new me is free of worries about what others think, and friends who aren't really friends." Mitch had chosen to be her friend not knowing her parents were filthy rich. He might just be the first friend she'd ever made where that was the case. The problem with friends who liked you because you had money is they didn't support you when things went sideways.

Mother made a scoffing noise. "Have you made any money?"

Her parents didn't know she'd been the beneficiary of Nanny Nonna's life insurance. They thought freezing her monthly allowance had her in the palm of their hand. "I just booked my first event. One thousand dollars for two hours. Not bad." Just a teensy bit of an exaggeration.

"Love, you're lucky Darren is willing to take you back. You destroyed the young man's self-esteem when you tossed him to the curb like yesterday's trash."

Darren was the parent-approved minion who'd done her parents' bidding and asked for her hand in marriage. When she'd discovered the true motivation behind his proposal, she'd broken things off. She'd been appalled when he'd come with them to Colorado to re-propose.

"He should be on the hunt for a woman who loves him." The only reason he'd proposed the first time was due to an over-the-top, modern-day dowry. She couldn't even imagine what they'd offered him to get him to propose again. Probably partnership in her father's practice. "He deserves someone who gets wet when she looks at him."

"Don't be crass. It's not ladylike."

The reprimand stung. While Luna had been close to Father growing up, her relationship with Mother had been a mixed bag of emotions. Mostly Mother preferred not to be reminded she had a daughter. Luna was a walking, talking memento of Mother's lost youth. Hell, she was probably secretly happy Luna had taken on a new identity. One that couldn't be linked to Mother as a reminder she wasn't as young as she'd like everyone to believe. Luna 1.0 would never show up on social media as any older than twenty-four, because Luna 1.0 had ceased to exist the day before her twenty-fifth birthday. "Mother—"

"I know you don't mind cutting me to the core with your juvenile grudge, but I can't believe you insist on continuing to punish your father in this way. We only did what was in your best interest."

Luna rolled her eyes. *Liar. Liar. Gucci pantsuit on fire.* Setting your daughter up to be the scapegoat—should it come to *that*—in a felony was not parent-of-the-year material. And, of course, it had come to *that*.

And when it had, dear old Mother and Father had had the audacity to ask her to trust them. They had a plan. A plan that would fix everything. A plan that involved a slick lawyer armed with a loophole defense.

A simple *I'm sorry* was all she had really wanted or needed from them after she'd been released on bail. Had they done that, she might have followed their instructions on how to beat the legal system.

"If there's nothing else, I should go. I have work to do."

"Your father wishes to discuss this with you in private. He'll send the jet to pick you up tomorrow morning. I know you don't mind letting me down, but you don't want to disappoint him."

"Actually, I no longer have a problem letting either of you down." Luna waited for a wave of guilt to smack her off balance. It didn't. Progress.

"I'm reluctant to tell you this." Mother sounded anything but reluctant. "But if you don't come home, your father and I have no choice but to cut you out of our will." A strident ring of triumph flavored her words whiskey sour.

Luna laughed. Not too long ago, that would have scared her spine right out of her back. She'd been raised to believe one needed lots and lots and lots of money to be happy. Not just a little money. A shit-ton of money. And a respectable husband. One with memberships to the best country clubs. Like Darren. "Did you know there are a gazillion stars in the sky?"

"The new will is drawn up." Mother's tone continued to spew black-hearted determination. "It's ready for our signatures."

A ripple of anxiety caused Luna's knees to wobble. But then, because her spine hadn't bailed on her, she straightened and continued down her own conversational path. "And you can see them all every night in Colorado?"

"According to your father—"

"And no one in Rocky Mountain Springs cares I'm wearing last year's labels." Sure, her inheritance from Nanny Nonna had allowed her to buy this place and become someone else, but it would be hard work that allowed her to continue. After all, Nanny Nonna hadn't been rich. She'd just had a nice life insurance policy.

"—if you're not back by the end of June, we will sign the will and disown you."

"And sitting under a tree and reading, while smoking a joint, is so much more fun than clubbing until three in the morning and drinking the latest cocktail concoction."

"If you don't meet with your father, all of your credit cards will be cancelled."

Triumph lifted Luna's lips. It wasn't often she got to one-up her parents. "Actually, I've already cut up my credit cards." Who would have ever thought saying those words would feel rich?

"Then how in the world are you paying your bills? You do know I can access your credit card statements and verify if what you're saying is true?"

"Go ahead. Verify."

"If you're not paying with your credit cards, where are you getting the money? Your father said you have a measly amount in your checking."

Luna didn't even bother to ask how they knew about her new checking account or its balance. Rich people could do a lot of things that poor people couldn't even imagine. Like circumventing the law and getting access to someone's finances. They'd probably bribed a poor teller. Or threatened his family with a frivolous lawsuit. Thankfully, she hadn't put all her money in that account.

"My finances are no longer any of your concern." Luna wasn't sure why she didn't want them to know about the insurance money, but she didn't. Maybe part of her feared they'd be able to pull strings and undo Nanny Nonna's listing of Luna as the beneficiary. Contest it somehow.

"Please tell me you're not funding your rebellion from a local loan shark?"

Luna's phone beeped. Another call. Possibly a customer. "I have to go. I'm running a business. I can't have my phone tied up with nonessential conversations."

"Then you'll get on the jet and come home?"

"I will not."

"Honey, your father's not going to like—"

"Goodbye." Luna would, and she could, make a success of this venture. She might not have a college diploma, but she did have ninety-nine percent of a college education toward a degree in Art History.

A degree not at all helpful when running a business. Which was just fine with her. She had a whole list of people to prove wrong about herself. A list including those at the university who had decided not to grant her a diploma after her arrest. The momentous event had happened during final's week, and she'd not been allowed to complete her finals. She needed to prove to them and her parents she had what it took to succeed in life without their stamp of approval.

"Hello, Luna's Goat Yoga. How may I help you?"

"I've been thinking about my implied contractual duties as your one and only friend in town," Mitch said.

She smiled. She had no idea what he was talking about, but his quirky personality was refreshing. "Implied contractual duties?"

"To make it official, we need to be seen together in public." Mitch's voice was so much more pleasant to listen to than the painful ring of Mother's. And kind of sexy over the phone.

Luna dropped into a chair. She'd never viewed a friendship as a contract. That fact that he did charmed the hell out of her. "What did you have in mind?" It would appear she finally had a real friend. The only string attached was that they must be honest with one another, which was barely a string at all. The most important thing was he didn't want her money or her body or her connections. Not that she had the first or last anymore.

"Dinner in Colorado Springs," he said.

Why Colorado Springs for dinner and not some place in Rocky Mountain Springs where there were people she wanted to like her? "That sounds like a clandestine-lover's date."

"It's a generic date between friends. You're not now nor ever will be my girlfriend. Acknowledged or otherwise."

She rolled her eyes. The guy did not understand her brand of humor. They would have to work on that. "Agreed. And since we agree, I propose we stop calling it a date, and instead refer to it as a meetup."

"I have no problem with that tweak. It will be a meetup between friends. But I'll pay."

"Only if I pay the next time."

He made a scoffing sound. "I believe in the custom that a man should open doors for a woman, and pay for meals, and publicly come to her defense no matter her culpability in a situation."

Luna's belly did a weird twisty thing. It could be their conversation that caused the internal commotion...or it could be because the last time she'd heard the word culpability in a sentence, she'd been under arrest. "So, you're not only a stickler about rules but also customs?" The idea of a man who held fast to behaving as an old-fashioned gentleman intrigued a quiet spot in her soul. A quiet spot she wasn't sure had existed in the soul of Luna 1.0. She quite liked Luna 2.0.

"Are you free Wednesday evening?"

Probably she should argue, but the desire wasn't there, and she wasn't going to force it. "I can rearrange my calendar." There was no harm in allowing him to be chivalrous.

"Excellent."

A thought struck her. An impractical, probably bad thought that resulted in a flicker of hope in her brain. "Just so I'm clear on what to expect on this outing, there's also a custom of kissing your date goodbye at the end of the evening. Is that something I should be prepared for at the end of this meetup?" She wished he'd never brought up his kissing abilities. Now it was like she couldn't get it out of her head.

"There will be no kiss." Just in case she didn't understand his words, he'd paired them with a tremendously tense tone.

Well, hell. "Excellent."

9

The Not Quite Sunrise Yoga class was halfway through its one-hour session. "Move into plank," Luna directed.

"Anyone have any fun plans for tonight?" Abby asked. She lived in Black Forest, a town that connected to Rocky Mountain Springs. She had been one of the first to attend Luna's early morning class. Happily, every time Abby came to class, she brought a new friend.

Today's new friend was a leopard-print-Speedo-wearing, pot-bellied man who sweated like a bullet-riddled hot tub. He said, "Darling, you're absolutely vicious to bring up the topic. You know I have nothing on my agenda for yet another night. Someone please tell me you do so I can live vicariously through you."

Luna grinned at the amount of drama one could put in their tone while planking. "I have a date with Mitch Johnson." Why had she gone and called it a date?

"You have a date with Mitch Johnson? *The* Mitch Johnson? The man who..." Abby trailed off.

Luna glanced her direction.

"Honey, you simply can't start to say something and not finish," squealed Speedo.

"Let's go into child pose."

Luna glanced up and watched as fifteen ladies and Speedo slid into position. Unfortunately, none of them resided in Rocky Mountain Springs. They'd all joined when she had run a flash sale. Three months for the price of one.

"Abby, you're killing us with the suspense," someone said.

"Forget I said anything," Abby replied, her voice muffled.

Luna stayed silent. If she tried to explain it wasn't a date but a meetup, that would require more details about her and Mitch. Details he'd probably prefer she didn't share.

"Oh, no. No. No. No," Speedo said. "It's simply savage of you to even pretend you expect us to forget."

God, it was nice to engage in girl talk. Out of all the things Luna missed about her old life, idle chitter-chatter ranked close to the top.

"Fine. Mitch Johnson used to be my best friend's fiancé."

The group sat up and stared at Abby.

Get out of here. No way. "You're kidding, right?" Luna held her breath and waited for a got-you laugh.

"Emphasis on used to be. Truly, I—"

"Used to be," Speedo interrupted. "Do serve this delicious scandal dish up with a side of titillation."

"Move into cat pose," Luna directed. "And let's leave Abby at peace." She recalled the brief conversation she and Mitch had had about him having a former fiancée.

"Peace! There will be no peace until we learn if you should go out with the dastardly Mitch Johnson." Speedo spoke in a tone of bravado like a knight who'd just pulled his sword and was preparing to duel.

His concern touched Luna. It had been a while since she'd felt genuine worry from anyone. Then again, Luna 2.0 didn't gossip. It was number three on her list of things Luna 1.0 had given up. "Class, you'll have to wait and get the info when I'm not around."

"What?" several students echoed.

"Oh, someone call a cute paramedic," Speedo said, "I'm dying of dismay."

Luna ignored Speedo's theatrics. "Mitch has a right to his privacy." She used her no-nonsense tone.

Could that be why he had wanted to go to Colorado Springs for their get-to-know-my-new-friend meetup? Had he purposefully chosen a location where the two of them could talk without worry of being overheard by the locals? Where he could privately reveal the details about his failed engagement?

Luna guided them into several additional moves before the class ended.

"Namaste," they all said.

"You'd like her." Abby said as she rolled her mat and stuck it into its black sleeve. Luna provided mats for everyone, but most brought their own.

Curiosity tickled the back of Luna's throat.

"I'm going to need specifics," Speedo demanded, stuffing his hot pink mat into a bag.

"She's super smart," Abby said. "Gorgeous. Driven. Sooooo driven. She's not one to ever settle for second place."

"I'm sure she's fabulous." Luna blew out the candles. "I don't get the impression he gives his heart easily." Or his friendship. She promised herself she wouldn't give him a reason to regret becoming her friend. Which meant not discussing his business with strangers. "I hope to see you all back tomorrow morning."

"If we can't talk about her, let's talk about this Mitch guy. Is he cute?" The question came from another of Abby's recruits, a freshman at the University of Colorado, and was directed at Luna.

All their gazes landed on Luna. "I think he's cute. But not in a bad boy way. More of a romantic comedy hero way. You know, the one who goes up against the hunky bad boy that the heroine has the hots for, and as a movie watcher you want the nice guy to win." Or at least that's how she found herself feeling lately.

"Oh, hell, I love cinnamon roll guys," College Freshman said.

"A what guy?" Luna glanced at her watch. Her next class was a goat yoga session. She really needed to walk her goats before it got started.

"A cinnamon roll guy," College Freshman replied. "Those that are sweet and nice as opposed to macho and broody. They're all the rage in romances at the moment. I'm learning about them in the creative writing class I'm taking."

Interesting. Mitch, initial prickliness aside, wasn't macho or broody—did that make him a cinnamon roll guy? If Mitch was indeed a cinnamon roll, it was just one more reason it was best they remained just friends.

When it came to all future boyfriends, she needed a guy who could handle Luna 1.0 on the off chance she sneaked out to play without Luna 2.0's permission. Luna 1.0 walked all over nice guys.

"Will you tell us all about your date tomorrow morning?" Abby asked. "I promise not to mention it to his ex."

"I'll tell you if our spending time together was fun or dull, but not the details," Luna said. "And I wouldn't dream of asking you to keep secrets from your best friend." If Luna ever had one again, she definitely wanted to be free to tell her—or him—everything going on in her new life.

"I demand you promise to at least tell us if he told you about his ex," Speedo said.

"I'll take your demand under consideration." She should really decide how much of her past to tell Mitch and how much to omit. No way would she tell him her whole truth, but if she did, she couldn't help but wonder how he would react. Her whole truth had a lot of ugly in it. Would he judge her? Of course he would. If the stiletto were on the other foot, she'd judge.

It was a good thing the only person she would ever unpack her skeletons for would be the love of her life. A guy who wouldn't judge.

But she'd do well to remember those skeletons alone were reason enough for her to not pursue anything more than friends with Mitch. Without a doubt, he'd find her past a love-relationship deal breaker.

10

Mitch's greenhouse was his brain's haven. Creating new hybrids while listening to classic rock never failed to take the snarls out of his thoughts. Today's knotted thoughts, though, kept resurfacing all tangled and messy. How would tonight's dinner with Luna turn out?

"Just...as Amahle predicted." Johnny's show-host voice startled Mitch out of his musings. Johnny wore a shirt advertising Mitch's shop. On the front were the words *Where Happiness Can Be Bought*. On the back, *Rocky Mountain High*.

Mitch flipped him off. "What did she predict?" He stood and brushed the dirt off his pants.

"That you'd be hiding in your playhouse and avoiding the fact it's time for you to go inside and get ready for your date."

Jesus. Was he late? Had he gotten distracted? Mitch quickly glanced at his watch then glared at Johnny. "I have three fucking hours before I pick up Bad Luck Luna." He frowned. He had to stop calling her that. "Besides, it's not a date—just friends having dinner."

"That's what I told Amahle, but she insisted I come this very fucking moment and remind you about your plans."

Mitch grabbed a towel off the bench and wiped his brow. With all the lights beaming down on plants and the moisture from watering, the space doubled as a steam bath. "I'm not likely to forget." He muttered the thought under his breath. Johnny's chuckle said he had heard.

Johnny picked up a newly repotted Chronic and smelled the leaves. "Says the man who forgot to show up to the church on his wedding day."

"Asshole." Mitch tried to sound annoyed and failed. It was his fault he'd done and said nothing to clear his name. "Screw up one wedding and suddenly it defines your whole life," he joked. There were some truths, no matter how much you wished otherwise, only others could bring to the light of day. That was one of them. Luna got it. Her omission caveat to his rule of friendship had shifted his opinion of her. In a good way. It had also left him obsessing over what untellable secret she held. And why was it untellable? For him, his truth omission was simple. If he told the facts, he'd paint someone else as a liar. The gentleman in him couldn't go there. Was Luna's reason altruistic or self-centered.

"As it should." Johnny pulled out his phone and pushed a button. It was on speaker, so Mitch heard the ringing.

"What took you so long?" Amahle sounded like Johnny had called to update her on the condition of a loved one undergoing life-saving surgery in a two-bit hospital.

"Hey gorgeous," Johnny drawled. "You were right. Found him in the greenhouse making love to his Chronic and gin. Want to talk to him?"

Mitch shook his head. "I don't—"

"Of course I want to talk to him," Amahle declared.

Johnny held the phone out to Mitch. "You heard her."

Mitch took the phone. "I'm not drinking gin, and I've got this."

"But do you?" Amahle asked. "Do you really?"

Mitch made eye contact with Johnny. Amahle's husband shrugged as if to say *leave me out of this.* "You do remember this isn't an actual date, right? I don't have to try and impress. If she doesn't like me or I don't like her, we'll reconsider our plan to become friends. No pressure. No weird first-date awkwardness." Definitely no first-date kiss.

"When did you become so glib about making a friend?" Amahle inquired sweetly. Too sweetly. "If I'm not mistaken, Johnny and I are the last ones you made an effort to become friends with. Other than Brandy, and that flopped."

Sweet my ass.

"So this is a big deal," Amahle continued. "Luna must have made an impression on you the other night for you to have taken the plunge and invited someone new into your life."

He hadn't invited her in. She'd crashed in unsolicited. "If you must know, I decided to pursue a friendship with her because it will do me good to have another female friend. Emphasis on *friend.* Someone—besides you—to help me navigate through the minefield of this Get Hitched dating app thing I'm now on."

"Ooh, any possibilities yet?" Amahle cooed.

"None." Or a ton. How in the hell was he supposed to know when he couldn't figure out how to work the damn app? "I'm handing the phone back to Johnny."

"Not yet. I have news."

"Front page news?" Mitch asked. "Or *Entertainment Weekly* news?" The first he'd listen to—the last was a waste of his life and the kind Amahle loved to terrorize him with.

"The kind one reads in *Cosmopolitan's* horoscopes," Amahle snapped.

"That's not news. That's garbage." Mom would have argued with him. Hell, that one summer when they'd lived by a library, she used to go every day of the week just so she could read her horoscope in the free newspaper.

Amahle harrumphed. "Do you want to know what it said?"

"Of course I don't want to know what it said. I would never encourage such a waste of one's intellectual abilities." Mitch disconnected and handed Johnny his phone.

"Fuckhead, you could have said *no, thank you.*" He slid the phone into the pocket of his shorts. "Women don't like when you make fun of their weirdness."

Amahle made fun of what she considered Mitch's weirdnesses all the time. His right ear's tendency to turn red. His freakish memory. His rule-following fetish. She shouldn't poke fun if she couldn't handle the throw back. "I'm sure she'll survive."

"I'm telling you, bro, you should call her back and let her read the horoscope to you. She read it to me, and it's loaded with potential."

Common sense told him not to ask. "What kind of potential?"

"The kind of potential men like to have where a beautiful woman is concerned."

Mitch turned back to a plant he'd been pruning. An exceptionally strong cannabis, which was why Johnny referred to it earlier by its slang term Chronic. "I'm not looking for that particular kind of potential with the town's newest resident." He and Luna were to be friends. That was what they'd agreed upon, and he wasn't the sort to go back on his word.

Therefore, they would not have sex. Would not fall in love. And for the love of a good high, would not get engaged. Been there, done that with his last neighbor, and it had ended as a clusterfuck.

Besides, he had a ball to attend, a business to expand, a life goal to realize, and an app that promised to set him up with women whose personalities were compatible with his own. Yoga nudists need not apply.

"Fine, but before I leave, are you still up for a day float on Sunday?" Johnny asked.

Mitch glanced back at him. "It's on my calendar." The last Sunday of every month, he closed shop. Floating down the Colorado River in kayaks with his best friends, all with coolers of beer attached to their boats, sounded like fun.

"Good. Good. One more thing."

"If you insist." Tomorrow, he'd set his repotted plants out on the deck so they could get some natural sunlight. Ever since discovering the soil from the Old Murphy Place was so much better than his own—something he'd discovered when Ms. Murphy had allowed him to plant on her land—and then figuring out how to replicate the pH of her dirt, his plants had been growing at twice the rate. He was constantly having to repot them.

He sighed. Just one more reason why he had wanted to buy the property. Original would always be best.

The sound of a goat's bleat off in the distance had him making a mental note to gate off his deck just in case Ms. Houdini came over for a visit. That damn goat was a pain in his ass.

"Amahle said to invite Luna," Johnny said. "She feels bad no one went to her sleepover."

"Or she wants us side by side when she grills us on how our evening went." Amahle was a romantic at heart. He didn't have to be a genius to know she had high hopes his and Luna's relationship would turn into something more. Which was crazy, because she of all people should understand why that was such a bad idea. She'd had a front row seat for how his life had tanked the last time he'd dated a neighbor.

"You're delusional, Fuckhead," Johnny said, "if you think she'll wait until Sunday to find out about your date. If I know my Amahle, she'll be on your doorstep when you come home. In fact, she'll invite Luna even if you don't, so don't bother putting up a fight. You'll lose."

11

Things *will appear grand but will end badly this evening.*

Like a dreadful movie trailer, Luna's horoscope looped in her thoughts as she walked slightly ahead of Mitch toward his red pickup truck, which sat prettily in the middle of her driveway.

His horoscope, on the other hand, had her struggling.

She knew his only because Amahle had mentioned it when she'd called earlier to invite Luna to a day of river floating.

Luna knew what her horoscope meant. Mitch would find her lacking in the qualities he required in a friend, and she would be disappointed.

But how would his come to pass?

Tonight, you will lose control of something you've been protecting.

What would he lose control of? If she had to guess, she'd say his patience. With her.

She wished she had no knowledge of either of their horoscopes. With knowledge came agitation. Starting with her second-guessing her decision on how to approach the evening.

Luna knew how to act on an average first date. Charming. Slightly uninterested. Mostly unimpressed. If at some point during the date she decided she would like a second date with the guy, she would toss in moments of unbridled enthusiasm.

She didn't feel bad about having first date rules. After all, men had their own.

Tonight, though, wasn't a normal first date. It was, to use Mitch's terms, an implied contractual date. An event meant to be a soft announcement to the world that they were friends. Soft because before making a loud announcement, they had to discover if they were friend compatible. Or at least, he had to decide if she qualified to be his friend. As far as she was concerned, she'd put up with anything for that tag.

She'd never in her life knowingly tried out for a spot on someone's friend list. It was terrifying because something told her if she didn't win him over, she'd never be accepted in Rocky Mountain Springs.

As far as she knew, there were no rules for this type of interaction. Other than be yourself. Ugh. Right now, she was a hot-mess mixture of Luna 1.0 and Luna 2.0. Sure, Luna 2.0 was trying to come out the victor, but, as with most things in life, success wasn't guaranteed. Hell, just this morning, she'd Googled Kate Spade and stared longingly at their latest collection of purses.

And after closing out of that site, she'd checked how much it would cost to have a maid come once a week and do all the gross things one had to do when they didn't have a maid. Like toilets. And trash. And cleaning the lint trap in the dryer. That thing gave her the heebie-jeebies.

Luna 2.0 wasn't the sort to waste time daydreaming of wealthy perks in her daily routine. That paragon would be totally Zen with chores because they gave one time to contemplate the important things in life. Like recycling. And mindfulness. And growing her own weed.

At some point tonight, Mitch would say, "Tell me about yourself," and she needed to have things to say. Truth be whispered, he pretty much knew everything she knew about Luna 2.0. The lady was a vegetarian yogi who loved nature and *Superman* movies. And liked to bake. And didn't gossip. End of story. Literally. End. Of. Story.

Luna was making Luna 2.0 up as she went. And it took time to reinvent yourself—that was, if you wanted to do it right. And she did. After all, she planned to live in her skin for the rest of time.

Which left her with her current dilemma. Did Mitch freaking need to know she was a work in progress? Was he a *one strike and you're toast* sort of friend?

She came to a stop in front of the truck and reached for the handle.

"Here, let me get that." Mitch opened the truck door. This after showing up with a bouquet of friendship wildflowers. So sweet.

"Thank you." She raised her long skirt in one hand and slipped into the seat as gracefully as she could manage.

She glanced down at her basic white T-shirt to check her bra straps weren't on display and rearranged her colorful skirt so its hem didn't touch the floor. Although the floorboard was pristine.

"You're welcome." He gently shut the door and strode around the truck, giving her a glimpse of his profile.

That jawline could sell sex to a nun. Luna hadn't lied when she told her Almost Sunrise Yoga Class he had the whole handsome-in-a-smart-guy-way thing going for him. Granted, his clothes could use a tweak. He totally played into the I'm-a-modern-geek-and-I-dress-like-one stereotype. Button up shirt, chinos, and cardigan sweater. Lucky for him, his ass actually looked cute in whatever he wore. Even pajamas. Okay, especially soft cotton pajamas.

She tore her gaze away from his ass and ran her hand over the smooth leather seat. White as snow. Mitch's truck was one of those vintage kinds you saw in Hallmark Christmas movies. All shiny and heartwarming.

Be still, my heart.

No, really, her heart needed to stop knocking around in her chest. She'd never make a good impression if she was all sweaty from nerves.

He started the truck and for three minutes said nothing as he drove slowly down the five-mile gravel road that led to the highway.

She searched for a conversation starter. Something that wouldn't cause her to stumble with half-truths. Nothing materialized. That had never happened to Luna 1.0 She'd just spout off shit about the stock market, or *Naked Runway*'s latest cover model, or the unfortunate outfit so-and-so had worn to the latest party.

Luna 2.0 had nerves tying her tongue and—gah—worry over making a good first impression twirling her insides. Oh God. Did he already think she sucked as a friend?

"Have you ever been to Big Slice?" He shifted the gears to go up a steep hill, drawing her attention to his hands.

He had nice hands. Not too small. Not too large. And his cuticles were well maintained.

Who emptied his lint traps?

"I haven't," she said. "Is it local?" Clean nails were on her must-have list when it came to boyfriends. If he asked, she'd mention clean nails as being one of her rules when it came to friendships.

"It's in Colorado Springs, but well worth the drive." He thrummed his fingers on the steering wheel.

She dragged her gaze away from his hands and stared out the window at the snow-capped mountain in the distance. Weird seeing snow in June on a seventy-degree day. And being in a truck with this guy. Who, by the way, smelled like an advertisement for seduction. Not from cologne, but the fresh musky smell of soap. "I have a couple of yoga clients who work in Colorado Springs. They love the town. Said it's *très* trendy."

"Do you wish you would've moved there instead of Rocky—" He slammed on the brakes.

The shift in motion sent her lurching toward the windshield despite her seatbelt.

Last minute like, his arm shot out to hold her in place. And his palm, fingers splayed wide, landed on her right breast.

"Oh." She gulped and waited for him to move his hand. He didn't. Like common trollops, her nipples hardened. And other parts of her body weren't any better behaved. They were all like FINALLY! It's *been ages.*

She doused her girly parts with a stern *false alarm* and then glanced around to see what had prompted the sudden stop. Nothing. Not even a road-crossing turtle. She smiled tightly. "You can let go of my boob now."

His hand didn't move. Instead, he eased off the break and pulled the truck over to the side of the road.

When it became obvious his brain hadn't registered his blooper, she began peeling his fingers one at a time off her breast.

As if coming out of a coma, he yanked his hand to the gear nob, and the tip of his right ear turned bright red. "Sorry. I wasn't... Sorry." He jerked the gear shift, causing a weird noise of distress from the truck, and then gripped the steering wheel with both hands.

She grinned. It was super hard to stay mad at a guy whose right ear changed colors when he was flustered. "Why did you stop? It wasn't to seduce me, was it? I mean, what's your plan here? Are you hoping we'll look into each other's eyes and declare ourselves friends with benefits?" she teased.

He surprised her by chuckling. And his ear went back to its normal color. "Your ego is the volume of the Colorado River."

Her lips twitched. Nice comeback. For a cinnamon roll guy, he had some game. "Says the man who goes around claiming kissing is his superpower." Damn. Why had she gone and remembered that? It was better forgotten.

He studied her lips. "Despite your point, and I agree you have one" —his voice was steady—"I didn't stop the truck to seduce you." He rearranged his rearview mirror.

"Then why?" She unhooked her seatbelt and twisted to glance out the back window. What had him so distracted?

"Your damn goats are following us."

She groaned. *For the love of sex.* She rolled down her window, leaned her upper body out, and shouted, "You three are in so much trouble." She'd specifically told them to stay in the backyard. "Go home. Right. This. Moment."

"Will that work? Will they go home on their own?"

She slid back through the window. "Probably not." Luna grabbed the handle, opened the door, and hopped out. "Ms. Houdini Linguini, shame on you. I know you know better, and yet here you are, being a bad example for Ms. Tinker Bell and Mr. JJ." She shook a stern finger at her goats as she went full angry-mom on them. "You turn around, young lady, and hoof it back home—and take your siblings with you. No oats for any of you tonight."

Ms. Houdini bleated but made no move to lead the group back where they belonged.

Mitch came around the front of the truck. "Imagine that. Goats that don't understand people talk." He reached into the back of the truck and grabbed a length of rope.

Ms. Tinker and Mr. JJ bleated and scattered.

"What the hell?" Mitch muttered.

"They're not fond of ropes," she explained. "Now that you've shown them the thing, they'll avoid you as long as they can."

Ms. Houdini sauntered up to Mitch and nudged his pockets.

"This hussy, on the other hand, has a crush on you," Luna said.

"Not on me, on my weed." Mitch rubbed the goat between her ears before hooking the rope to her collar. "I'll lead Ms. Houdini back, and hopefully the others will follow."

"But that's over a mile away." These damn goats were ruining their evening.

He handed her the keys. "Turn the truck around and bring it to the house."

"I can't drive a stick shift." So, this was how her horoscope would come true and her evening would end badly. Her get-to-know-Mitch outing had been thwarted by her goats.

"You're smart. You'll figure it out." Mitch strode away, Ms. Houdini keeping pace beside him.

He thinks I'm smart. Not wanting to disappoint his faith in her brain, Luna pulled up a YouTube video on how to put a stick-shift in reverse, and then how to move through the gears, and then what in the hell was a clutch.

By the time she'd mastered the beast and arrived back at the house, Mitch sat on her front porch looking tattered. Dirt smudged his cheeks and shirt.

Ms. Houdini stared moodily from the front tree to which she'd been tied, and the others kept her company.

Luna screeched the gears into park and, with the engine still running, jumped out of the truck.

Mitch stood and stomped toward her. "You need a fence. If you're going to be a pet owner, you have to be a responsible adult." He hopped in the truck and turned it off, then climbed out and scowled at her some more.

She fidgeted with the bracelets on her left wrist. "I can see how you would come to that conclusion."

"I'm. Serious. Lock them up."

Cold prickled her skin. That turn of phrase gave her the I've-been-to-jail willies. "I'll have you know I own a playpen with a latch. I just haven't put it together." She spoke quietly. Mr. JJ and Ms. Tinker would run away for sure if they thought they were about to be put behind bars.

He gave a clipped nod. "I didn't know they made playpens for goats. Aren't those for kids?"

Despite the real concern she had for her goats' mental well-being, she laughed.

He didn't.

She cocked her head. "That was funny?"

His eyes crinkled to slits.

"Oh, come on. Don't tell me you didn't mean for it to be funny?"

"Obviously, I didn't."

"Then let me explain." She pointed toward the trio of troublemakers. "Baby goats are called kids, and you said kids. And Ms. Houdini and her siblings aren't babies even though they're small and look like babies... Never mind."

He still didn't crack a smile.

Tough audience. "I special-ordered a pen for small farm animals."

Now he smiled. "Of course you did."

The prick of condemnation in his tone stung. "What does that mean?" There was absolutely nothing wrong with buying a product meant for a specific purpose. The world did not have to be viewed as one fence fits all.

"Nothing." He sighed and glanced at his watch. "If you don't mind, let's stay here and order pizza. I can put your goat contraption together while we wait on the food to arrive."

Irritation tried to build a good head of steam inside of her, but she cut it off at the belly. Luna 2.0 could allow another to have the last word even if the speaker used words that made it clear he thought her ridiculous. "That is so sweet of you."

"Not sweet. Just practical."

Determined to salvage the evening, she nodded her agreement. "Just so our non-date night isn't a total bust, why don't I set up a projector and screen while you build the pen?" Luna 2.0 might not need to win every argument, but she had no problem changing the subject to move an evening forward. "That way, when you're done, we can watch a movie under the stars."

He glanced up at the sky. "Deal. I'm going to run home and get my tools."

"See you in ten." Luna went inside and grabbed a sheet out of the laundry basket. Outside, she used a roll of duct tape to attach one side to Mildred the tree and the other to the side of her house. Instant movie screen. A trick she'd learned on TikTok.

"I ordered you a vegetarian pizza and myself a ranch chicken," Mitch said from behind her as she added the last strip of duct tape.

She turned to acknowledge his arrival back on the scene of their date.

A breath got lodged in her throat.

Woah!

He wore a form fitting white T-shirt and snug faded jeans. Super sexy. That visual deliciousness wasn't even the icing on the cake. Oh, hell no. The icing came from his prop.

An old, battered toolbox. Vintage like his truck.

A burst of lust slid up her throat. "That will work." She must have not gotten the desire all the way down because her voice came out sounding like a frat boy sucking helium after one too many beer bombs.

His brows skidded around on his forehead like he couldn't decide what emotion this moment warranted. They landed on neutral. Not up. Not down. Not squished together in the middle. They just sat above his eyes like well-behaved toddlers. "Where do you want the playpen set up?"

"Where do *you* want to set the playpen up?" She used a Luna 1.0 flirty tone. *Ugh. Stop it. This is a friendship.*

He glanced around the backyard as if he either had no clue he'd just been accidentally flirted with, or he was choosing to ignore it. She glanced at his right ear. Not red.

"I'd suggest there next to my fence." He pointed. "It's the flattest area of your yard."

She cleared her throat. Clearly, she was the only one slipping off their just-friends, non-date slide. "Not there." She breathed a sigh of relief that her voice was back to normal. "It's where I host yoga on the days the weather is good."

"And when it's not good?"

She pointed to the barn. "I've been cleaning out Ms. Barnetta."

"Barnetta?"

"That's what I named my barn. I plan to turn her into a goddess-shed."

He rubbed his temples.

She recalled his horoscope. *What would he lose control of before the evening ended?*

"Is a goddess-shed anything like a she-shed?"

She nodded. "But for goddesses. Mind you, I'm not an official one, but Nonna—a former nanny—was, and she made me an honorary one."

His eyes flashed open wide right before he looked down at his shoes. "How do you turn an old barn into a shed for a goddess?"

What had she said that caused him surprise? Did he not believe one could be deemed an honorary goddess? If he didn't believe that, he'd never believe her if she were to tell him how Nanny Nonna occasionally spoke to Luna in her dreams. "You hire a contractor. Mine, once I can afford to pay him, will knock out the wall that faces east and replace it with floor to ceiling windows so my students can see the mountains while they are doing yoga."

"That's not a bad plan. In fact, it's rather brilliant." He scratched his head. "You'll have a million-dollar view. A drawing card to get out-of-towners to come for a session while they are here vacationing."

She stared at the back of his head. He totally got it. "The contractor will also lay a wooden floor. I've already purchased the yoga mats and yoga props to complete the area. Plus, there will be a lovely sitting area for reading when it's snowing. And a gas fireplace." Why was she rambling? He didn't care about her plans to be an overnight success.

His gaze made it back to her. "I can set the pen in the other corner if that works for you?"

She considered the spot. "Great idea. It will provide the goats a lovely view of the bubbling brook and wildlife."

Thirty minutes later, he had the contraption laid out and began systematically putting each piece together.

Unsure what to do with herself, because staring didn't seem like a good idea, she went live on Instagram. "Hi, this is Luna of Luna's Goat Yoga. This guy behind me is Mitch." She watched him use a silver L-shaped tool to turn a screw. A smile lifted the corners of his lips as he worked. Funny how his change in clothing had messed with her equilibrium. Whereas in his normal good guy clothes, she'd found him nice on the eyes, in his faded jeans and form fitting T-shirt, she found him disturbingly masculine. Just proving clothes really do make a man.

"Mitch is my neighbor. Tonight, he's assembling a new play gym for my goats. By the way, he's single. So, if you know anyone who's looking for a super-sweet guy, join the Get Hitched app. He's on it." She pointed the camera toward Ms. Houdini. "If you're wondering why goats? It's because I own a goat yoga studio. That is Ms. Houdini. The sleeping one is Ms. Tinker. And the all-black one is Mr. JJ. They are quite friendly and will never get any bigger than they are now, which makes them perfect for goat yoga." Eventually, once her business grew, she'd get more goats.

Flipping the camera back on herself, she said, "If you're interested in booking a session, message me. Signing off. Luna of Luna's Goat Yoga." She quickly added several hashtags to the post. One of them #MitchJohnson. Why, she wasn't sure.

"Could you come hold this for me?" Mitch called.

He turned on the phone's light feature before holding it out toward her. Ms. Houdini stood next to him, nudging his leg with her head. No doubt in search of weed. Luna snapped a quick pic.

"Any time now." He sounded downright grumpy.

"Okay. Okay." Who knew grumpy paired so well with sexy?

Putting her phone in her back pocket, she walked toward the man.

No matter how hot he was, there was no way she was going back on their agreement about being only friends.

12

Mitch glanced across the weathered picnic table at Luna and watched as she nibbled daintily at her pizza in a manner so at odds with her full-of-life personality. What the fuck was that about? He would have bet his right to privacy she ate like a lumberjack.

Not that she wasn't feminine. Hell, her naked body had left zero room for argument that she was one-hundred percent female perfection.

Total surrender to a good time appeared to be Luna's life's motto, so it would stand to reason she'd have the same approach with food. Not nibble at it like a girl trying to make a good impression on a boy. So why was she doing exactly that?

Unless... He shook off the fantastic thought. She'd made it quite clear he wasn't her type. And he believed her. Her nibbling had nothing to do with him. Was she watching her weight for her next date? Did she have another date already lined up on the app? If she did, the guy better fucking not stand her up.

"You're staring." She laid the barely touched slice on her plate. "What are you thinking?"

An easy smile lifted his lips. One he hadn't had to remind himself to make like he normally did when around anyone new. Early in their relationship, Amahle had told him he was too serious and to lighten up. That didn't come easy to him. But somewhere between knocking on Luna's front door to pick her up tonight and this moment, he'd relaxed and let his guard down. Something he rarely did. Bad Luck Luna was easy to be with. "What did one ocean say to another ocean?"

She wiped at her full lips with a cloth napkin. "I don't know, what?"

"Nothing. They just waved." He took a hearty bite and waited for her to laugh.

Her features remained immobile.

"Don't you get it? Waved. Ocean waves." He waved at her.

"I got it." Her nostrils lightly flared. "I'm just wondering where it fit into the conversation we were having?"

I'm a fucking idiot. "One of the rules of friendships is to make each other laugh." He immediately regretted the words. They painted him a nerd all the way down to the *Star Wars* boxers he owned.

He blamed this ego-bruising moment on his friends who had introduced him to the rules of small-town friendships. They told him to arrive at every gathering armed with at least one clean joke, one dirty joke, and one politically incorrect joke. "I'll try again later when you're not suspecting." A lame finish to a lame opening.

Luna laughed. "That's funny."

He liked her laugh even if it was at his expense. It screamed of honesty. "I was being serious."

She reached out and placed her hand on his arm. "Your honesty made me laugh. Not a contrived joke. What other friendship rules do you strive to follow?"

He moved his arm out from under her hand. "We're not allowed to talk about politics, religion, or old flings while high or drunk during our first year of friendship."

Luna gave him a smile that beamed brighter than a thousand lightning bugs stuck together in a Mason jar. A smile he couldn't quite decipher, but it did all kinds of things to his ability to breathe.

"Fuck the last rule," Luna said too loudly. "I always talk about old flings when I'm high. You should try it sometime. It's great therapy."

"I don't believe in therapy."

"Get out of here! Why not? As my Nonna used to say, once you share a bad memory, it won't have the power to chafe your ass as bad."

His muscles bunched and not just because she'd once had a nanny she had obviously adored who'd helped her navigate life while he had basically raised himself. But also because he hated the thought of someone hurting her. He rubbed his neck to release the tension. "You want me to believe *you've* actually been hurt in a relationship?"

"Why do you say it like that? Like I'm not capable of being hurt? Do you think of me as a stone-cold bitch? Is that what you're implying?" Anger was clear on her face and in her voice.

"Fuck, no." Why so touchy? "I'm implying that I can't imagine a man who had your love tossing it away. It's far easier to imagine you doing the tossing."

Her expression softened. "I'll admit, I have done most of the heart crushing. And I'm not proud of that. Not anymore, anyway."

"Are you saying there was a time when you were proud?"

She grimaced. "Not proud, but there was a time I simply didn't care."

"What changed to make you care?"

Her eyes widened as if the thought of answering scared her. Then she shrugged. "I guess I grew up. Saw the world through the eyes of another and realized I didn't like me so much."

He had no idea how to respond. Inside his happy-go-lucky neighbor lay a deeper side. One that didn't paint her not-girlfriend material.

She gave him her full attention. "Your turn. You mentioned you have an ex-fiancée. Do you want to talk about her?"

"God, no. I'd prefer to talk about our new friendship."

A brilliant smile, one that moved the freckles around on her nose, lit up her face. "Holy Batman. I like the way you think."

He loved that *Holy Batman* came out of her mouth with such ease. She really did have a thing for comic characters. Not just a ploy to get the man. Like Brandy and her supposed enjoyment of small-town living. She'd never planned on their living in Rocky Mountain Springs after their marriage. She and her father had cooked up a whole scheme for Mitch Johnson. "I'll remind you of that the next time you disagree with me."

Luna picked off a pepper and set it next to a growing pile of mushrooms. "Since I exposed one of my darker sides, and I'm feeling quite vulnerable as a result, I think it's only fair you share something shocking-ish about you. Then I promise we'll get back to our friendship."

"What makes you think I have anything shocking to share?"

She raised her eyebrows and lowered her chin. "We cannot be friends if you don't."

Her answer intrigued him. "I turned out to not be the kind of man my fiancée wanted."

The fact his announcement didn't appear to shock her hit him in the gut. Like she could completely understand why a woman would come to that conclusion.

"And what man did she want you to be?"

"Someone who would spontaneously agree—the night before our fucking wedding—to give up my livelihood and move to Manhattan to work." He couldn't believe he had just told her his wedding story. A story he'd not even shared with his real friends.

Her brows slammed together. "You have connections in Manhattan?"

"I don't. She does. That's where she's from. We met when she moved here to work on her master's." He watched as Luna's brows slowly returned to their normal position, but if he wasn't mistaken, her breathing was slightly elevated like someone who'd received a fright. "Do you have something against Manhattan that I should know about?"

She huffed out a breath. "What could I possibly have against a city that's over-populated, over-polluted, and over-hyped?"

He relaxed. "On that we agree."

"Is that why you were against going to work for her father? Did the atrocities of the city outweigh your love for your fiancée?"

"My need to rule my fate, something she knew about me almost from day one, outweighed my love for my fiancée. You can't be in charge of your fate if you're working for someone else. They can fire you at any time, and you can suddenly find yourself homeless and jobless." That was another of his reoccurring nightmares. Pulling out his wallet to pay for something and having no money and the clerk calling the cops and Mom shouting *run*. Thus, his rigid need to be a business owner. In charge of his income.

Luna tugged at her bottom lip with her thumb and index finger, drawing his thoughts back to her.

"Need for security aside, she should have known you weren't the kind of man to make a spontaneous life-altering decision," Luna mused. "I barely know you, and I know enough to know you're not ever going to be impulsive."

He studied her expression. Having been raised by a spontaneous woman, he'd had his fill of the *ain't-this-fun* bullshit. Mom's spontaneity had leaned heavily toward running out on the check and the rent and, eventually, her son. "After the wedding rehearsal, we called the wedding off because she said she could never marry a man who wouldn't put her happiness first. Then she begged to be the one to tell all our guests the wedding was off because she said it would be less embarrassing." He paused and swallowed. "Then the next day, fifteen minutes after the wedding should have started, I received a text saying she'd changed her mind, and to hurry to the church for our nuptials. When I got there, I discovered she'd never cancelled the wedding. She had allowed the guests to show up. Allowed them to assume I simply arrived late to my own wedding."

"That's a bit bizarre. Then what happened?"

"She walked down the aisle and whispered in my ear that if I loved her, she knew I would change my mind."

"OMG. That is not playing fair. What did you say?"

"I whispered back, 'The answer will always be no.'"

"Then what?" Luna prompted.

No turning back now. "She slapped me and ran down the aisle, telling all those in attendance I was late because I had gotten sidetracked while reading a comic book."

She gasped. "And you never set the story straight?"

"A man doesn't—"

His phone rang, and they jumped like kids caught whispering in class. Who in the hell was calling him? No one other than Amahle and Johnny ever did. And they knew not to tonight.

"My apologies." He pulled out his phone. "I should've put it on do not disturb."

She pushed her hair behind her ears. "Friends answer phones in front of other friends. It's no big deal." Sincerity filled her eyes.

He glanced at the caller ID and balked. "It's Brandy! My ex."

Luna sucked in a breath and must have swallowed a bug because she hacked up a rough-sounding cough.

He gently slapped her back to help open her airway. He rejected the call and then blocked Brandy's number. He had no idea why she had called, but it didn't matter. He no longer cared. "It's like we conjured her or something," he joked.

"Ummm...about that."

"I'm tired of talking about Brandy." She'd not been on his list of things or people to chat about tonight.

For a moment, he thought Luna would insist they continue. But then she gave him an understanding smile. "Enough therapy for one night. What non-therapy topic would you like to discuss?"

"The dating app."

She cocked her head. "What about it?"

"I can't figure out how to navigate the program to show me who I've matched with. Want to help me choose my first date?" It was time for them to get the night back on the friendship track.

13

The next day, Luna elbowed thoughts of Mitch to the rear of her over-active imagination. She did not need to know if he'd called Brandy after he'd left her house last night. Because of course he'd called her. Even if he'd acted like he didn't care two cents about her out-of-the-blue call. *Out of the blue, my ass.*

And she didn't need to know what Brandy wanted. Without a doubt, she wanted to try again, even if she didn't come right out and tell him. And, of course, she wouldn't.

But that's why women called men they've broken up with. Oh, they might pretend it's just to check on them or a butt call, but that was a bunch of poppycock pot pies. As Mitch's new friend, Luna didn't want to see him get hurt again, so the idea of him calling Brandy back had her agitated.

But today wasn't about Mitch and his ex. Today was about Luna and her being one step closer to financial security. "I did it. All on my own." Well...with some help from her secret insurance windfall. "Thanks, Nonna."

She glanced at the sky as if expecting to see her former nanny floating on a cloud, waving at her. She wasn't.

It was a perfect day for the event—sunny and in the low seventies. She scanned the picturesque setting she'd created for her first goat yoga spa day affair. Colorful yoga mats and yoga props, like blocks and blankets, were strewn on the ground. All to be used by the bride and her six bridesmaids.

An antique tea pitcher sat in the middle of the table, surrounded by place settings with mismatched glasses. A fat-bottomed crystal vase of colorful wildflowers also adorned the table—a leftover from friends-night-out with Mitch. She leaned down and sniffed the flowers. They smelled like hot sunshine and lazy happiness.

Did Mitch have rules for what type of flowers he brought to a woman? Wildflowers for friends? Tulips for casual dates? Roses for fiancées? Knowing him, he probably did.

As Luna puttered around the picnic table, her thoughts drifted back to the night before and Brandy's unexpected call. Abby must have told Brandy about Luna's date with Mitch, and, for obvious reasons, Brandy had purposefully timed her call to interrupt them. Which was fine. After all, Luna hadn't asked Abby for a pinky swear to keep their plans a secret. She'd not asked for one very important reason. The most she and Mitch would ever experience was some form of friendship. Even if he were her type, and he wasn't, as long as she planned to live under an assumed surname, she couldn't pursue any type of relationship. It wasn't honest. And had all the markings of turning into something messy at best and ugly at worst.

She yanked her thoughts back to the present. Today would set the stage for her future. Success breeds success. She had to make Luna's Goat Yoga profitable. Just like Mitch, never again did she want to be at the mercy of someone else for her survival. Her parents had thought she'd forgive and forget. They were wrong.

And revenge aside, she just wanted Luna's Goat Yoga to be popular. What had started out as spite, a way to get back at her parents for what they'd done to her, had turned into something different. Something sparkly on the outside and giggly on the inside.

A breeze whipped around the house and caused the doilies she'd placed on the empty ornamental platters to blow away. She sighed and went to anchor the rest of them. The dishes were awaiting the chocolate cake and finger cookies she'd baked with love this morning. Okay, *love* was the wrong choice of word. The first two batches of cookies had burnt and set off her smoke alarms. To add insult to injury, the first batch of cake batter she'd whipped up she'd dumped on the floor while trying to pour it into the pan.

By the time she'd managed to get edible items out of the oven, all love for the activity had evaporated.

She should have paid more attention those times when Nanny Nonna had insisted Luna learn her way around a cookbook and a kitchen.

At least she had paid close attention to how to make candles. And candles were a product she planned to sell at Luna's Mercantile—a project which would happen in phase two of Luna's quest for financial independence.

"Stop eating that," she admonished Ms. Houdini, who was chowing down on a wayward napkin. Luna had taken special care in dressing her goats for the event. Ms. Houdini flaunted a pretty pink ribbon in her hair with matching pink lipstick. Ms. Tinker had a sunny yellow flower tucked behind one ear. And Mr. JJ sported a dandy looking orange vest.

The sound of car doors slamming caused Luna's belly to jump. She took a deep breath and mindfully exhaled. *First impressions make bank.* She had no doubt the group of women would post about their time at Luna's Goat Yoga.

Squaring her shoulders, she padded barefoot around to the front of the house. "Hello. Welcome to..." All the air left her lungs. The women filing out of the white limousine, with the words *Bridal Weekend* written on its side windows, were not strangers. Luna knew all seven of them. Quite well.

"What are you doing here?" she croaked. How in the hell had they found her?

The one dressed in all white yoga gear and wearing a bride sash across her chest stepped forward. "Sweetie, is that anyway to greet your long-lost best friend?"

Tabs wasn't Luna's long-lost best friend. She was her long-lost ex-best friend. The one who had blabbed to the tabloids everything she knew about Luna the moment Luna's life became fodder for tabloid bottom dwellers. And since they'd been friends since birth, she'd had a lot of material.

Luna scowled. "Who told you how to find me?"

A pained expression flittered across Tab's face. "Your father. He said you were in the mountains pouting over the fact you were no longer Manhattan's golden child, and he simply begged me to come and talk some sense into you."

"Is it true?" asked Summer, a petite brunette. She was Tab's little sister. "Did you come all this way to mope?"

"Please, tell us it's not true," Tabs said. "After all, you were never really the golden child of Manhattan. But you were my best friend, and I want you back. Clubbing is just not the same without you."

Luna didn't react. She'd been naïve to think Father wouldn't strike back when she'd refused to get on the plane and come home. "And are you a bride-to-be? Or is that a lie?" What exactly did her father hope to gain by telling her old crowd where to find her?

"I'm almost a bride-to-be. My fiancé is simply waiting to be out from under a tedious contract," Tabs said.

"Do I know him?" Luna led them around to the back of the house. They were here. They'd paid. They might as well do some yoga.

"Darren," Tabs said.

Luna stopped walking but didn't turn. Thank God none of them could see her face. After she'd broken things off, Darren had been in an accident. One where he'd driven off the road and blamed the accident on his being distracted by his overwhelming grief. Had that been a lie? A lie which had resulted in a whole new deluge of articles being written about her?

And what in the hell did Tabs mean he was under contract? Was she referring to some document he'd signed with her parents to ask Luna to marry him? As lawyers, they loved them a good contract. If that were the case, she did not feel sorry for him. Served him right if he had to squirm to get out of the legal agreement. She'd felt truly awful thinking she'd caused him so much pain.

But how did one react when one's ex-best friend has just announced she's semi-engaged to your ex-fiancé?

She weighed her options. Luna 1.0 wanted to reply with piss-and-vinegar sarcasm. Tell them to get the hell back into the limo and get off her property. Luna 2.0 refrained from being a bitch. She needed the income. "I hope the two of you find your happily ever after. Now, pick your mat, and we can get started."

She'd purchased the mats online and then embellished them with paint and flower stencils. Crafting, she'd discovered, made her authentic self happy.

While the bridal party selected their spots, Luna let the goats out of their playpen. Funny, the lock wasn't latched. She could have sworn she'd secured it.

"Ladies, meet Ms. Houdini, Ms. Tinker, and Mr. JJ. They are Nigerian Dwarf goats, a breed who are known to be quite lovable and petite. One fun fact about this breed is you can walk them like you would take a dog for a walk."

"Where are their horns?" Tabs asked.

Had Darren actually proposed to another woman while still telling Father he was waiting for Luna to come to her senses? That would not bode well for him if Father found out. "Their prior owners had them removed."

"Will they bite?" Sally asked. Out of all of them, she'd always been the nicest. The only reason she'd been invited into their group was because her father hosted Botox and filler parties.

Sally was who Luna 2.0 had been modeled after. Morally speaking. "They may lick you to see if you have anything tasty hidden in your clothes, but they won't bite." At least, she hoped they wouldn't. They never had up until this point.

"How did you teach them to do yoga?" London and Paris asked at the same time. They were identical twins and often simultaneously spoke exact phrases.

Luna looked away and rolled her eyes, and then glanced back at the ladies. "They don't actually do the yoga. But you will find that they like to join you in your poses. Especially when you're in a position they can climb on top of you. Like a plank. Or Downward Dog."

"That's disappointing." Tabs bristled. "I was under the impression they did yoga beside us. I'm not sure I want a goat to climb on me."

Goats weren't people. They might walk with you, but you couldn't teach them to actually do yoga. "It was in the brochure I sent your assistant...who told me you were coming from California."

They all laughed sheepishly.

"Sorry we didn't give you a heads-up," Sally said. "Your father made us promise not to say a word."

"I see. Well, I'm sure you'll enjoy the experience. I've never had an unhappy customer." Granted, she'd never had an out-of-state customer. Just the semi-locals. No one but her needed to know that detail.

Watching her former friends interact with one another cracked open a heart-wound Luna thought had healed. The one caused when all her childhood frenemies, these ladies, had abandoned her the moment they heard of her arrest.

Luna walked over to the music and turned it on. "Shall we start by bowing to the flag?" She had an American flag hanging from Mildred. After being arrested and facing the possibility of losing her rights as a citizen, she had gained a new healthy appreciation for the freedom the flag stood for. "And to one another."

Luna led them through an advanced level workout. One that included planks, headstands, and backbends.

An hour and a lot of sweat later, Luna bowed and said, "Namaste." As usual, her mind had quieted, and she no longer felt attacked by being tricked into hosting her old peeps. Although one of them could have at least given her a heads-up.

They bowed back and said, "Namaste."

Luna picked up the towel and wiped her brow. "That concludes this portion of the event. You may wash your hands at the spicket." She pointed toward the waterspout on the side of the house. Next to it, on a small three-legged stool, she'd placed a wicker basket filled with hand towels, wash cloths, and soap. "After that, make your way to the picnic table, and I'll bring out the food. You're welcome to sit there and eat, or you can take your refreshments and sit in the chairs under the tree that looks out over the mountain and the burbling river below." She glanced toward the mountain and thought of Mitch. What would he think of her old acquaintances? They were nothing like Amahle and Johnny.

Luna doubted seriously Mitch's friends would ever turn their backs on him during a crisis. Not the way her friends had. Which further proved she'd done the right thing by leaving her old self behind and starting fresh. She wanted friends. The right kind of friends. The kind who liked you for no other reason than they liked you. Like Mitch liked her.

"You're an excellent instructor," Tabs said.

"Thank you." Luna resisted an urge to quiz her over Darren. Anything she said, good or bad, would be met with skepticism.

"How high are we?" the twins asked in unison.

"I don't know. How much weed have you consumed?" The lame joke slipped out almost as if Mitch had just controlled her mouth.

They all stared blankly at her.

She sighed. "It was a joke. Weed's legal here."

Still blank stares.

"Never mind. You're eleven thousand eighty-eight feet high. Or to put it in simpler terms, if you walked from the bottom to the top of Manhattan, that's how high up we are. Around two miles."

"Eww," squealed Tabs. "I hate to walk."

"That's why God created chauffeurs," the twins replied.

By the time Luna returned with the cake and cookies, they'd all gathered under the tree with their phones and glasses of tea. Luna glanced around for her goats. Ms. Tinker and Mr. JJ were under the table. Ms. Houdini was nowhere in sight. Ugh. Where had she disappeared to this time?

"Ladies." Luna set the food on the picnic table. "Your treat for putting in the hard work."

They all looked up as one. "Please join us," Tabs said.

Luna did, only because she didn't want to give them any reason to leave a bad review of Luna's Goat Yoga. "What are your plans for the rest of the day?" What was Father's reason for sending them here? Had he hoped seeing them would make her homesick? If he had, it had backfired. She felt more confident than ever that she'd made the right decision.

"We're staying in Colorado Springs," the twins said.

"There's absolutely nothing for us to do in Rocky Mountain Springs," Sally added. "Believe me, we checked it out before we came. We'd be thrilled if you came with us. Partying just isn't the same without you there helping us to get into trouble."

"I'm not that person anymore. I've grown up. I love living here in a small town. I enjoy what I'm doing. I don't miss the night life at all. I hope Father didn't bribe you with a big payday if I came back home with you."

Tabs jumped up. "Get over yourself. We don't need your father's money. We were just trying to save you from yourself. I mean, look at you! The changes in your appearance are hideous."

Hell. What had she been thinking pushing any of their buttons? They had the power to out her. "I'm sorry you feel that away," Luna said in a conciliatory tone. "But I happen to like the new me."

"Like!" Tabs all but shouted. "Your hair's a mess. You're not wearing shoes, and when was the last time you had a mani-pedi? It's like you've been brainwashed into believing you're poor. Like in that movie *Overboard*. I insist you come with us, or we'll be forced to tell everyone where you're hiding."

Terror ripped through Luna. She couldn't let that happen. But the only way to keep them from ruining her new life was to push them all off the cliff. Or...reciprocate with her own brand of blackmailing. "I would think my staying here, incognito, would be something you wanted, Tabs. After all, if I return, I'm certain Darren would re-re-propose. And he'd insist none of you were invited to the wedding of the decade, which would forever label you as has-beens."

Tabs's face turned blotchy red. "Like we have nothing better to do than to bring you up in a conversation. You are dead to all of us." Tabs looked at her friends. "Isn't that right? We'd rather be ugly than allow your name to ever leave our lips again."

The cheap shot caught Luna in the ribs like a well-aimed spear. In their circle, it was the ultimate insult.

They all nodded.

Luna met their nods with an unblinking stare.

Tabs gave Luna a cocky smile. "Come on ladies, we're leaving. I don't want what she caught to rub off on any of us."

"I guess that means we won't be air kissing goodbye," Luna said in a tone a tad too snide to belong to Luna 2.0, and yet a tad too humorous to be Luna 1.0. It was like the Lunas were merging.

The rest of the fake wedding party stood, looked from Tabs to Luna, and then back to Tabs. Not a one of them gave Luna another glance before traipsing to the limo and climbing inside.

Unwelcome emotion mud-masqued Luna. It was one thing to know you'd made the right decision, but another to watch the bad decision walk out of your life. That group of ladies had the power to destroy her new life and there wasn't a damn thing she could do about it. She could only pray she'd gotten her bluff in on them.

Once the car had disappeared down the road, she grabbed a leash and went in search of the travelling Ms. Houdini. She'd barely made it to the end of her driveway when her phone dinged. She glanced at the screen. Her stomach clenched. Fuck. Luna's Goat Yoga had seven new reviews. This was not going to be good. She opened the link and read.

1. *Worst experience of my life. Luna's Goat Yoga ruined my bachelorette party.*

2. *Luna's Goat Yoga has stinky goats.*

3. *Luna of Luna's Goat Yoga isn't nice. She makes fun of her students.*

4. *Don't pay extra for the food. Luna's Goat Yoga serves her customers food that even her goats won't eat. The cake tasted like salt.*

5. *Luna's Goat Yoga...*

Unable to stomach any more, she shoved her phone back in her pocket, along with thoughts of revenge, and went in search of Ms. Houdini. Mean girls had to have the last laugh. If you didn't give it to them, they became dangerous.

Luna knew enough to allow her old friends to think they'd won. And for now, they had. But they hadn't crippled her. She would find a way to rise above their vicious sabotage of her business. If nothing else, she would rebrand under a different name.

She sniffed back tears and kept walking.

Mitch stood quietly in his greenhouse and observed Luna stomping up his sidewalk to the deck. If the stomping wasn't hint enough, the mutinous set of her profile confirmed something had her mad as hell. Was it Ms. Houdini for slipping away again? The damn goat had been sleeping on his deck for the past hour.

"Houdini Linguini Parker! Shame on you." Luna shook a finger at the goat. "I've told you this house is off limits. Off. Off. Off limits." Her voice shook as much as her finger. Like maybe she'd been crying. Had she been crying? He couldn't tell from this angle.

Ms. Houdini, of whom he had a clear view, bleated but didn't look the least bit sorry. She never did.

Luna sniffed loudly, scrubbed a hand down her cheek, and then knocked on his back door.

Fuck. What could have happened to make her so upset? Had someone in town been rude to her? He knew there were those who were keeping their distance because they blamed her for his possibly moving his business elsewhere, but he hadn't heard of anyone being mean to her face. Just aloof.

"You're lucky Mitch is at work, or he'd be demanding you never be released from your pen," Luna said to Ms. Houdini. "And trust me when I tell you that is not a situation you want to find yourself in."

He smirked. Like Luna knew anything about the wrong side of a set of bars. Her warning to her goat was equivalent to him saying *trust me when I tell you that wearing high heels all night after a long day at the office is not a situation you want to find yourself in.*

Then again, what did he really know about Luna Parker? Nothing, really. Other than the fact that she was eccentric.

Luna leaned down and scratched Ms. Houdini's head between her ears. "What's this?" She held up a cannabis leaf.

Mitch grimaced. He hadn't realized the four-legged menace had gotten into any of his containers.

"Holy Batman," she said. "Mitch should be more careful about leaving his plants lying around. They might be bad for a goat."

Unbelievable. Her goat had escaped and gotten into his product, and she blamed him.

Luna glanced at his back door and then her goat. "Just between us, I kind of wish he was home. I mean, I know he's a little awkward in social settings, and he's a little rigid, but I don't mind. I'll take that any day over a guy who pursues you for personal gains."

The loneliness in her voice caused his heart to tighten. Who had pursued her for personal gains?

She clipped the leash to Ms. Houdini's collar.

Mitch placed his hand on the door and was about to make himself known when he heard her say, "Young lady, I have a date tonight, which means you must be on your best behavior. No following me."

His hand dropped away as he processed the comment. It bothered him more than it should, but he couldn't decipher why. They were friends who were going to experience the joy of app dating together. Which reminded him, he should ask someone out. Luna had helped him find three women who'd shown interest in him that he thought might be okay. He pulled out his phone. It was time to act. He chose the first name on the list, Olga, and sent a message asking if she'd like to meet for drinks. The action didn't result in any sort of eager anticipation in his gut, more like nausea. But at least he'd moved his plan to find a date for the ball one step forward.

14

Twenty-minutes after Luna had left with Ms. Houdini, Mitch still stood in his greenhouse, queasy.

It was moments like this he despised everything about his childhood.

Amahle and Luna were dead-on with their descriptions. He was fucking awkward in social settings. Not because his brain didn't work right, the way Mom claimed, but because he'd seen enough growing up to make it hard for him to trust. And when you don't fucking trust, you suck at making friends.

Last night he'd been able to push past his scars and work at making a new friend, but it had taken every fucking ounce of his energy. With each forward step, he'd had to draw upon perseverance and his reluctant willingness to try something that did not have a high probability of turning out in his favor.

As a result, today, when Luna had shown up on his deck, he'd had nothing left to give. If he'd made himself known, he would have been worthless to her. As much as he wished otherwise, there was a reason he only had two real friends in town. Yes, he could make friends. And keep friends. But only with people who weren't in a hurry for him to go all in. Only with people who saw his quirks as endearing. Only with people who stuck around long enough to get to know the real him.

The him he could be when his walls were down, and his quirks eased up, and his scars faded.

"There you are!"

Mitch jumped at the unexpected sound of a voice. Relief lowered his pulse once his brain registered it wasn't Luna. It was Mayor Regis. Mitch turned toward the man. "What brings you over today?"

The mayor was not a friend. He was an acquaintance. Mitch didn't trust him.

But he was Mitch's landlord, and he ruled Rocky Mountain Springs. Thus, Mitch treated him with the respect he was owed. Not deserved, not earned, but owed.

"I'm dropping off the packets to those hosting booths at the Summer Festival," Mayor Regis said.

Mitch nodded. "I guess that is right around the corner."

Rocky Mountain Springs held the festival once a year during the influx of new students coming to nearby campuses for college visits. It helped to bring those students and their parents to their town to see what it had to offer.

"This is not for public knowledge, but a very important businessman will be in attendance. It's imperative we shine."

"I'm sure he will be impressed," Mitch said. "Business is up for everyone. The new bakery and Luna's Goat Yoga has helped to bring in even more customers. I'm sure their booths will add extra shine to an event that is always well received."

Regis fluttered his fat hands. "Your neighbor applied to have a booth. Of course we turned her down."

"Why?"

"The official answer is..." Regis leaned in and whispered, "She missed the deadline, and there's no space available."

"And the true answer?" Mitch did not lower his voice or try to hide the disapproval in his tone. He didn't like games that affected people's lives. His mom had played more than enough of those with his own life until he'd reached adulthood.

Regis adjusted his bow tie. He had an impressive collection of them. Today's sported yellow polka dots. "I've done a little checking into her background. I mean, after all, she waltzed in here and—from what you've reported—on a whim bought a prime piece of our real estate right out from under you. Land, I will remind you, I would have bought but didn't because I have a soft spot for you. It never dawned on me you would screw up the opportunity handed to you on a silver platter."

The disdain in the mayor's voice cut. Mitch prided himself on being dependable. And he, as well as the whole town, knew Regis had looked the other way when the land had come on the market just so Mitch could purchase it. The soft-spot comment was a bunch of bullshit. Rocky Mountain High had brought in a record number of visitors ever since its grand opening. The mayor's good deed had been a calculated move to keep Mitch and his business in Rocky Mountain Springs. Nevertheless, Mitch conceded he had fumbled the opportunity. "I thought my preapproved amount was more than enough to win the house."

"One should always be prepared," Regis snapped. "Which is why I've done some checking. Did you know Luna Parker didn't exist six months ago?"

"Are you implying aliens dropped her on earth six months ago, and before that she lived with them on their planet?" Mitch asked, attempting to lighten the mood with a joke.

The mayor frowned. "I'm saying I did a background check, and there's nothing to check dating beyond six months ago."

Mitch was intrigued as hell, but he chose his words carefully. "She has the right to privacy." He'd offered Luna friendship and with that came allegiance.

"Son, it's my primary duty as Rocky Mountain Springs's mayor to keep our town safe. Thus, I always conduct a background check on new citizens."

Disbelief shot through Mitch. "That seems like an unnecessary expense for the town's coffers."

"Not when you remember criminal types like to hide out in small towns. Watch a few episodes of 20/20 and you'll know what I mean." The mayor rubbed his bald head with a handkerchief that matched his tie.

Before moving to Rocky Mountain Springs, Mitch hadn't realized small-town caricatures existed outside of fiction. Once he realized they did, it had given him great amusement to pick them out as he met his neighbors. The mayor was the most over-the-top. "Isn't there a law against running a background check on someone without their permission?" While Mitch silently made fun of others for their caricature personalities, he'd be the first to admit he was one himself. The nerd.

"My right to do so is in the small print of the application to open a business, which she filled out and signed. Not that I needed to go to that extreme with Luna. As it turned out, the information was sent to my office via an anonymous letter. Dropped off, not mailed."

Mitch paced. He could think better when in motion. "What did the letter say?"

"That Luna Parker didn't exist until recently."

"Besides that?" The conversation was giving Mitch a migraine.

Regis checked his faultlessly manicured nails. "Nothing of much use."

Mitch took a seat on the step and sifted logically through the possibilities. "You're shunning her from our town based on an anonymous letter?" One of those could come from anyone. An ex. A competitor in the yoga industry. The possibilities were endless.

"What more do I need?" The sly smile that tilted Regis's lips turned Mitch's stomach sour.

"Did you stop to consider that maybe it's as simple as she didn't like her birth name?" Or she'd had a lousy childhood like him and wanted a fresh start?

"Or maybe she's in witness protection. Or maybe she's running from a stalker," Regis countered.

The hairs on the back of Mitch's neck rose as he tried to recall Luna's comment to Ms. Houdini—it had been something about being locked up. "Those reasons sound farfetched, don't you think?" Mitch argued on Luna's behalf. And even if they were farfetched, if true, the mayor could be endangering Luna by digging into all of it.

Was Luna Parker in danger? Did that have anything to do with her earlier tears?

"As mayor, I can't afford to overlook any possibility. Hell, if Ms. Parker has a stalker, it could have been him who left the note."

"If that's the case, instead of shunning Luna, the town should be making plans to protect her."

A smirk hooked Regis's mouth. "You want us to protect someone at the expense of the whole town? Did I mention she tried to kill me with her damn muffins?"

Mitch laughed. "She didn't try to kill you. She's just not much of a cook. And yes, I believe we should do our part to protect her if she's in trouble."

A vein bulged in Regis's cheek. "That's why I'm the mayor and not you. I can't afford to play nice. I've been elected to do what's best for the town, and what's best for the town is to eliminate potential problems."

"If Luna discovers your methods, she could sue you."

"The only way she'll find out is if you go and tell her," Regis said in an icy tone. "And I can't think of one good reason why you would do that. Can you?"

Mitch could think of plenty but didn't rush to reply. He'd learned a long time ago that when faced with an authoritarian trying to bully you, silence was your friend. It was less confrontational.

"I see." Regis swept off the step with his hanky and took a seat beside Mitch. "Maybe I can help you come up with some reasons to remain silent."

The veiled threat didn't go unnoticed. *Time to calm the waters.* "Surely there's a way to protect both the town and Luna without pushing her out of Rocky Mountain Springs."

"In the movies, you'd be right. But last I checked we don't live in the movies," the mayor admonished, not sounding the bit calmed down. "Let's say she's running from a stalker. What do you see as the worst-case scenario should the stalker decide to harm her?"

Mitch's pulse picked up and his stomach tied itself in a knot. "She dies." He stood, needing to put space between him and the mayor and the idea of losing Luna to violence.

"That's not the worst case. The worst case is her stalker tries to kill her in the middle of our town, and a stray bullet harms you or me or any of the other citizens who don't know to be aware of possible danger." Regis stood and pulled two joints out of his suit pocket. He offered one to Mitch.

Mitch declined. He needed to stay alert. "You're being a little over-the-top, don't you think?"

Regis lit his joint and inhaled deeply and then exhaled. "Danger aside, let me explain this to you from a money standpoint. While I own ninety-three percent of the town, I answer to my financial backer. A guy who makes my background searches look like kids' play. If word was to reach him that our town is in danger, he could decide to liquidate the town...so to speak."

What in the hell kind of guy had he borrowed money from? People didn't just liquidate towns. "Rocky Mountain Springs is thriving. He'll see no reason to shut her down." The more he thought about it, the more he was certain the mayor was bluffing.

The cheek vein bulged even more. "I've seen him liquidate a town because they failed to have his appetizer of choice—caviar—available at their café."

"That's ridiculous." Mitch rubbed his palms on his pants. Regis was describing the kind of guy who used to do business with Mother.

"Maybe. But it is what it is. Please tell me you understand the predicament we're in, and you're on board to do your part."

"My part?"

"Help our Luna to decide to leave our storybook town."

Mitch frowned. That wasn't his part. It couldn't be his part. There were rules when it came to friendships. "I won't pressure her into doing something she doesn't want to do."

The mayor studied Mitch through narrowed eyes. "Perhaps you need a stronger personal incentive to get her to leave." He stuck his joint in his mouth and inhaled, held the smoke, and then exhaled. "I'll tell you what, you run her out of town, and I will keep to myself the information I have on your past. Information that may or may not tarnish your pristine reputation should it become common fodder among the gossips."

Mitch stilled. "I've done nothing wrong."

"Oh, but your mother has. She's a felon, isn't she?"

Panic engulfed Mitch, causing cold sweat to run down his back. Just hearing the term *felon* was enough to set him into what mother called his demon spiral. He clenched his hands and fought to keep the demon at bay. Mitch knew from experience if the demon was allowed a voice, it would spew nothing but ugliness.

"Who's to say your shop isn't a front for you and your mom to sell illegal drugs out of the back?" the mayor continued. "I wouldn't put it past those friends of yours, Johnny and Amahle, to be involved in it all either. In fact, that would explain the rumor I recently heard."

Mitch narrowed his eyes. "What rumor?"

"According to my source, a couple who'd gone on one of their rafting expeditions never returned home from their vacation. One could speculate those poor vacationers stumbled across sensitive information about your dubious dealings, and you had your business associates dispose of them."

Harsh laughter erupted from Mitch. "You know that's not true."

"But do I?" Regis asked smugly. "Johnny certainly looks the part of a hardened criminal."

Blood pounded in Mitch's ears. "You shouldn't say things you can't prove."

"Here's the thing, son. I don't have to authenticate anything," the mayor countered. "I've seen both individuals and businesses ruined as a result of a plausible rumor. And let's not forget one of the stipulations when the town granted you your license was that you would maintain a reputation beyond repute."

Regis wasn't wrong. When filling out the paperwork at the state level, Mitch had had to reveal the names of any known felons he'd ever associated with. He'd listed Mother. The licensing board had called him in for a formal review. He'd been forced to relay to them all the ugliness of his past and detail what he'd done to remove himself from the situation. In the end, they'd granted him a license but with caveats.

"I see I have your attention," Mayor Regis said. "I take it you'll help me get Luna out of town?"

Mitch owed it to Johnny and Amahle not to put their livelihoods in jeopardy. But growing up on the streets, he knew giving into a bully only led to more bullying. If you didn't show them some type of strength, they owned you. He raised his chin and bartered for the only thing he knew would cause the mayor pain. "If I do your bidding, I expect you to sell me my home and my shop, and you will leave my friends alone." His voice came out strained but at least his words weren't controlled by the part of his brain that operated on pure fear and made no sense.

Regis frowned. "I don't believe you're in a position to make demands, but because I like you, and I'm feeling generous, I'll sell your home to you once you rid the town of Luna Parker and her damn goats."

"And you'll leave my friends alone?" Mitch pushed.

"Yes. Yes, I'll leave them alone."

"How much for my home?"

"The same as the amount the bank offered to loan you to purchase the old Murphy Place plus ten percent."

Even though his house sat on a smaller parcel of land, the price was fair considering the location. "I will require an iron-clad contract." Perhaps if he was honest with Luna about everything, she'd agree to move elsewhere. Somewhere that no one knew her secret.

The mayor put out his joint. "I thought we trusted one another to strike deals with nothing more than a handshake."

Mitch sneered. "And I thought someone who is the mayor of a town would never resort to blackmailing me to get his way."

"Fine," Regis snapped. "If that's what you require, yes."

"It's what I require, and I meant it when I said I won't take any action until I have one in hand." The latter was a stalling technique. If he knew Regis, the guy would drag his feet forever before signing a contract. Asking the mayor to give up a piece of his empire was like asking a mother to give up a child. Or at least a normal mother. And while Regis procrastinated, Mitch would brainstorm ways to defeat the bully.

The mayor pursed his lips. "You drive a hard bargain. Now. I must go. I've several more packets to deliver."

Mitch watched him leave before slumping to the step and putting his head between his knees and gasping for air. All his life, since he'd barely been out of diapers, Mother had told him it was his job to make sure she never got caught for her crimes. She said if the police ever found her, they'd charge her with felonies, and they'd take her away, and he'd be forced to live with monsters.

When the night had come that the authorities finally caught up with her, he'd run and hidden under an old truck like the one he owned now and silently watched them drag her out of the junkyard in handcuffs. He'd continued to hide, surviving on the streets, until he was no longer considered a juvenile.

During all that time, he had daily promised himself he'd someday get a real education, own a home, and would live a rule-following life.

He shuddered out a hard breath. Right or wrong, he couldn't lose everything he'd worked so hard to achieve.

All he had to do was talk Luna into selling her home.

It wouldn't be easy. Then again, it wasn't impossible or improbable. Right? *Absolutely right.*

A thought scraped his brain and wouldn't shove off. Could he live with himself if Luna's happiness was the price for his peace? Even if he went about everything with honesty?

His absolutely right might actually be absolutely wrong.

He shook his head roughly as if the thought were tangible and could be dislodged and destroyed. As long as he didn't use trickery to get Luna to sell, then her decision would be her decision.

And besides, if he didn't do Regis's dirty work, the guy would go after Johnny and Amahle.

15

Twenty-four hours after Luna's friendship date with Mitch, she sat across from her Get Hitched date, Ronnie, and tried to be a good listener. Really, really tried. But if she had to endure one more story about why today's youths were doomed because they were never disciplined and as a result had no respect for their elders, she would scream.

And not an internal half-assed yelp. It would be out loud and at top volume. Worthy of being called a shriek.

"I take it your parents ruled you with an iron fist?" she offered as her part of the conversation. What other reason was there for a guy to turn out so judgmental?

He straightened and gave her a smug look. "They didn't have to. I was an obedient child." He picked up his strawberry daiquiri, took a delicate sip, and then gracefully wiped his lips with his napkin.

She swirled her swizzle stick in her Old Fashioned. "Are you an obedient adult?" She could think of nothing more boring. "Like...do you ever color outside the lines grownups are told to stay within?"

"Never. It's so uncouth." He gave her a searching look. "Don't you agree?"

She downed half her drink and contemplated her next words. She could blow smoke up his ass and pretend to agree for his ego's sake. Which was how she'd been raised to treat men. *Stroke them like a cat, and they'll give you your heart's desire.* That had to be the worst advice ever. Thank God Luna 2.0 treated men with the same honesty she wanted them to give her. "I strongly believe life is much more fun when it's occasionally lived outside the lines. That's where all the action is."

When she'd said yes to Darren's marriage proposal, it had been her stroking his ego—and just basically not being a bitch. Hell, the guy had proposed on one knee in front of a room full of his peers and both sets of parents. And it didn't help that her life had been in tatters at that moment.

Yes had been a bad decision on her part. Just one of many she'd made that year.

Of course, if she had known then what she knew now about the damn proposal, she would have kicked him in the balls while he'd been down on one knee.

"I don't understand," Ronnie said.

"For instance," Luna said, "just the other day, I did yoga in the nude in my backyard and got caught. Had I worn clothes, that encounter would've been boring, but instead it exuded tension."

Ronnie's face froze in horror.

Luna waited for it to thaw.

"I see." He glanced at the waitress and mouthed *Check please.*

Luna dropped her swizzle stick. "Are we done?" She had not seen that coming. "Is the date over?" They'd only had one drink. The plan had been to have a couple and then order dinner.

Ronnie looked down his long nose at her. "I believe in cutting my losses early on outings like these when it becomes obvious things could never work out."

"Oh." Not an unreasonable plan of action. And it wasn't like Luna wasn't happy to have the evening come to an end sooner rather than later. In fact, it sounded like some rule Mitch would have. "It was nice meeting you."

"You, too." Ronnie stared hard at her. "Before I leave, I must ask. Have you been in the news lately? Ever since seeing you in person tonight, your face has felt familiar. I've been racking my brain trying to recall where I've seen you before. I know it wasn't in person, which has left me with the conclusion it must have been on some news broadcast. That's all I watch."

Holy Batman. Since getting new contacts that had changed her eye color and altering her hair style, and adding a few freckles here and there, she'd not been identified as the old her. What should she say? "I don't—"

"Luna, is that you?" said a warm male voice. One she recognized. One that glided over her like hot fudge on cold ice cream. *Thank God for an interruption.*

She turned and watched as Mitch strode toward her with a genuine-ish smile on his face. What in the devil was he doing at her date restaurant?

"I thought that was your laugh." He stopped at their table.

"Hi." He looked quite dashing in a black cardigan, form-fitting black T-shirt, and black jeans. He would make some woman a great piece of arm candy. "I didn't know you liked this place." Did he have a Get Hitched date tonight as well? What were the odds they'd choose the same restaurant? Well...not that long, considering there were only so many super nice restaurants to choose from.

"Pardon my interruption." Ronnie stood. "Luna, thank you so much for having drinks with me. I wish you the best of luck in your search for the perfect partner."

"You as well." How had they matched up on the app? He wasn't anything like the type of guy she'd said she wanted to meet. Was there a flaw with the app?

He picked up the bill holder and stuck money in it. "I paid half. I would pay for all of it, but I feel like you misrepresented yourself on the app." With those words, he rushed away.

Mitch gave her a quizzical look. "Did you lie?"

"What the hell?" She downed half of what was left of her drink before giving her attention to Mitch. "I'll have you know I answered every question honestly. There should have been no confusion in what type of man I'm looking to meet." Damn it. It should've been her who had left Ronnie sitting at the table. He was the one who'd been a bad date. And he had to go and dump her in front of Mitch.

On the bright side, she wouldn't have to dodge any more of Ronnie's questions about where he'd seen her in the past. She'd thought she'd changed her appearance enough not to be recognized by the public at large. Maybe she should change her hair color again.

Mitch took a seat next to Luna instead of across the table. He picked up the bill, glanced at it, and stuck a twenty inside. "His loss."

How sweet. "Damn straight."

Mitch had sat so close, their knees touched. And for some reason the contact made it hard to think. Or maybe it was the half drink she'd just gulped. That was a more logical explanation.

He gave her an intense stare, as if looking for an answer to a question she didn't know, and then he blinked. "Sorry it didn't work out."

She shifted her knees to the left so that they no longer touched his. "I'll just have to add it to all my other app-dates-gone-wrong entries in Ms. Rosie Nosey." She picked up her swizzle stick and went back to stirring her Old Fashioned. She should have ordered a double.

"In what?" he asked.

"My journal where I keep a running account of my dates-gone-wrong."

"That's right. You name inanimate objects." Mitch took his cardigan off and laid it on the chair Ronnie had occupied earlier. Getting comfortable as if ready to settle into an evening in her company.

"Aren't you meeting someone?" she blurted. "Like a date? Oh wait, don't tell me... You have a rule about showing up super early for a date? And you plan to pass the time with me. Am I right?" Why was she being rude to Mitch? It wasn't his fault a guy had just ditched her in front of him.

Mitch's lips twitched. "I don't have a rule about showing up super early. Tell me about your other entries in this journal."

"If I tell you about them, will you promise not to use it as fodder to make fun of me?"

He frowned. "I was thinking more along the lines of using your missteps to not make the same mistakes on my future app dates."

"Did you get dumped tonight as well?" For some reason she'd kind of sort of thought he'd never get around to actually making an app date. That he'd talk himself out of the idea. And she had been weirdly fine with that.

His right ear turned red. "Not hardly. Olga and I met for drinks at the bar across the street. When I was leaving, I saw you through the window and thought I'd come over and say hi, since we're friends."

Olga...not Brandy. Now would be the perfect opportunity to ask what had become of the out-of-the-blue call. Or was that the type of question you had to be friends for years before you could ask? "How did it go?" Real friendships couldn't be shoved inside a greenhouse and forced into early maturity. And until she felt at one with Luna 2.0, she needed to navigate relationships carefully and avoid relationship-ending missteps.

"Let's just say I'm glad we only made plans to have drinks."

She gave him a ruthful smile. "That will be my new rule of app-dating. First dates—drinks only." It would be fun to commiserate together about their dating ventures.

He cocked his head. "Luna Parker, are you drunk?"

Had she slurred her words? "Of course not. Why would you say that?"

"Because the Luna I'm friends with would never embrace the art of living by rules."

She blinked. He'd made a joke in a very unawkward way. In fact, he'd done so in a sexy way. She'd not seen this side of him. "Very funny. If you're going to tease me, the least you could do is offer to buy me dinner."

A smile spread across his face. "There's the woman I know. The one who breaks rules. Rules like the man should do the asking out on dates, not the woman."

"Oh, for the love of sex, that rule is about as outdated as the one that says men and women can never be just friends."

"There are exceptions to every rule," he said. "But most rules are rules because time has proven them accurate more often than wrong." This was delivered in his uptight voice.

She sighed. What had she said to get him out of his comfort zone and back into his rigid zone?

His gaze briefly shifted to her lips before jerking back up to her eyes.

Her breath caught. Was that desire she saw in his eyes? She quickly glanced away. They were friends. She didn't want to mess that up. Dates were a dime a dozen. Friends, for Luna 2.0, were like rare diamonds. While it might be intriguing to color outside the lines with him, she knew she'd regret the choice in the morning.

She should say something to squash any romantic ideas he might have. "You and I will be a casebook study of how men and women can be just friends. A study so fantastic some psychiatrist will use it in their future best seller that debunks the theory opposite sexes can't be just friends."

The slight tightening of Mitch's lips followed by the downward jerk of his head was his only response.

Luna waited for the thrill to materialize over having done something very Luna 2.0.

Luna 1.0 would have never made the mature choice to keep Mitch in the friend zone.

The thrill never hit. *Ugh. What is wrong with me?*

16

Thirty minutes after Mitch crashed Luna's date and then became her replacement date, they had ordered drinks and were waiting for dinner to arrive. They'd chatted about many things. Even managed to avoid the topic of her awful attempt at making muffins but not what he wanted to speak about. What he needed to talk about. Her selling her property.

Now that their conversation had come to a natural lull—after she'd commented on the cuteness of the baby being held by her daddy two tables over and he'd agreed—it was his chance to subtly introduce the subject. "So, where do you see yourself raising a family someday? A big city or a small town? A home with a dangerous cliff in its backyard or a home with a white picket fence?"

Her eyes crinkled at the corners. "Look at you, forgetting we're not on an actual date and there's no need for you to work that particular early-in-the-dating question into the conversation. Was that just a memory-muscle question your brain told your mouth to ask?"

While having someone bust his balls for screwing up in the conversation arena wasn't his favorite thing, he found it refreshing that Luna did so in a manner that didn't sting. "Guilty. I always try to ask this by the second date with a woman, and since this is our second non-date, you're probably right about the memory-muscle. You, of course, don't need to answer."

She laid a hand on his and squeezed. "I don't mind answering." She moved her hand away. "I grew up in the city, and while it has its perks, I think if I ever have children, I'd love to raise them in a small town."

"But not necessarily Rocky Mountain Springs?" he pushed, resisting the urge to ask her about her name change. She should have the choice of when and with whom she shared that secret.

"It depends on if our being friends helps me to make additional friends." She thrummed her fingers on the table as she spoke. "If it doesn't, I'll move. While I'm not afraid to put in the work to prove I'm likable, I'm also not a glutton for punishment. Life is too short to be around people who don't like you."

Her answer should have thrilled him. Under the right circumstances, she was willing to sell. Those circumstances were exactly what he'd been blackmailed into making happen.

All he had to do was stop being her friend and influence others to continue boycotting her both personally and professionally and she'd move, and the mayor's threats would dissolve. Not to mention, he'd have the opportunity to buy his home.

Only if he went about getting her out of town via manipulation, he wasn't sure he could live with himself. It wasn't honorable. Then again, the mayor's threat affected more than Mitch. Regis had gone after Johnny and Amahle. The honorable path would hang them out to dry.

It's one thing to take the high road when you were the only one facing severe consequences. It was entirely a different thing to take the high road when the well-being of others was also on the line.

As much as Mitch hated to admit it, he had no choice but to get Luna out of town. The only thing he had a choice in was if he did so with honesty or dishonesty. Fuck. Why in the hell had the mayor gone and investigated his background? The thought of Mayor Regis knowing about his mother's criminal history made Mitch edgy. Sensing a pending panic attack, he changed the subject.

"What is your test to know when a friend is a good enough friend you can tell them your secret fears and secret desires?"

Luna's eyes widened at his awkward, out-of-left-field change of topic. What he wouldn't give to be a smooth operator at least once in his life.

"Oh. Wow." Her slender hand fluttered to her throat. "You're going deep."

"I've been accused of that before."

She laughed.

He felt his ear heat. "That's not what I meant."

"Sorry." She didn't sound sorry. "Drinking brings out my gutter brain."

He took a gulp of his drink and told his brain to absolutely not think about going deep inside of her. She'd made it quite clear she was only interested in friendship. If she'd said something flirty, it was only because she'd had a couple of drinks. "I can ask a different question."

He didn't want to ask a different question. He liked this one. If his plan was to use honesty to get Luna to leave, the path forward would require him to tell her his fears. All of them. And there was no way he could share those until he trusted her not to use them against him.

"Not necessary," Luna said. "I have an answer. My test to know when a friend is one I can tell my secrets to is when they've proven they won't turn their back on me in a moment of crisis."

Her response was as perfect as it was sad. He reached out and laid his hand on top of hers. "Have you ever had someone do that to you?"

She pulled her hand away and fidgeted with her bracelets. "That answer is for another day. How about you? What is your test of a true friendship?"

He sat back. "Someone who accepts my brain glitches as part of who I am." Having a mother who had been embarrassed by his personality, he placed high value on those who thought his weirdness was part of what made him fantastic. Like Amahle and Johnny.

Luna's lashes fluttered, veiling her eyes. "Tell me about your date."

It took him a moment to process her own awkward change of topic. Had he said something inappropriate? He didn't believe so. "What about my date?"

Her eyes met his with an intensity he didn't quite understand. "Are you going to ask her to be your plus-one at the weed ball?"

Hell. That was a whole other problem in his life. "She had prior plans for that evening." He was pretty sure her plan included washing her hair, but plans were plans. "I...don't suppose you'd consider being my plus-one?" He hadn't meant to ask the question but found himself glad he had. That was, until Luna closed her eyes like he'd just asked her to give him her last good kidney.

Did her reason for looking so pained have anything to do with why she was in hiding? Why she had changed her name?

"I can see you wish I hadn't asked. Don't worry about it." The last thing he wanted to do was to put her in a position that might be dangerous. "I'm sure with enough begging, Amahle will be my plus-one."

Luna jolted like maybe he'd jerked her out of an unpleasant daze. "Not necessary. I'd love to be your date. It's the least I can do for a friend. And I consider us friends." She placed a lot of emphasis on the last word.

Fuck. How in the hell would he juggle being her friend with the mayor's threats? "My offer to be your friend doesn't come with strings attached. Don't feel like you're under some type of obligation to say yes."

"I disagree. On our first outing, you mentioned the reason for inviting me to dinner had to do with the implied contract of being someone's friend. And you were right. A friendship is an implied contract to be there for one another. And my answer is a firm yes. I'll go with you to the weed ball."

They traded a glance. A glance that spoke volumes without words. Or at least his imagination manufactured a whole conversation that went along with the glance. "Thank you. It means a lot."

She gave a sharp nod as if to say *you're welcome.* "And, seeing as we're talking about what it means to be a friend, will you give me your honest opinion of the muffin I left for you?"

Not the muffin. He glanced around the room for a distraction. Finding none, he resumed eye-contact with Luna. "Why do you ask?"

She bit her bottom lip and studied him as if deciding if she could trust him with the answer. Then she shrugged. "A bad review...or seven...on my website for Luna's Goat Yoga. One of them said my food was awful."

He swallowed hard. He should have told her right away. He'd known of her plan to serve food at her yoga spa day events. "The thought is what matters, and your leaving that muffin for me and a half dozen for the mayor was very thoughtful."

"But?"

"But they weren't the best."

She slapped her palms on the table. "Why didn't you just tell me? It would have saved me so much embarrassment."

He felt his right ear heat. "My apologies. Next time your cooking sucks, as your new friend who places a high value on trust, I promise to be honest and mention it. We'll just consider that one of the rules of the implied contract that comes with our friendship."

"You better. What good is a friend if they don't tell you when your dress is in your underwear or your muffins need a taste fluffin'?"

"Deal."

Her eyes lit up. "I have a brilliant idea."

He swallowed hard. "Dare I ask?"

"If you're up for something fun after the ball, what do you say to the idea of us having a friendship ceremony in my backyard underneath Mildred?"

"A what?"

"A friendship ceremony. You know, like a wedding ceremony only not."

"That's a thing?"

"Absolutely. And it will be grand if we have one. Ms. Houdini can be my goat of honor, and Mr. JJ can be your best goat. Ms. Tinker can be our goat witness. It'll be a hoot."

He dragged a hand down his jaw. "Has anyone ever told you you're not normal?"

She shrugged. "Normal is highly overrated."

17

One week later, Luna and Mitch were at the ball.

She studied her date while he glanced around the room. The pulse in his jaw had started twitching the second he'd laid eyes on her which had only been a few moments ago. Because of schedule complications, they'd met at the ball instead of him picking her up and bringing her like the *rules* said he should.

She adjusted the bohemian headband she'd made for tonight's event. It was embellished with black antique jewels. The adornment went perfectly with her long black lace dress and its nude-colored silky slip. She cleared her throat. "As much as I wish I could, I can't read your mind. What's wrong? Did something happen before you got here or have I done something to set you off?"

"I'm upset because from a distance, you look nude."

She rolled her eyes. "Is that all? Don't be such an old man. I'm fully clothed. It's a false impression. No one actually thinks I'm nude."

He made a noise that sounded something like a growl. "I can assure you every man at this event is fantasizing just that." His right ear turned red as he spoke. "Even the valet made it a point to tell me I'm one lucky son-of-a-bitch to have you as my date when you walked out to meet me at the car."

She reminded herself why she was here. To be his friend. Not to teach him how to lighten up. Still. To be lectured about what she wore was beyond infuriating. "Considering we're just friends, why do you care what other men are thinking? You can't possibly be jealous."

"Of course I'm not jealous. I just care about your reputation. As your friend, it's my job to protect it, and if someone says something lewd, I'll be honor-bound to kick his ass. And you do recall my telling you that I have to maintain a spotless reputation to keep my license to sell?"

She placed a hand on his arm. "Under no circumstances are you to sully your reputation trying to defend my honor." For the life of her, she couldn't imagine him in a fight. Then again, he wasn't the type to say something he didn't mean. The guy puzzled her. It had been a long time since a man had done that. "I'm sorry I made the wrong dress choice, but it's too late to change, so let's put your disapproval aside and make the most of being here." She glanced around. The room buzzed with excitement. Especially at the bar, which had been strategically situated in the center of the ballroom.

Those gathered there were heartily laughing as if being entertained by professional comedians. "What is our goal tonight?"

If this were one of her parents' parties, she'd be cynical and assume the people creating the stir were hired party energizers. Those whose job was to give the event the feel of high energy.

But this wasn't one of Mother and Father's events. And she couldn't be sure energizers were even a thing in Colorado.

She continued to survey the room. Whoever had set up the party knew a little something about entertainment. The tables were tall and contained no chairs, encouraging interaction. People who sat didn't mingle. People who stood moved around a room.

"I need you to help me make a good impression. Help me make contacts."

She laid a hand on his arm. "Then all you need to do is act yourself, and they will adore you."

He gave her a look of bemusement. "I'm not exactly an excitement kind of guy at these types of events."

She straightened his tie. "Then it's lucky for you that you have me as a friend. If you'll trust me, I promise by the time the evening is over, everyone will remember your name and consider you an asset on their contact list."

His nostrils flared. "I have no doubt you can pull that off. Hell, you managed to win me over, and I had no desire to be won over by you."

She grinned. "I did, didn't I?" Winning him over was a testament that Luna 2.0 attracted real friends. And if she could win over Mitch Johnson, she could overcome the damage done to her business by her ex-friends. She'd been following them on social media to see if they mentioned her. They hadn't. But there were a lot of vague posting about a mysterious new friend they'd recently met. One they couldn't mention by name...yet.

"You also won over Johnny and Amahle," he added.

She pushed the thought aside and focused on Mitch. "I like them as well. Now, tell me, what kind of personality do you believe will impress tonight's clientele?"

He rubbed his jawline with his thumb and index finger. Obviously giving much consideration to her question. Finally, he said, "Yours."

Warm and gushy feelings swept through her, making her toes curl in her pinchy-toe heels. She'd bought them secondhand. "Then let's get busy. Point out the big shots, and I'll get us in on their conversations."

"The guy in the black top hat is the president of The Colorado Cannabis Growers Association."

"Are you a member?" she asked.

"Of course."

"Follow me." She poached drinks for them from a wandering waiter, handed one to Mitch, and then made her way to the top hat guy.

The wearer was an exceedingly handsome gentleman, conversing animatedly with a group of three men and one woman. His tuxedo was not off the rack. Nor was his Rolex a knock-off. Things Mother had taught Luna to discern early in life. *If you don't know the difference, you might someday fall for a fake rich man.*

Luna and Mitch stood on the outside edge of the group while she waited for a lull in the current conversation, which revolved around best-selling edibles. Who was having luck with what? When a moment of silence happened, she jumped in. "I am new to the world of legalized cannabis, but I have to say I find it fascinating how creative you all are in the kitchen."

"And you are?" the top-hat wearer asked.

"I'm Luna Parker, date of Mitch Johnson." She pulled Mitch closer to her side. "Darling, is it okay if I tell them about the edible you're working on? Or do you want it to stay a secret?"

Mitch stared, stupefied. She resisted the urge to kick him in the shin the way Amahle would. Instead, she squeezed his arm, and that did the trick. "Not at all," he said.

Well crap. She'd sort of planned on him telling her no. They'd have to work on their schtick. She squealed and gave the gathering a smile. "Mitch is working on a new edible that, well, let's just say it's going to blow your mind." She leaned in slightly and lowered her voice. "In fact, I'd go so far as to say if he perfects it, all fifty states will legalize weed within the year."

Mitch choked on the hors d'oeuvre he'd just popped in his mouth.

"What makes it so special?" asked a woman as she looked Mitch over as if he were a morsel she'd like to nibble.

Luna tightened her grip on Mitch's arm. She told herself it was to give him moral support. That was her story, and she was sticking to it. Just as Mitch didn't need to be jealous of men looking at her, she didn't need to be jealous of women looking at him. She gazed up at Mitch with an adoring smile and waited for him to reply.

He cleared his throat and took a sip of his champagne. "Umm. That's a secret."

Luna glanced merrily at the group. "I can't say another word, but you should all get ready to have your jocks and panties knocked off."

Almost everyone laughed at her outlandish declaration. Mitch being the exception.

The president gave him a good look. "Mitch, I'm looking forward to talking to you about this edible when you're ready to put it on the market."

When Mitch didn't immediately respond, Luna squeezed his arm.

The pressure broke him out of his dismay. "Thank you."

"I do believe I see Amahle," Luna said. "Let's go say hi before she sneaks out of here."

"Amahle's not—"

"Supposed to be here. I know. I wonder how she managed to get a babysitter." Luna pulled him with her through the crowd as she spoke. Once they were out of sight and earshot of the group, she stopped and stared at him. "Friend, you've got to do a better job of playing along."

18

Mitch stared into Luna's eyes and fought for a calm he hadn't had all night. Hell. A calm he hadn't had since meeting her. "I thought you said I could trust you."

She blinked, and the grip she had on his arm loosened. "You can."

"Says the woman who just made a promise I can't deliver?"

Luna grinned. A smile so large it reminded him of an accomplice ready to celebrate a well-played crime with her delinquent cohort. "Sure you can."

"You have them all believing I'm going to create an edible that's so special every state is going to legalize cannabis?" What had she been thinking to make that kind of promise?

She raised her hands in a what-can-I-say gesture. "Go big or go home. That's what Father taught me."

"Your dad taught you that if you're going to lie, make it unbelievable?" Was that a legit kind of thing fathers taught their daughters?

Though hell, if he were ever a father, what kind of father would he be? He'd had no fucking role model growing up. Scratch that. He'd had plenty of role models, and they'd all been fucking assholes.

Her smile slipped. "That's not what I said. He taught me not to think small when making a lasting impression."

Mitch sighed. He knew she meant well, and she couldn't help it if she had an all-or-nothing personality. And to be fair, that's one of the things he liked about her even though it often gave him hives. "It's impossible to make an edible so good all the states will legalize cannabis."

"That's likely true if you have a negative attitude."

"My attitude is realistic."

"Poppycock potpie. It's full of negativity. If you like, I'll help you create the perfect edible."

He laughed. "You're not exactly known for your cooking."

Her cocky smile slipped. "Hey, just because my muffins aren't up to snuff doesn't mean the rest of my cooking is bad."

"Shall we go home?" he asked.

"Already? Why?"

He had no idea why he'd said that. Other than the fact she still brought out the awkward in him. The guy who couldn't handle situations full of uncertainty. "Because it's obvious I bore you as your date and that's why you said something so outlandish."

She grimaced. "What are you talking about? I'm not even a little bored. I like hanging out with you." Without asking his permission, she reached up and grazed her lips on his cheek.

Desire coursed through him. Desire he didn't welcome. He took a step back, putting some distance between them. "Friends don't kiss."

She cocked her head and shook it. "Hanging out with you, Mitch Johnson, is like eating chocolate while wearing white linen."

"Do you have any sayings that actually make sense?" he asked.

She straightened. "In other words, you're socially correct all the way down to your no-doubt starched boxers, but get you out of those babies, and you're full of potential danger."

"I do not wear starched underwear." He glanced around the room. "This is important to me. Was I wrong to invite you?"

A line formed between her eyes. "Mitch, I promise my methods will achieve the goal you're after. There was a time in my life, before I discovered the joys of simple living, that I attended events like these. I know what works and what doesn't work. That's why I asked you to trust me."

"Then you do you come from money?" he asked.

"Ooh, there's a woman surrounded by others over there." Luna spoke in a cheerful tone as if they weren't having a serious conversation. "She must be important. Let's see what her group is talking about."

Luna's evasion of the question gave him her answer, which made sense. You couldn't buy a home on a whim if you don't have money. And someone her age didn't have that kind of funding in the bank unless they came from wealth.

The bottom line, she had more in common with Brandy than she did with him. And he, as-is, hadn't been enough for Brandy. The thought gave him heartburn. "Why don't we call it a night?"

"Give me another chance to be useful to you."

"I don't know."

She stepped closer and stood on her tiptoes and peered intently at him. "Please. I'll do better this time. I don't regret you offering to be my friend. The last thing I want is for you to regret being mine."

He leaned his forehead down on hers and took several breaths. Underneath her personality quirks, Luna Parker had a good heart. She couldn't help it if she had been born into money any more than he could help being born into poverty. "Okay." He straightened. "But don't say anything about my edibles."

A wayward grin lifted her lips. "Never twice in one night. It's simply unheard of in polite company."

He chuckled. Damn. Being her friend would never be boring.

19

Two hours later, Luna sat unbuckled in Mitch's truck, in her driveway. She turned in her seat and bestowed upon him her full attention. "That went well. Thank you for trusting me."

They'd stayed until the event had ended, which was not late. He had eventually relaxed and had been fun...in his trademark awkward way.

Once she'd stopped trying to be the center of attention, something Luna 1.0 would have never done—*stopped*, that was—Luna 2.0 had enjoyed herself. One of the perks of being Mitch's date was watching him interact with his peers. Around them he was a different man. In charge, knowledgeable, and easygoing. He hadn't needed her at all.

Now she watched as Mitch twisted on the truck's bench seat so that his body angled toward her. The fact he'd said nothing didn't even surprise her. He wasn't one to speak without weighing his words.

While he studied her, she noticed things she hadn't noticed before. The ridiculous length of his eyelashes. The sexy way his throat moved when he swallowed hard. The slight flare of his nostrils. Why were his nostrils flaring?

A peculiar sense of lightheadedness swam over her. What was that about? "Any day now."

"When you started talking about the legitimacy of aliens, I almost called it quits."

Oh yeah. She had done that. But only because the wife of one of his cohorts had introduced the subject. "The look on your face was priceless," she teased. He'd looked like she'd announced the world would be better off without legalized cannabis.

"I'm still getting used to your sense of humor."

"Oh, I wasn't being funny. I stand by my words. Aliens are totally a thing."

He reached out and tucked a curl behind her ear. "Have I mentioned before that you're weird?"

She turned her face toward him to respond. Instead of dropping his hand away, he opened his palm and cupped her jaw. After a half-beat of registering how good his touch felt, she teased, "Then it's a good thing you like weird. Just as it's a good thing I like uptight rule followers."

He jerked his hand back to his lap. "I'm glad you went as my plus-one tonight. You were quite delightful. Even if I'm now in the impossible position of creating an edible that will knock all their jocks and panties off."

She slid her headband off and fiddled with it while she processed a proper retort. And processed the weird stirring in her stomach caused by his hand on her face. Probably the result of a tad too many flutes of champagne. "Are you ready to do our Friendship Ceremony?"

He raised his eyebrows and gave her a WTF look. "We're still doing that?"

She gave him a WTF look right back. "Of course."

He opened the truck door. "Then, let's do it." He hopped out and came around the cab to her side where he opened the door and helped her out.

When he tried to let go of her hand, she held tight. "Close your eyes."

"Only for you would I close my eyes."

His trust felt good. She hoped she never did anything stupid to lose it. Determined not to, she carefully led him around to the back of the house. "Okay. Open them." She stood aside and waited for his reaction. Mildred was decked out in fairy lights, and an arch stood proudly under the tree. An arch! She'd fashioned it out of old wire she'd found in Ms. Barnetta instead of ordering one on Amazon.

He took his time taking it in, his expression a study in multiple poker faces. Then he smiled and shook his head. "Fancy. I wasn't expecting... Truthfully, I have no idea what I was expecting."

As ideas went, it was an odd one. She knew that. But it was fun and carefree and very Luna 2.0. "Excellent. Let me get the goats dressed while you light the candles on the picnic table. Feel free to help yourself to a flute of champagne. Once our Goat of Honor, Best Goat, and goat witness are ready, we'll hold the ceremony."

Twenty minutes later, they stood facing one another under the fairy lights. Ms. Houdini stood next to Luna. She had on a black hat that looked like something out of the 1920s, blush, and seductive red lipstick. Mr. JJ stood by Mitch. He wore a black bow tie. Ms. Tinker laid on the ground in front of them. Her only accessory, gaudy pearl clip-on earrings.

"Now what?" Mitch asked.

Luna could tell by the mellow in his eyes and the sweet scent in the air that he'd smoked a joint while she had gotten the goats ready.

"I recite my vows to you promising to be a good friend. And then you do the same."

"I haven't written any vows."

She blinked. Why hadn't he written vows? She pulled hers out of a hidden pocket in her dress. "Then you'll just have to wing it." She opened her speech, cleared her throat, and began. "I, Luna Parker, being of mostly sound mind, do hereby declare my unwavering friendship to Mitch Johnson. I promise to have your back in any public situation. If I believe you to be wrong, I will tell you so in private. I promise to be there when you need to talk. To say nothing when you just need my presence but not my opinion. I promise to laugh at your bad jokes at least once a month." She folded up her speech, stuck it back in her pocket. "And I promise to help you create an edible that will make all fifty states want to legalize cannabis." She waited for him.

He said nothing.

"It's your turn."

"I know. I'm just trying to come up with the right words for how I'm feeling at this moment." He pulled at his collar.

"Then as your friend, I'll stand here silently and wait for you to speak."

Many seconds later, he cleared his throat. "I, Mitch Johnson, clearly being of unsound mind for being a part of a friendship ceremony, do hereby declare my freely given friendship to Luna Parker. I recognize Ms. Parker's weirdness and never-ending antics as a part of who she is, and I embrace the idea of bringing a friend like that into my life. Together, I believe we will balance each other out. I...shall strive to always have her back in any given situation. And to occasionally put aside my rules if the result brings a smile to her lips." He stopped and glanced at the goats. "And I promise to protect her from those who would try and harm her. Oh, and eat her muffins without complaint."

She laughed.

"Now what?" he asked.

"Well, in a wedding ceremony, this is where you would kiss the bride. So, I do believe, in a friendship ceremony, this is where you should hug your friend."

20

M itch's thoughts were caught between common sense and desire. Desire shoved common sense and all its negativity on its ass.

"If it's all the same to you," he said. "I do believe something as solemn as a friendship ceremony should be sealed with a kiss."

He stood quietly and provided her with time to say no. As he did so, he recounted the freckles on her nose. Nine of them. Hadn't there only been seven the last time he'd counted?

The pink tip of her tongue swiped her parted lips, scattering his thoughts.

"Now is when you should say something," he said.

"Like what?"

He'd never known her to be at a loss for words. "Like *yes, no, are you fucking crazy, Mitch?*"

Her smile was a flash of light. "Why on earth would I say no to kissing the dude whose superpower is kissing?"

He shook his head. "I can't think of a fucking reason."

"Stop talking and for once in your life, just do," she whispered as her eyes drifted shut.

"Yes, ma'am." He slid a hand over her jaw and tipped her head back. He slanted his mouth over hers and gently touched his lips to her perfectly unpredictable mouth. The contact unleased an appetite in him like none he'd ever experienced. Still, he fought hard to keep the kiss tender and simple.

As if in disagreement with him, her fingers curled into his jacket, and she flattened herself against him and opened her mouth inviting the hunger he was trying to keep at bay. Giving into his desires, he groaned and pushed her lips wide so his tongue could taste her.

Of course, she tasted of chaos. Hell. She personified chaos. His new best friend was more chaotic than Jack Nicholson in *Batman*. But it was more than chaos he tasted. There was also the sweet flutter of butterflies and the tangy galloping of desire. God, he could become addicted to her taste.

The thought yanked him back like an unexpected ice bath in the desert, and he disengaged from the kiss. He couldn't afford to become addicted to Luna.

"I wasn't done kissing," she said in a throaty voice.

Her words made him smile, yet he clenched his hands at his sides to keep from touching her again. "I need to rationally consider my next move. I can't go down—"

Her eyes popped wide. "Who said anything about going down? We're friends—"

"I was talking about love, not oral sex." His right ear heated.

"Be still, my heart." She plopped her hand over her chest. "A guy who brings up the L-word before the O-word. And at a friendship ceremony to boot."

Her teasing should have saved the moment. And it would have, had his brain been able to get control of his mouth before he opened it and said, "The last time I fell in love, it ended in an engagement, which ended in humiliation. I can't do that ever again." Fuck. Why was he talking love? What in the hell was wrong with him? That had been a kiss to seal their friendship.

She lifted her hair off her slender neck and waved a hand as if to cool herself. "As your new best friend, let me point out, friends don't fall in love with one another. It would ruin the friendship. The kiss was truly just a kiss."

He shook his head, causing his glasses to slip down his nose. He shoved them back into place. "A kiss that caused my brain to crumble like a poorly designed sandcastle."

She scoffed. "I do believe you're high, and thus I will not allow your words to cause me to get a big head or my heart to knit intricately woven thoughts of our falling in love."

He ran a hand over his face. Kissing his ex-fiancée had never made him spin out of control. "I apologize for having the first bad idea in our newly cemented friendship."

"Not that I plan on keeping count of who accumulates the most bad ideas in our future relationship, but by my account, I now have one freebie due me."

He laughed. "If I could bottle you up and put you in an edible, that would absolutely cause all states to legalize cannabis."

"Aren't you just the smoothest-move operator?" she said with a wink.

She thought he was flirting. He wasn't. "Seriously. Just one taste would be all it took to have every consumer voting for the right to enjoy their own Rocky Mountain Luna High."

21

Twelve hours later, Mitch raised his hand and knocked on Luna's door. When the door swung open, he was not ready for what he saw. "Damn it to hell." The four words had to squeeze out of his clenched throat. "Where are your clothes?" How in the fuck was a guy to stay sane around her?

She rolled her eyes. "Not trying to scar your sense of properness. I was in the shower and forgot to grab a towel and was on my way to the utility room to get one when you knocked. I didn't want you to think I wasn't home, so I answered the door because, you know, it's not like you haven't seen me naked." She stepped back.

"Come on in and make yourself comfortable while I get dressed."

Those words coming out of the mouth of any other woman wouldn't have been believable, but Luna was clearly not answering in the nude as a form of seduction. Her expression shouted nonchalance about nudity just like it had the day he'd seen her doing yoga in the nude. "Parker, I can come back later."

"Nonsense. I have a project I need your help with." Luna removed a raincoat from the coatrack by the door and slipped it on. "Oh, by the way, I've decided on a nickname for you."

"And that is?"

"Captain Suck Face."

"You're hilarious." For the love of a good high, the woman was making fun of him for suggesting they kiss to end their friendship ceremony.

She blinked. "I wasn't trying to be funny. Last night you proved to me that kissing truly is your superpower. So, it only stands to reason you need a superhero nickname."

"And Captain Suck Face is the best you could manage?" Amahle would laugh her ass off when she learned of this moniker.

"I would have gone with Captain Smooch Lips but couldn't because—"

"Shut up already." A grin tried to lift his lips. He had to force it away. "I don't know why I even like you."

She laughed. "I like you, too." Her tone was as cheerful as the smile she flashed. "A lot. Although I don't know why either, so don't ask me to explain."

She turned and padded barefoot into her kitchen.

Thoughts of their kiss had kept him up all night spurring him to show up this morning in the hopes of talking about it. Unfortunately, thoughts hadn't clarified his reaction to the kiss. Why had something as simple as a kiss unleashed so many wants that he absolutely could not act upon? They'd decided to become just friends for valid reasons. His reasons had not changed. And they were further complicated by the mayor's blackmail.

Hell, that kiss need not ever be mentioned again.

Which left him scrambling for a reason as to why he was here, should she ask. Maybe to borrow butter.

In the kitchen, he noticed her refrigerator was now covered in sticky notes. "Is there a story behind all those things?" He resisted an urge to grab one and read it like she'd done with his invitation to the ball.

"My upcoming appointments. I've misplaced my planner...again. And business has exploded since I went live on Instagram and asked those considering booking a spa day at Luna's Goat Yoga to please not let the recent reviews spook them away. I explained that, like so many of us, I'm a work in progress, and blah, blah, blah."

He'd read the reviews. They were scathing. Her method of addressing them impressed him. "Good for you." He noticed something yellow peeking out from under the refrigerator and leaned down and picked it up. A sticky note which had lost its sticky. On the front it said, *Wednesday at 3:00 for six.* "You forgot to put a date on this one. How will you know which Wednesday it refers to?"

She grabbed the note and pondered its content. "It's for the first Wednesday after the first full moon after the summer equinox."

"What's so special about that day?"

"It's the best day of the year to send a request for forgiveness into the universe to those you've done wrong. I'm hosting an Instagram live Forgiveness Yoga event that morning, and six of my regulars are participating."

Did she have someone she needed forgiveness for? And did that person have anything to do with her living under an alias? He settled into the thought. Perhaps that's why she was possibly in witness protection. She'd reported a crime committed by someone she knew, someone dangerous, and… "If you made that up off the top of your head, I'm impressed." He strode to the window and stared out. The goats were in the pen, but the gate hung open. Why have a gate if you're not going to utilize the latch? "What did you need help with outside?"

"You'll see. But let me change first. This raincoat is hot."

He yanked himself around and fell into her green eyes. Kissing her last night had been a monumental mistake for two people who wanted to prove men and women could be just friends. But honestly, he didn't regret the lapse in judgment. "Okay."

Five minutes later they stood in front of her barn. She'd put on a pair of soft blue sweats and a white T-shirt.

"Thanks for waiting. By the way, do you know how I can reach the last person who lived here?"

He got a sudden case of indigestion. "I guess now is as good a time as any to mention my ex-fiancée used to live here."

"Oh. I'll have to sit with that knowledge for a while before I can speak as to how I feel about learning that."

He didn't know how he'd expected her to react, but definitely not calmly. Maybe with a bit of jealousy. Which made his ego way too big for his body. Of course she didn't care. It wasn't like she had romantic designs on Mitch. "Why do you ask?"

"There was a box of essential oils tucked behind a wheelbarrow. Half of them were broken. The other half intact. I just thought I'd make an effort to get them back to their rightful owner. They're not cheap, you know?"

He snorted. "I'm sure they belonged to Old Lady Murphy. She's the original owner." She'd been the town's lovable drunk. "She never mentioned them, but she was the sort to use them."

"And what sort would that be?" Luna asked quietly.

"The sort who went through life believing black and white answers didn't exist. I could tell her my name is Mitch and she'd say not in a previous life. You know...that sort."

"My Nanny Nonna was like that. She believed you could interact with those in the afterlife. And she wasn't wrong. On more than one occasion, she's come into my dreams and given me guidance on decisions I'm facing."

"I see." He wasn't even a little surprised to learn Luna thought she could communicate with the dead. Because of course she thought that. "Someday I'd like to hear more about your nanny."

"Absolutely." She turned toward the barn and pointed up at the trap door. "Speaking of dead people, would you mind pulling the ladder down for me?"

He waited for her to elaborate on the opening of that sentence, but she didn't. Instead, she busied herself grabbing a dusty bucket and emptying it of its contents.

"What does my pulling the ladder down for you have to do with speaking of dead people?" he finally asked.

"Oh, that." She flipped the bucket over and placed it beneath the attic opening. She stood on it, reached for the stairs, and came up several inches short. "In a recent dream, Nanny Nonna told me to get my ass up in the rafters of Ms. Barnetta and check out the contents of its freezer."

22

Luna watched as Mitch processed her words. The myriad of expressions playing across his face was comical. She knew he'd finished when his face went perfectly blank.

"I can assure you," he said, cabernet sauvignon dry, "you won't find a freezer. Is there even power out here?"

"Of course, there is. Now, if you don't mind, I'll just give it a quick look-see and verify the freezer's existence with my own eyes."

Ever since last night, she'd kept telling herself she should just tell him her story. The felony part. Get it over with. If it was a friendship deal breaker for him, wouldn't it be better to discover that now than later?

Definitely. But telling him meant divulging her parents' murky little secret. The secret that was all tied up in her felony. And, according to Nanny Nonna, family trumped friendship when it came to one's loyalty.

Closet skeletons of those you love should always be left in the attic. In other words, Luna could not bring her parents' skeletons out for show and tell, because like them or not, she loved her parents.

Nanny Nonna had whispered that little gem in Luna's ear during another of her dream visits—a pop-in that had occurred right after Luna's big bad arrest. Those words, words she'd heard loud and clear in her dream, had steered Luna to plead guilty to a crime she hadn't committed. Well...she had technically done it. That dream had ultimately led her here. To this barn, staring at a guy whom she found herself liking. A lot.

So until she knew she could trust Mitch to never repeat her secrets, she wouldn't tell him.

She waved toward the ladder and gave him a smile. "Be a doll."

He pulled the ladder down and stepped back. "Go on. Check for your freezer. I'll stand here with a *friendly* I-told-you-so ready to burn your cute ears."

Her cheeky smile turned into a real one and then she scrambled up the wobbly ladder. What would she find left behind by the previous owners—other than a freezer?

So far, the bottom half of the barn had netted her all kinds of fun objects that had not been sold at auction because of a stipulation of the owner. According to the auctioneer, it had been predetermined that the person who bought the house got the barn and all its contents. Luna had been particularly excited over her discovery of a butter churner and an old-fashioned ice cream maker. They tied in nicely with her super-secret project idea. One she couldn't wait to initiate. Just as soon as she made a success out of Luna's Goat Yoga. She needed the income from that to fund her super-secret project.

Nothing that she had discovered so far compared to what met her gaze when her head broke above the trap door. She swayed and grabbed the opening to keep from tumbling backward. "Ho-ly Batman!" Excitement swept through her faster than a pregnancy rumor at a private middle school. What she saw had mystery written all over it, and she loved a good mystery.

"What?" Mitch asked. "Is there really a fucking freezer?"

"Duh. But that's not what has my thong in a twist."

"Is it a spider? If it's a spider, I'm not killing it."

Was that because he was afraid of spiders? Or because he didn't feel the need to kill a creature simply trying to live its best life? Or because his love of superheroes and Spiderman wouldn't exist if it weren't for a spider? Knowing him, it was the last.

She pulled her gaze away from the sight and forced it down on him. "Not a spider. Come and see for yourself."

"That's okay." He took several steps. Backward. Toward the exit. "I'm afraid of heights."

"For the love of sex, are you kidding me?"

"I assure you," he said stodgily, "acrophobia is a legitimate fear, and you shouldn't mock people who have phobias. And *for the love of sex* is not an appropriate phrase to use in times of distress."

Whatever. "Acrophobia or not, you're going to want to see this."

"Not happening."

She told herself not to judge him. All superheroes had a weakness. "Suit yourself." She scrambled over the edge and surveyed her discovery.

It was some type of lab. Complete with cauldrons and beakers and tongs. And a James-Bond-worthy safe with a massive combination lock. She walked over and fingered the lock. Flipped it over to see if the combination was taped on the back. No such luck. Yep. A mystery. She pushed on the vault to check its weight. It didn't budge. Interesting. If she wasn't mistaken, the darn thing was attached to the flooring.

She glanced at the books on the table. Soils. Chemistry. Ancient medicines. Then she walked over to the freezer. *Please don't let there be dead bodies inside.* Prepared for the worst, she closed her eyes and flung open the lid.

Cold air blasted her, causing ghost shivers to dance down her body. They started at her neck and ended at her toes.

Luna Parker, for heaven's sake, if there are dead bodies, they're dead. They can't hurt you. That was Nanny Nonna whispering in her ear.

Luna opened her eyes and took a picosecond glance. And then a microsecond glance. And then she hardcore stared. At black trash bags. Bulging black trash bags.

The hairs on the back of her neck woke up. She swallowed super-duper hard. *People don't put things in a freezer that don't require a temperature-controlled environment.* This came from her brain...not Nanny Nonna.

Things like dead bodies required temperature control to prevent the smell of rotting flesh from giving away a killer's secret.

She really should just open one and check. But, if she did, and a dead body popped out, her fingerprints would be on the bag. Then again, Nanny Nonna would never set her up to take the fall for a murder. Her parents, maybe. But not Nanny Nonna.

Luna shook away the shivers, carefully unwound the strings, and pulled open the top bag, all while demanding her eyes remain open.

Air whooshed out of her lungs. "Oh, thank the Universe." Her eyes relayed to her heart what they were seeing, and the organ did a happy dance.

Her freezer was stuffed to the brim with perfectly preserved pale pink flowers from a blooming Thundercloud Plum Tree. From Mildred. The bestest, most wonderfulest sight in the world. They were what she needed to kickstart her super-secret project. Well...that and money.

No wonder Nanny Nonna was all aflutter wanting her to look.

And it appeared Nanny Nonna wasn't the only one who knew Mildred's golden secret. Which so explained why Nanny Nonna had directed her to attend the auction on a day Luna had planned to spend plotting her new life while maintaining a low profile at an Airbnb two towns over.

"Is this a ruse on your part?" Mitch yelled.

"Nope." She retied the bag, grabbed a notebook off the table, and thumbed through the pages. Dates and numbers with the occasional written word. "Was Ms. Murphy a scientist?"

Mitch didn't reply.

Luna poked her head over the opening and looked at him. "Well?"

He scratched at the side of his head. "I guess you could say that...in an uneducated way."

Keeping her focus on him, she said, "Those are the best scientists."

Luna clambered down the ladder. This could only mean one thing. Nanny Nonna and Ms. Murphy were in spiritual cahoots. Which could also only mean one other thing. The two of them wanted her to use the contents of the bags in the freezer to jump-start her super-secret project. "Grab the sides of the ladder and take it one step at a time. I'll be right behind you."

"Not happening." He turned and, as he'd done on more than one occasion in their short acquaintance, stalked away.

What the actual fuck? "Aren't you the least bit curious what I discovered in the *working* freezer?"

"Not particularly."

"Ms. Murphy has a science lab up there." She omitted the part about the safe. No reason. Just did. "Why do you think that is?"

He walked to the picnic table and plopped down. "She wanted to find a cure for alcoholism."

"And?"

He rubbed his hands on his pants. "At one time, she thought pot was the answer. That's how we came to be friends. I helped her start her own weed garden."

Hmm. "And?"

"We discovered her soil has a different pH than mine, and the product that comes from her dirt is night and day better than what I can grow."

Luna relaxed. "Is that why you wanted to buy this property and bulldoze it? To maximize how much of its soil you had to grow your product?"

His eyes hardened. "I never planned to bulldoze the land. That was a bad joke referencing the fact Brandy had lived here. I wanted the land because I want to be a homeowner, and there's not a lot of options in Rocky Mountain Springs for one to own property."

"Oh. If that's the case, why did you quit bidding? From what I've heard, I got it for a bargain price."

"I was preapproved for a set amount by the bank. When it went above that amount, I had to call and get it raised, only my phone didn't work and by the time I got a hold of my banker, you'd won the bidding."

She wrinkled her nose. "On the bright side, you now have a new friend, and I have a real friend."

A vein popped out on his forehead. "Are you not used to having real friends?"

"Unfortunately, I've recently discovered that people I thought were my friends weren't."

"Why weren't they?"

"I can't say for sure, but my working theory is they were using me for things I had that they didn't."

He frowned. "I'm sorry."

She shrugged. "Don't be. It all worked to bring me to this point in my life, and I'm loving this point in my life."

"You love it here?"

She nodded.

"Even though the locals aren't friendly?"

"They'll come around. But enough about that. Tell me about the soil on my land. Should I bottle it up and sell it to other pot sellers?" she teased. "Or do you want to enter into a contract with me that only allows you access to it?"

He wiped his palms on his pants again. "Not funny."

She studied him. "Something bothering you?"

He went and sat at the picnic table. "Kissing you has me out of whack."

She liked that he was honest about last night's kiss. She, too, had been thrown by it. Hell, more like knocked on her ass. The guy had the lips of a Greek god. "I have an idea. It's an out-of-the-box type of idea."

"Do you ever have any other type?" Amusement flickered in his eyes.

A ribbon of excitement loosened her tongue. "We could finish what we started last night. Get it out of our systems. Then the mystery of it will be behind us, and we can go back to being friends. Complication-free friends. Because that is what we both agree would be the best type of relationship for us to have. And I kind of like having you as a friend. Lovers can be found in most any bar, but not friends."

He considered her long and hard. "Do you think that will work?"

Breath rushed out on a happy note, and she nodded. "Does that mean you're considering my proposal?"

"Now that I've gotten used to you, I don't want to mess up this friendship," he replied.

"Is that a no or a yes?" she asked.

His nostrils flared like they had last night in the truck. "Let's do this. I trust you."

Trust. Why had he gone and used that word? It reminded her of what it meant to be a friend. Luna 2.0 wanted friends she could trust, which meant being a friend others could trust. Before they had sex, she had to tell him about her felony. Family loyalty be damn. "Before we do...it..." She trailed off as Luna 1.0 tried to shut Luna 2.0 up.

"I'm listening." His voice was coated in dark chocolate and soaked in fine whiskey.

Get a grip. She was allowing sexual desires to get in the way of common sense. It wasn't the right time to tell him about her felony. While there was nothing left for her to be charged with, there was for her parents. Before she could tell Mitch about her run in with the law, she had to know one hundred percent he—in the name of following rules—wouldn't go to the authorities, which meant she had to come up with something on the fly. "I need to tell you my theory on the soil."

"Can't it wait?"

"Where did Ms. Murphy plant her weed?"

He sighed. "Next to the barn. East side."

"That's what I figured." She tossed him a grin. "That's where the broken essential oil bottles were."

"So?"

For a smart guy, he had some glitches. "Obviously, the oils soaked into the soil, and that is what made her soil so much better."

His brows furrowed. "You might be on to something."

She grinned. She really might be. The other thing she was on to was that truths didn't have to be told immediately. She and Mitch could have sex today, and on another day, she could tell him her truths. "Well, Captain Suck Face, are we going to just stand here, or are you going to take me somewhere and blow my mind with your sexual prowess?"

23

Mitch stood naked in front of Luna. A gloriously naked Luna.

She kept opening her mouth to speak but words failed to spill forth.

"Not what you expected?" He should have prepared her. She'd never seen but one side of him. The rule-following Mitch Johnson. But there was a time in his life he hadn't been a rule follower. He couldn't be if he'd wanted to survive in the neighborhoods in which he'd lived. And when he was naked, that old side of him became obvious.

"You have tattoos."

She'd found her voice. A good sign. The shock was over and now the questions would erupt. "I do." They covered his chest and crawled over his shoulders to his back.

She ran a finger along the ink of a fallen angel. "Tell me everything about them."

"Later. Right now, I'd prefer to talk about your perfection." Of course, he'd seen nude Luna before. Twice. But he'd never been able to openly take in the sight. "You don't mind if I just stare for a while?" She had the perfect combination of curves and strong lines. And barely there tan lines that had him salivating to trace them with his tongue. A tremble went through him.

"Excellent idea." There was a hitch to her voice. A hitch that told him she wasn't nearly as confident as she'd like for him to believe. A hitch that told him inside Bad Luck Luna, who was really not bad luck at all, existed Vulnerable Luna.

He chuckled and lay back on the bed, tugging her with him. He really wanted to explore Vulnerable Luna.

As if mocking his view of her vulnerability, she reached between them and ran her palm along his length.

He hissed. "If I say something stupid, it's because all my blood has left my brain and gone there."

A soft hum vibrated from her throat. "I'm pretty sure my blood has also left my brain and travelled south."

Fuck. He rolled so that he was on top and straddled her. Her eyes widened and her lips parted in invitation. An invitation he could no longer deny himself. He leaned forward and grazed her soft lips with his own.

"I'm just wondering something," she said between their mouths.

He ran kisses down her jaw and to the indent of her throat. "What are you wondering?" He inhaled her scent. She smelled of rose petals and excitement.

"Why are both of your ears red? Surely having sex with your best friend doesn't cause you to be embarrassed."

Best friend? He liked the sound of that. "Nerves."

"What are you nervous about?"

His right ear was the bane of his existence. A neon sign when he was nervous. But he'd had enough practice to know how to please a woman. His awkwardness hadn't followed him into the bedroom in quite some time. What did it mean that he was nervous now? The answer was obvious. "If we're only doing this once, I want it to be the best you ever had. Friend or no friend." He moved his lips over her collarbone and to the creamy round top of one breast. He flicked the rosy tip with his tongue.

She shuddered and moaned.

He did it again, and her hips arched into him. He dragged his lips lower over her flat stomach, pausing at her belly button to flick it with his tongue several times. She grasped his shoulders and dug her nails into his back. Kitten noises greeted his ears as she pushed up into the pressure of his mouth. He glanced up at her. "I love the way you purr."

Her eyes were closed but a frown wrinkled her forehead. "I most certainly do not purr. I'm not a cat."

She really was beautiful in a wholesome way. He loved that in her day-to-day life, she didn't seem to bother with makeup. "I'm pretty sure I heard a purr."

Her eyes opened, and her pupils were dilated. "Whatever. Your ears are red."

Laughter rumbled in his chest. "Shut up." God, had he ever laughed during sex? The fact they were teasing with one another made the experience ten times more intimate. They weren't just having inter-course—they were having an experience. The kind you take your time with so you can savor it later in your memory banks. "Has anyone ever told you you talk too much during sex?"

"You started it." Her words were punctuated with a mischievous grin.

Mitch's heart lost its balance and tumbled around in his chest. "You're killing me, Parker."

She rolled over on her stomach and went up on all fours. "Fuck me."

The command robbed him of breath, and he groaned. His gaze locked on the image of her full ass cheeks dancing in front of his face. A desire to do just as she requested burned through him like hot coals going down a slide. But fucking her was only one of the things he wanted to do. He ran his hand down her spine. The satiny smoothness of her skin weakening his resolve to go slow. He gritted his teeth, afraid he might come like a teenage boy if he weren't careful. "Your ass is fucking artwork. I've wanted to touch it since the first day I saw it naked." He palmed a cheek and squeezed as he spoke.

She shivered. "Please tell me my boy scout neigh-bor has a condom?"

Again, he chuckled. She wasn't wrong. Up to this point in their relationship, he had been the boy scout, and she was the bad girl. "Johnny insisted on giving me several to put in my wallet before I met Olga the other night. You know, just in case that went well."

She rolled over on her back and wrinkled her nose. "Ugh. A simple yes would have been enough."

"Sorry." He sat back on his heels and grabbed his pants to retrieve a condom from his wallet. "You make me nervous. Like it's my first time or something. And in my defense, I told you my brain's not receiving any oxygen."

"Slide that thing on and let's see if I can't get you over your nervousness."

"If you insist."

Much later—maybe hours, maybe days—they both lay flat on their backs staring up at her ceiling breathing hard.

"Holy Batman." She rolled over and leaned up on one elbow and gave him a saucy smile. "You should definitely change your pickup line. The next woman you want to make all tongue-tied, tell her sex is your superpower."

Fuck. His ears were red again. He could feel them. They were burning like they'd been lit with a torch. "That good, was it?"

"Like I said...holy Batman."

He leaned up on one elbow and kissed her softly. "Glad you liked it. Give me a second to dispose of this condom, and we can do it again. Did I mention I have several?"

As he walked to the trashcan on unsteady legs, it hit him. He'd forgotten to tell Luna about the mayor's blackmail. That should have happened before sex. Now he'd have to find the right time to bring it up and hope she didn't hate him for not telling her sooner.

Luna didn't want to break the comfortable silence between her and Mitch as they both came down from the exertion of an afternoon of great sex. But at the same time, she wanted to talk. To discover more about this man who'd just given her the best orgasms of her life while his ears burned red. Starting with his tattoos. Experience told her men didn't like to chat after surrendering their ability to think straight to a woman. Which meant she should resist the urge to converse. Ignoring the hell out of conventional wisdom, she whispered, "What happens now?"

He reached for her hand and laced their fingers together. "I thought we might talk."

"Oh. God. Yes." She scrambled into a sitting position, leaned against the headboard, and pulled the covers up under her arms. Who would have thought he was a man who liked to talk after sex? She started with an easy question. "Did you and Brandy do it in this room?"

He sat up, retrieved his glasses from the side table, and then settled in beside her, leaning against the headboard as well, pulling the sheet up over his lower half. Leaving her with an excellent view of his naked torso. Tattoos aside—and there were a lot of them which were sexy all on their own—the guy had a body that made her body sigh with happiness. *Biceps and triceps and abs, oh my.*

"I take it the fact you're asking means you've had time to process how you feel about knowing she lived here. Does it bother you?"

Does it bother me? Yes. Yes, it does. Why? I don't know. It wasn't like she was in love with Mitch, which seemed like the only logical explanation of why it should matter. Never in her life had she been the jealous sort. In her old days, she had been the queen of open relationships. Her relationship motto had been *a girl should always keep her options uncluttered.* "Is that silly of me?" She chose to stare straight ahead. Conversations weren't as intimate when you weren't looking at each other.

"Parker," he said softly in an after-sex voice that was really, really nice.

Slowly, she turned her head. "What?"

His eyes filled with warmth. "It's not silly at all. But I can promise you, ever since meeting you, she's not been able to live rent-free in my brain like she had been doing for far too long. You, my darling nemesis, evicted her."

That was a sweet thing to say. "What did she want the other night?"

"I have no idea. I didn't return her call. I can't think of one thing of importance we have left to say to one another."

"Oh." She didn't allow herself to follow up with another question. His past relationships weren't any of her business.

"New topic," he said. "The night of your sleepover, you said something, something that escaped me until a few minutes ago, and I want to ask you about it before I lose it again."

She tensed. Knew before he even said it what he was going to say. "What would that be?"

"You said, 'I'm not really me.' What did you mean?"

Yep. She had said that. Recalled it clearly. She'd been about to spill her truth, because while high on weed, it had seemed imperative she be transparent. Now, not so much. But, since he had asked, what should she say? *I could lie. Tell him it was nothing more than a high statement.* But she didn't want to lie. According to him, truth was his everything. She took a deep breath and exhaled. First, she'd go with a diversion tactic. "Luna Parker is my real name. But not my first and last name. Luna Parker are my two middle names. What's your middle name?" She held her breath and hoped he didn't ask why she went by her middle names.

"I don't have one."

Holy Batman, this guy was made for her. "You won't get this because you don't know all of my flaws, but that might just be the best answer ever." As failings went, it wasn't a big one, but her inability to remember the middle names of the guys she dated wouldn't become an issue with Mitch.

"That kind of cryptic comment makes me want to get to know all your flaws. I can't imagine they're any worse than the ones I've already discovered."

"You're so *not* funny. Which is one of your many flaws."

He shifted so that his body slanted toward hers and caressed her jaw line with the pad of his fingers. "What's your real first and last name?"

She sighed. They had, for better or worse, fallen out of the casual hookup mode and slid straight into *this could be something* mode. For the sake of their friendship, she had to steer them back to what she'd promised. An uncomplicated hookup. "Luna Parker is now my real first and last name. I made it legal before moving to Colorado. I'd prefer not to say any more about it...yet. Is that a friendship breaker for you?"

His hand fell away. "Are you in danger?" he asked quietly.

"Not danger." Why in the world would she be in danger? "I simply came to a point in my life when I realized I didn't like who I was. Didn't like the woman I'd become. I've worked hard to erase that person from existence. I'm afraid if I mention her name, it will open the gate to allow her to get her hands on Luna 2.0."

"Luna 2.0?"

"I think of my old self as Luna 1.0 and my new self as Luna 2.0."

He laughed. "Let me get this straight. Rule-breaking, impulsive, naked yoga Luna is an improvement over Luna 1.0?"

"Big time."

"Lord help us." He smiled. "Jokes aside, when I went to college, I did the same. I didn't change my name, but I took on a new personality. One of a man who took education seriously, who limited the amount of peopling he had to do, a man who had hobbies that had nothing to do with putting food on the table at no cost. A respectable man in charge of his future."

She unpacked his words and found it full of hints about young Mitch. Hints she wanted to explore. But if she allowed him to keep his secrets for now, then it should be okay for her to keep hers. It wasn't a matter of deceit but a matter of waiting until their friendship deepened enough to allow such privileged information. "How did you decide on that man?"

He didn't answer right away. She liked that about him. Liked that she could trust that whatever he said, it wouldn't be off the cuff but something he'd thought about and meant. "I firmly believe he's the man I would have become had I been given a fighting chance growing up. I've never met my dad, and Mom was...is...a junkie."

A desire swept through her to wrap him up in a bear hug and squeeze all the sadness out of him. Sadness that dulled the spark in his eyes. She reached over and placed her hand on his. "I kind of like that you're a man who follows rules and has one for everything, and yet can be friends with someone who has been known to break a few." And she absolutely adored how his ears turned even redder during sex.

"Speaking of broken rules, this should have never happened."

There was her big nerdy teddy bear. "And that, my dear sir, is why the freedom to break a rule should always be left on the proverbial table." She ran a finger over one of his tattoos—an image of an angel with a broken wing. "Or are you suffering from rule-breaking regret?"

He raised his hand and stilled hers. "Truthfully...the only brain currently working in my body—especially with you touching me—has absolutely no regrets."

The unusual sensation of heat filling her cheeks caught her off guard. Since when did she blush? She shook off the weird reaction and gave him a sassy smile. "As it should be, Captain Suck Face."

"That is the worse nickname ever."

She turned completely toward him. "Agreed. It doesn't come close to doing you justice. How about I change it to Captain SOS?"

"SOS?" He stood, reached for his T-shirt and pulled it over his head, hiding his tattoos but giving her a great view of his male parts.

She gave an appreciative sigh. The guy was definitely well hung. "Stands for Smooching Orgasmic Superhero."

He laughed. A deep belly laugh that wrapped her up in joy.

"Since you're okay with my keeping my first and last name a secret with you, why don't I share another secret I have as a thank you?"

His laughter disappeared. "I'm listening." He sat on the edge of the bed.

Hopefully Nanna Nonna wouldn't haunt her ass for telling. "The spring flowers from Mildred, when mixed with the right ingredients, become a powerful aphrodisiac." Luna knew this, thanks in part to an inherited cookbook she'd been given by the lawyer who'd told Luna about her insurance inheritance. And in part because of a dream she'd had in which Nanny Nonna had told her to take a look at the recipe on page 139.

A pulse jumped to life in Mitch's jaw. "Were you on that just now? Is that why you were so aroused?"

And there was the sweet Mitch. The good guy. The one not quite sure of his charms and skills. "You were my aphrodisiac. But if we were to continue and the day arrived where I needed a little extra help, I could take a drop of the mixture and within five minutes, I'd be just as ready as you are. Or vice versa."

"If your blend does what you say it will do, why haven't you bottled it up and put it on the market?"

"That's why I bought this place. Why I didn't want Mildred to be knocked down. When the time is right, I plan to market the secret formula, but in the interim, I can share a vial of the stuff with you."

He scoffed. "Not necessary. Even on the worst of days, I'm not going to have any problem being aroused by my neighbor."

"Aren't you sweet? Dumb but sweet."

"Enlighten me, oh wise ass one."

"Use the formula, dummy, in the edible you create to prove to your cohorts you weren't just blowing hype at the ball."

He stilled. "What's in it for you?"

An answer popped into her brain. A ridiculous answer that had to do with love. A chance at love. Which made her laugh softly. Obviously, her brain still lacked oxygen. She went with the next idea. "Let me share your table at the fair. City council told me they didn't have any open spots available when I requested one."

His phone rang.

"For the love of sex," Luna snapped. "That had better not be Brandy."

"I told you I blocked her number." He pulled his phone out of his pocket, glanced at the screen, and grimaced. "Sorry, I need to take this. It's the mayor."

"Ooooh. Maybe he has the power to get me my own table. You should ask him."

Mitch glanced away and mumbled, "I'll see what I can do." With that, he hurried out of her bedroom. No kiss goodbye. No lingering look. No awkward hug.

"Hi, Regis," she heard him say right before her front door shut.

She plopped back on the bed and sprawled her legs and arms. Holy Batman. She'd just had sex with her best friend. And liked it.

24

Three days later, Luna and Ms. Houdini took in the sights as they strolled down Main Street. This was Luna's favorite part of Rocky Mountain Springs. Well, that and a certain superhero. The businesses were lined up elbow-to-elbow and their storefronts were painted in a kaleidoscope of colors. It was a happy place, and the perfect setting to host the town's fair.

In front of the businesses, tables were set up. Behind the tables stood local entrepreneurs who were preparing to meet and greet fair attendees.

Not wanting to give the locals anything to disapprove of where she was concerned, Luna had chosen to dress conservatively. Which meant she'd had to dig to the back of her closet to find something. What she had settled on was a summer dress whose style and flowered material beckoned back to the frontier days of Laura Ingalls Wilder.

Ms. Houdini had also dressed for the event. She wore her best floppy straw hat, and her favorite trollop-red lipstick. She proudly pulled a red wagon behind her. Luna had invited Mr. JJ and Ms. Tinker to come, but they had been too lazy to take the required bath. In the wagon were the brownies Luna had made to sell at today's fair, plus new beds for all three goats.

Moments earlier, she'd purchased the oversized dog beds at the first booth on Main Street. It belonged to Mr. Henson, a dear man with some rough edges. He'd been very grumpy when she'd first stopped by but had offered her the slightest of smiles as she'd passed over a hundred-dollar bill for her purchase and told him to keep the change.

As she continued making her way down the main thoroughfare toward the table she and Mitch would share, she smiled and waved at anyone who would make eye contact.

Moments earlier, she'd run into Amahle and Johnny. They were taking a group of college boys on a rafting excursion. She'd been delighted when they had stopped to say hi. Now, she paused in front of Mitch's table and ran a hand over her hair to make sure it wasn't sticking out at weird angles. This was the first time they would see each other since they'd spent an afternoon exploring each other's body. She cleared her throat to get his attention.

He turned, looked at her, blinked, then looked at Ms. Houdini and scowled. "I see you brought your trouble-making goat and left the rule-following ones behind."

"I did." She glanced at his right ear to see if it was red. It wasn't. Was his heart not racing like hers was?

She wiped her palms on her dress and held out a hand. "If I forget to say it later..." For the love of sex, why had her voice just wobbled? If he wasn't nervous, she shouldn't be nervous. It's not like she'd never been in this situation. Well, not this exact situation. "Thank you for allowing me to share your reserved space."

He shook her hand. "You're welcome," he said stiffly.

She grabbed her fresh-baked brownies—the only item he'd allowed her to sell—out of the wagon. A blue ribbon divided their table down the middle. On his side were rows of perfectly aligned pot brownies. "Look, we must have used the same type of brownie pan. Our brownies all look alike." She'd bought her bakeware at the local market because it allowed every brownie to come out uniform and with yummy edges. She plopped hers on the other side of the ribbon.

"That's what happens when you live and shop in a small town," he said dryly. "Not an overabundance of options."

She nodded and then busied herself removing the harness and rope from Ms. Houdini and replacing it with a pretty red leash. She attached one end to the leg of the table.

Once she was done, she stood and smiled. "Your brownies are fully loaded with dope. Mine with hope," she blurted.

"Hope?"

She studied him. Was it her imagination or was all the goodwill they'd built with each other gone? His whole demeanor said he once again wished she didn't exist in his life. "You know, hope the townspeople will give me a chance, now that we're friends. Hope they lead to more business, so I'll make a profit this year. And other assorted hopes." Like the hope Mitch would continue to like her once she told him her whole truth. A truth she had planned on telling him tonight but wouldn't if he didn't relax.

He ran his hand through his hair. "I'm glad you made it. I'm sorry I didn't invite you before this morning."

"Why exactly was it you didn't?" She would have asked him when he called at the crack of dawn, but he'd hung up before she could.

"I had asked the mayor, and he said no. And you know me and how I like to follow rules." He pushed one of her brownies back to her side of the table.

The mayor had said no. That stung. Not being liked sucked. "If you ask me, the mayor's a prick. And the rules set by pricks are always fodder for rebellion."

He startled. "Shush. You can't call the mayor a prick in a normal voice. Small towns have big ears."

The rebuke chafed, but since he'd done it in private, she didn't argue. "If he said no, why did you invite me?"

"Because we're friends."

She went soft inside. "Thank you." She didn't care how awkward he was; as long as he always had her back in public, they could be friends. "I'm excited to be a part of this fair."

Ms. Houdini bleated, drawing Luna's attention. "I bet all the children are going to love you." She arranged Ms. Houdini's new bed on the ground so the goat could see all the action but still be in the shade, then poured her some water in a small dish.

"I just hope the visitors aren't afraid of her," Mitch mumbled.

She studied his tight lips. "You're kind of grumbly today. Did I do something wrong?"

He made a scoffing noise and raked a hand through his hair. "It's nothing you did. My mood is all on me." He situated a sign advertising the price of his brownies in front of his merchandise.

"What did you do?" she urged.

He straightened and gave her his full attention. "Standing next to you, I'm discovering just how stupid my idea was to wait and see...slept together while in the midst of a crowd."

She heartily agreed. "I thought about dropping by to see you and getting the first meet over with, but I knew you probably had some dumb rule about the guy contacting the girl, and I vowed, when I can, to honor your rule fetish."

He glanced around as if to see if anyone appeared to be paying them any attention. "It had nothing to do with rules. I didn't contact you because I didn't know how to tell a woman that sleeping with her was a..."

"A what?" She bent down and rubbed Ms. Houdini between the ears. "A blunder? Is that what sleeping with me was?"

"Is that what you thought?" He bent down so that they were at eye-level.

She tried to read his face. What did he think the correct answer was? When in doubt, fall back on what you know. Less room for embarrassment. "Of course it was a blunder. I mean, even I realized—after the fact—that friends don't sleep with friends. Especially if they want to remain just friends, and that's exactly what we agreed to want to do."

"We did agree to that." He swallowed hard, and she saw his Adam's apple move. "And it's important not to say things you don't mean. Which is why I let you rope me into the friendship ceremony," he said. "I take the vows we said to one another seriously." He stood.

She straightened. That's not what she wanted at all. But he was right, and even if he was like a hot superman with his secret tattoos, she had to stick to their original agreement and stay friends. End of story. She faked her most sincere smile. "I totally agree, and now that we've dismissed the awkwardness, do you have a blank piece of paper? I need to make a sign for my brownies."

"You didn't bring one?"

"Considering the short invitation, I'm lucky to be wearing matching bra and panties." She *was* wearing matching ones, wasn't she? She moved his sign so that it sat in the middle of the table. "Never mind. I'll sell mine for the same price as yours."

"Yours should be cheaper. Mine are laced." He moved the sign back to his side of the table.

"Mine are from a secret, secret, secret semi-family recipe." She moved it back to the middle. "They are worth as much as your laced ones." They'd been made from a handwritten recipe that had been stuck inside the cookbook she'd inherited.

His lips flattened. "Did you put an aphrodisiac in them?"

"Of course not. We're saving that for you to unveil in your edibles." That recipe had also been included in the cookbook.

He left the sign alone. "Should I sample one of yours to make sure they're edible? I don't want people making fun of my friend."

Damn. That hit the gooey middle of her heart. Which shouldn't be gooey at all considering he thought sex with her had been a blunder. "Aren't you the sweetest thing ever?" She opened a brownie and handed it to him.

"That's what I've been told. What's your bottom line on your brownies?" He took a bite.

"I have no idea. How about you?" She waited for him to exclaim over her brownie.

"Three dollars and five cents."

"Well?"

"*Well* what?"

She fisted her hands on her hips. "How's the brownie?"

"It's very tasty. Like extremely tasty. I'd keep that recipe."

"Why thank you, kind sir." She opened a brownie and tried it for herself. Yum. Once she'd swallowed, she said, "How much of your dollar investment per brownie is the cost of the weed?" She opened another brownie and popped it in her mouth. She'd been slowly learning the importance of one's bottom line.

"Just price your brownies at fifty cents. Consider them a loss leader." His grumpy tone was back.

What had she done this time? She saluted him. "Yes, sir, Captain SOS. Have you sold any yet?"

"No. But do me a favor. When we do get customers, please don't bring up aliens, jocks, or panties."

She giggled. "I won't if you promise not to bring up your newly identified superpower with any of our customers."

A smile lifted his lips. "Trust me, from here on out, that will just be our secret."

Several female college-aged students stopped by their table, all wearing the same sorority shirt and white shorts.

"Good morning." Luna handed them adorable pink business cards that she'd had printed at a bargain price. "I'm the owner of Luna's Goat Yoga and Spa. When you get stressed out with college or your last crush, give me a call, and I'll set up a relaxing spa day for you and your sorority sisters."

"More like current crushes," one of them said, and they all snickered. "How much do you charge?"

"For college students, I give a hefty discount. Contact me later in the week, and we can discuss prices and dates that work for you." College students became working citizens who eventually got married and looked for fun ideas for bachelorette parties. A discount now could turn into a profit later. And if they stayed local, daily yoga class customers.

So far, Mitch hadn't jumped into the conversation. She elbowed him.

"Hello." He handed them business cards. "I'm the owner of Rocky Mountain High. It's a—"

"Oh. My. God. I've heard about your brownies," the lone guy in the group enthused. "They. Are. Legendary." He leaned in closer and whispered, "They may be why I chose to attend University of Colorado."

Mitch didn't respond. His eyes were focused elsewhere.

Luna repressed a sigh. "You and about half the student population from what I've heard."

They laughed.

"Enough with the small talk." She picked up one of Mitch's brownies. "Show me your ID and your money and let's make a sale. Everything on his side of the table is ten percent off."

Mitch, who'd been staring off in the distance, jerked his gaze to Luna and frowned.

Before he could say something rude, she added, "All Rocky Mountain High asks in return is you send your friends over here to buy more."

Neither of them said a word until the students were out of earshot.

"Why did you—"

"Your people skills are asleep at the wheel."

He grimaced. "You're right. I have stuff on my mind."

"What kind of stuff?"

"The kind of stuff that makes me antsy."

"Like taking me to bed again?" Well, that had just popped right out of her mouth.

He shushed her with his eyes. "Remember, I'm not your type, and that's for the best. And, for future reference, you can't sell my merchandise at a discount without prior permission."

"Stop trying to change the subject before I get my turn at a rebuttal."

He rubbed a hand down his smooth jaw. "Have I told you today, you look lovely?"

She bit back a grin. The guy was impossible to fight with. Then again, she didn't really want to fight with him. "Thank you." She surveyed the crowd. "Who is that group of people standing together at your three o'clock?" One of them, a very pompous looking dude, kept looking their way and frowning. Next to him stood a guy who looked fierce and expensive. Who the hell were they?

"Could you narrow it down?" Mitch asked. "There are several clusters at my three o'clock."

"The ones walking toward us right now."

Before he could reply, they stopped at their table.

"Mitch." The pompous one nodded stiffly at Mitch and ignored Luna. "How are you doing, son?"

Mr. Fierce and Expensive stood off to the side with his back to their booth.

"I am doing mostly well, Mayor Regis," Mitch said firmly. "And you?"

So that's the infamous Mayor of Rocky Mountain Springs. But who the hell was the other guy? A bodyguard? A mafia prince? A bar bouncer?

A woman stepped forward, blocking Luna's view of the man who was ignoring them, and gave Luna a pinch-faced look. Then she focused her attention on Mitch. "Your application to the Chamber of Commerce requested a solo booth, and we accommodated your request and denied your request to turn it into a table for two. What happened?"

Mitch tugged on his ear. "Ummm."

"He owed me a favor," Luna said, "and I collected. I'm Luna Parker." She held out a hand to the mayor who kept glancing back at the man.

Mayor Regis stuck his hands in his pockets. "Yes, yes, yes. Of course we know who you are."

She lowered her hand. She hadn't felt this unwelcome since the day of her infamous arrest. "It's so nice to meet all of you in person." Killing them with humanity felt like a squirt of cheap perfume to the eyeballs, but she didn't lose her smile as she struggled to regain her dignity. "Hopefully next year I'll have a table assigned to me, and I won't have to favor trade for an invite to the party."

"We're so sorry we weren't able to accommodate your request this year," the mayor said. He looked like he wanted to hurl toothpicks at her eyes.

Luna shivered. This guy had no reason to hate her. Dislike her, maybe. But not the kind of hate she felt coming out of his pores. What the hell was his problem? "Here, have a brownie. No charge. I've used my Nonna's secret recipe." Sometimes the best defense was niceness.

"No, thank you," they said in unison.

"Mitch," the mayor said, "I'm disappointed in you. Why don't you drop by the office on Monday, and we will discuss the ramifications?"

"Certainly," Mitch said.

Luna studied her friend. Something in his tone just now worried her. Something tight and angry.

"Excellent." The mayor did an abrupt turn and glanced around. "Over there. Let's go see how those booths are doing, shall we?"

His entourage nodded and left without a goodbye to those manning the brownie booth.

"You okay?" Mitch asked her.

How kind of him to ask. "I'm fine." Not a lie. She was. But her feelings not so much. They hurt. "What was that whole ramification comment about?"

"Nothing of any importance. Just the mayor being the mayor. I'm sorry none of them had the good manners to accept your generous offer of a brownie."

She shrugged. "Who was the scary guy in the nice suit that stood with his back to all of us?"

Mitch glanced toward the man in question and studied him. "I'm fairly certain that's the man who has bankrolled all of the mayor's land purchases here in Rocky Mountain Springs."

Interesting. "How much of the land does the mayor own?"

"I've been told over ninety percent."

She blew out a breath. With that kind of hold on the community, the mayor wasn't just a figure head in town. He had real power. "Does my owning property in town have anything to do with why he hates me?"

"It's a complicated story, but yes," Mitch said. "One I need to share with you sometime when we're alone."

"Well, that sounds ominous." Without warning, tears exploded and rolled down her cheeks. She madly wiped them away.

"Why in the hell are you crying?" Mitch huffed.

"I don't know. Maybe it's because you're the only person in this town who likes me."

He reached out, briefly linked fingers with hers, and squeezed. "Don't let them see you cry. It gives them pleasure." He squeezed her fingers again before letting go and stepping back.

She pushed her tongue to the roof of her mouth and held it there until the need to cry passed, and then said, "Thank you."

"That's what friends are for. Shall we move on to a new topic? One that doesn't upset you?"

She gave him a watery smile. Him and his new topics. "Tell me, Mitch, since we're going all in with our friend-status, what do you want most in life?"

He opened folding chairs and they both took a seat. "Financial stability."

"Why?"

The tendons in his throat tightened. "Because it means I never have to worry about being homeless."

Horror shot through her. Not only had he grown up with a drug-head mother, he'd also been homeless. Growing up in Manhattan, she'd seen her share of homeless people, but she couldn't fathom one of them being her sweet, grumpy Mitch.

"What do *you* want more than anything in this life?" he asked.

It took her a moment to move her thoughts away from his more-than-anything and contemplate her more-than-anything. If he was going to be painfully honest, she could as well. "To be loved for who I am."

"I would think that's a want you shouldn't have a hard time getting fulfilled." He glanced out at the festival goers. He waved at someone who waved back. "The right guy will find you very lovable."

"And that's not you?" she quizzed. "You don't find me lovable?"

"I find you lovable, but we wouldn't work as a love match. We're the very definition of opposites. We'd be a disastrous couple. Hell, even the Get Hitched App must agree since it didn't match us."

She rolled her eyes. "That damn app is flawed. One that knew what it was doing would have never matched me with a guy like Ronnie."

"Or me with Olga," he replied.

They fell into silence and let the minutes tick by as they sat with their own thoughts.

He sold six brownies. She sold zero.

She stood and paced. Why wasn't anyone buying her brownies? "Going back to our previous topic," she said. "I also want—more than anything—for my obituary to end with *hashtag: no regrets.*" Regardless of what happened in the future, she did not regret buying her house at auction.

"What would that even mean?" Mitch asked.

She came to a stop in front of the table and leaned against it. "It would mean everything I did while living, I did it because it's what I wanted to do. Not because it's what somebody expected me to do." The table wiggled under her weight, so she straightened.

He frowned. "Sometimes we have to conform to the wishes of others in order to obtain our greater wants." Today he wore shorts and a T-shirt with the name of his company on the front and a cannabis plant on the back. Under the plant were the words *This Bud's 4 You. Sharing is Optional.*

"I'm not sure I agree. Can you give me an example?"

He surprised her by suddenly standing, practically knocking his chair over in the process. "I need to stretch my legs. Would you mind staffing the booth?"

Alone? Panic swept through her. What if the mayor came back and demanded she leave? *Nope. I'm not going to let that man intimidate me.* She plastered on a smile. "Should I run a sale on your brownies while you're gone? They don't seem to be going over as grand as mine."

He chuckled. "You haven't sold any."

She feigned ignorance. "I haven't?" Of course, she hadn't. Why weren't her brownies selling?

Mitch laughed again. It was as if he was going out of his way to make sure the locals thought he enjoyed being around Luna Parker.

Then he winked at her.

He was truly doing his part to help her fit in. The realization brought a fresh set of tears to her eyes.

Luckily, he turned and walked away before he saw them.

Ms. Houdini noticed him leaving and jumped up to follow. Unfortunately, her leash got caught around the leg of the table. The resulting tug on the table caused half of its legs to collapse.

"Ms. Houdini!" Luna admonished in a low whisper as she adjusted the table legs. "You've got to be more ladylike." Luna scrambled to untangle the goat.

"Problem there?" a man said. Not just any man. The mayor. He'd come back.

Making brief eye contact with him, Luna shook her head. "All's good." She frowned down at Ms. Houdini, who was now tugging like a wild beast at her leash.

"It doesn't look all good," the mayor insisted. "I'll tell you what, why don't I watch your table while you see to your goat? Perhaps she needs a restroom break."

Luna eyeballed the guy. Why was he being nice? And where were his groupies? "I'll wait until Mitch returns. He'd be beside himself if I left his product unguarded."

The mayor fiddled with his bowtie. "Nonsense. I'm perfectly capable of protecting this table from underage consumers. Go before your goat makes a mess on our streets and causes a stench."

Luna cringed. That would put Mitch over the edge. "You're a doll." She grabbed her pooper scooper out of the wagon. "I won't be long." She quickly walked Ms. Houdini behind the nearest building and allowed her to do her business. Then Luna rushed back to her table. "Thank you," she said to the mayor, who had his back to her and was busily straightening the ribbon that lay between the two types of brownies.

He startled and glanced at her almost as if guilty of a crime. "That was quick."

"She just needed to do number one." Something was up. Off. But Luna had no idea what. She pointed to the table. "I appreciate your straightening everything."

The mayor frowned. "I did it for Mitch. He likes order." With those remarks, he pivoted and ambled away.

Isabella shuttered. Her gut told her something was wrong, but glancing at the table, she could see no apparent problem. She'd mention it to Mitch when he returned.

A woman came to a stop in front of the booth distracting Luna's thoughts away from the mayor. "Hi. Are you local?" Luna asked, holding out her hand. "I'm new, so I haven't met everyone."

The woman gave her a warm smile and shook her hand. "I'm not from this town. I belong to a church group. We jump into our church van every chance we get and travel to the local fairs. I have to say, we're impressed with the variety of booths."

"Which booth is your favorite so far?" Luna asked.

"I found the crystal booth to be enchanting. Have you been in her store?"

Luna nodded. "I spent way too much in there just the other day."

The woman held up a silk drawstring pouch with the store's name embroidered on the front. "Me, too. Just a moment ago."

"Can I interest you in a brownie?" Luna pointed to Mitch's side of the table. "These have a little pick-me-up in them. And these are my Nonna's secret recipe. They do not include weed."

The woman dug her billfold out of her purse. "I'll take six. No weed. It probably wouldn't be appropriate if the church ladies got stoned."

Luna laughed. "You could be right." She handed the lady six brownies. "That will be three dollars."

The woman handed her a five-dollar bill. "Keep the change. You've been charming."

"Thank you." Luna handed several of her business cards to her friendly customer. "One for you and extras for you to share with each of your friends. If you and your church family ever want to participate in a goat yoga spa day, give me a call."

The woman glanced at the top card and then stuck them in her purse. "I'll do that."

Luna watched as she went from one booth to the next, nibbling on a brownie as she did so. Nanny Nonna had been a habitual church goer. One who belonged to Bible studies, and book clubs, and, of course, the church choir. But then, she'd also believed in other things. Things quite prevalent in her home state of New Orleans. Things like voodoo, and ghosts, and superstitions. Things she'd carefully taught Luna. Which was why Nanny Nonna was able to come into Luna's dreams.

Luna really hoped Nanna Nonna didn't pop into her dreams tonight—after Luna told Mitch about her felony—to scold her for not keeping the family skeletons in the attic.

25

Mitch hadn't made it past more than five booths when he heard his name being called by a voice he knew. He pretended not to hear and moved at a quicker pace.

She called out again, her tone shrill. Like it had been when she'd darted down the aisle without him on their wedding day.

Reluctantly, he stopped and turned. As if unaware he wasn't thrilled to see her, Brandy waved before carefully making her way across the stiletto-eating cobblestone monster, AKA Main Street.

Two steps away, she suddenly went catawampus, her arms wildly windmilled, and to his dismay she landed against him, her hands clasped behind his neck for balance. It took several seconds, seconds in which he was pretty sure the whole town watched, to disengage from one another. As soon as he could, he stepped back.

"Sorry about that." Her eyes were wide, and a glint of humor touched her smile. "I can't believe I just lost another heel to these damn rocks."

"Hello, Brandy." He didn't bother to match her cheerful tone or ask her why she'd worn those heels if she knew she was going to be on Main Street. She knew better. She'd lost many a pair here.

She bent down and slipped off the broken heel and, placing a hand on his shoulder for balance, stood in front of him on one shoe. She let go of him long enough to push her platinum blonde hair behind her ears. "So formal. We've had sex, you know."

Sex? That seemed to be the word of the day. And his thought of the day had been he wanted to have sex with Luna. Again. And to find more things he had in common with her to put on his Luna Parker Pros and Cons list. "We have. And now we're acquaintances at best."

Her smile mutated into a pout. "I've been trying to reach you. Why haven't you returned my calls?"

"Isn't that obvious?" He didn't have to glance around to know they were the center of attention.

She scraped a pale pink fingernail down his jaw. "Enlighten me."

He nudged her hand away. "Rules of engagement with one's ex-fiancé clearly—"

"You and your stupid rules," she snapped. "Newsflash—"

"I'm well aware of your opinion of my rules." It was one thing for Luna to make fun of his rules—she did so with a twinkle in her eyes—but entirely another for Brandy. She no longer had the right to criticize anything about him. "Did you need something?"

She huffed. "You're not going to make this easy for me, are you?"

He smiled. Not because he was happy, but to throw those watching from afar off balance on what they assumed was going on. He'd prefer everyone thought they were having a friendly conversation instead of verging on another fight. "Considering I can't imagine what it is you want to talk to me about, I can't answer your question one way or another."

Her nostrils flared like a bull seeing red. Sort of how she'd looked on their wedding day.

"I'm sorry," she said. "I was wrong to walk out on our wedding."

"No shit."

"And I was wrong to let everyone think it was your fault."

"Can we just cut this short, and you tell me why you're here?" He should have stayed at the booth. At least there he would have had Luna around to help him deal with Brandy.

"Isn't it obvious? I want to try again. You're a hard man to replace." His ex ended her stilted speech with a flutter of her fake lashes.

This was a woman he'd once thought himself in love with. Why didn't it make his heart stir to hear her say *I'm sorry*? Hell. The two of them had had fifteen things in common. Fifteen had seemed enough. "I no longer love you." It was hard to love a woman when your heart was busy trying to convince your brain you were in love with another. One who thought sex with you had been a blunder.

"Silly boy. Of course you still love me. Perhaps it will help you to get over your hurt pride if I tell you Daddy said he'd buy us a house for a wedding gift. As in, he'll buy *your* house for us, if that's the one you have your heart set upon. In fact, he's already approached the mayor about the property. You see, you win. We can even have it titled in your name only. You've always wanted to be a homeowner. I'm going to make your dream come true. Marry me, and we can live here in your tired little town in your tiny little house and run a business together."

Brandy's father wielded power like an evil comic book character. Kind of like the mayor but on a larger scale. How had the mayor handled the request? Had he admitted he'd already promised to sell the land to Mitch in return for Mitch running Luna out of town? Was that what the mayor wanted to speak to Mitch about?

"I don't need your father to buy me a house." He shuddered at the idea of being indebted to Brandy's father in any capacity. "I'm capable of doing that on my own."

Brandy hesitated. "I know we were being very forward to inquire into the purchase before I had a chance to speak with you, but you know Daddy. He always likes to be ten steps ahead."

Mitch rubbed at the headache starting between his eyebrows. If he didn't want to have a scene for all Rocky Mountain Springs to witness, he needed to stay calm. "Mayor Regis and I have already worked up an agreement for me to buy my house. I don't need a handout from your father." Would the mayor skirt their verbal contract for a more lucrative offer from Brandy's father? Was that why Regis had not produced a written contract?

"The mayor owes Daddy a favor. I'm not sure your wishes will come into play if Daddy wants to buy the house you're living in."

Mitch's headache grew ten times worse. "Then you need to change his mind."

"You know Daddy. He doesn't often change his path once he's decided to do something. Especially when he thinks it will make his little girl happy."

Mitch glanced toward his booth. Toward Luna, who now stood in front of their table while a small child played with Ms. Houdini. Dressed in a yellow flowered sundress and wearing flowers in her hair, Luna easily caught the attention of everyone walking by their brownie stand. Especially when bathed in sunlight. Mostly because of her beauty, partly because she hadn't worn a slip under her dress. Something he hadn't noticed until just now.

"Is that the woman you recently took out on a date?" Brandy asked.

"It wasn't a real date." The last thing he wanted was for Brandy to take a disliking to Luna. She could make it harder for her to make friends in town. He hadn't realized just how much it bothered Luna to not be liked until he'd seen her tears today. They had tightened his heart into a knot. "More a contractual date." An implied contract that came with a friendship.

"A contractual date," Brandy purred. "That sounds absolutely desperate on her part."

He glanced at his ex. What had he said that made Luna sound needy? "That's not—"

"I'm happy to hear you haven't been busy falling in love with the homely creature."

In what universe would someone call Luna homely? Still, he didn't correct Brandy's observation. To do so was to invite trouble. For Luna. "Which doesn't change the fact I'm no longer in love with you." He glanced back at his new friend. Truth be told, there was a damn good chance he'd left his heart back at Luna's house the day they made love. That's why he hadn't called her. He didn't know what to say. He'd promised her nothing but friendship. And she'd made it more than clear that's all she wanted from him. As she had done again today when he tried to bring it up.

And yet...he'd probably fallen in love with her. And why wouldn't he? The woman showed him so much patience. And despite all his flaws, she appeared to relish being his friend.

Brandy placed a hand on his face and turned his gaze back to her. "I'm sure you're saying that because I hurt your pride."

He wiggled out of her grasp. "My pride survived."

"Given time, you'll remember how good we were together."

He shook his head. "The mere fact you're saying that shows how little you ever knew me. I don't say things I don't mean."

Brandy's bottom lip trembled. "I understand. I'm too late. Forgive me for believing we were worth another try."

A tear dropped on her cheek. He knew from experience she could call them up at will. And thus they were wasted on him. "Your tears are going to ruin your makeup."

She scowled. "Be a doll and carry me to my car." She placed her shoeless foot on the ground and winced. "I'm afraid I twisted my ankle when my heel broke."

Ready to call bullshit, he glanced at her ankle. Damn. It was swollen. Not something she could fake. He sighed and swept her up in his arms.

She linked her hands behind his neck and laid her head on his shoulder. "I parked in your driveway."

That meant going back the same way he'd come. Past Luna. Which shouldn't matter since she only desired his friendship. Maybe it would keep Luna from guessing his true feelings. And wasn't that for the best? As friends their differences worked. As love interests, they'd be what Mom liked to call a long shot. And Mom's long shots never paid off.

The conclusion settled like a rock in his stomach. He waited for his brain to find the flaw in his practicality. It didn't.

As he walked past his booth, he stupidly paused and glanced at Luna.

Her attention was fully on him and Brandy.

"Mitchell, you always did know how to sweep me off my feet," Brandy said, drawing his gaze back to her just in time for her to soundly kiss him on the cheek.

Luna made a strangled noise.

He whipped his gaze back to her, and the pain he saw twisted his gut. Hell. Had he been wrong? Did she want to be in a relationship?

A slow-paced clap gained his attention. A crowd had gathered. They were eyeballing him and Brandy. Their expressions told him they thought two lost lovers had reunited. And of course that would appear to be a fairytale ending to a tragic love story.

Brandy perpetuated the image by waving at her audience.

"Stop it," he hissed.

Amahle stepped forward. Unlike the others in the gathering, anger stitched her eyebrows into a menacing unibrow. "Damn it, Mitch. What about Luna? Your date went so well."

Brandy laughed merrily. "Didn't you know," she spoke in a conspiratorial tone, "it was a contractual date. He was forced into going out with Luna."

Mitch groaned. Fuck. "I was not forced."

A loud gasp from Luna caused him to once again meet her gaze. He wanted to explain why he'd told Brandy that, but to do so would leave Luna vulnerable to Brandy's anger. He tried to convey in his gaze how sorry he was, and he hoped like hell she'd remember to trust him.

"Luna, is she telling the truth?" someone called out.

"I think she's crying. Is she crying?" someone said.

"If she's crying, it must be true," another said.

Luna straightened. "Mitch and I are friends." She spoke the words with her gaze glued to his. A gaze that pleaded with him to come to her rescue.

He grappled with how best to handle the situation. Not for himself, but for Luna. If he came to her rescue, how would Brandy react? Would she unleash her brand of hell on Luna? Would she make it her mission in life for Luna's Goat Yoga to fail? His gut told him she would do all those things. As much as he hated leaving Luna hanging, it was best for his friend if Brandy didn't see her as a threat.

"But is she right?" someone persisted. "Did he take you out because of a contractual obligation?"

"Mitch," Luna said.

Fuck. The pain in her eyes felt like a poker to the heart. "Luna, you don't need to answer their questions."

"Honey, let her speak," Brandy purred. "Confession is good for the soul."

Luna's gaze whipped to Brandy. Her eyes narrowed, and her nostrils flared.

Mitch held his breath. He wouldn't blame Luna if she lost control, but he silently urged her to remain silent.

"Listen, bitch," Luna said, removing any hope Mitch had to keep things from escalating. "You're obviously under the misconception I'm someone you could steal a man from. Let me set you straight. If I wanted Mitch, he'd be mine. Not because I forced him with a contract, but because I'm the kind of woman men fall in love with. The kind of woman who knows how to get her man without manipulation. The kind of woman a man damn well shows up on time to their wedding for."

There were several gasps from the crowd.

"And yet, it's me who is in his arms," Brandy snarled.

More gasps and a few snickers.

Luna raised her eyebrows. "Because I told him in no uncertain terms the only thing I want from him is his friendship. Isn't that true, Mitch?" She ripped her gaze from Brandy to his.

He cleared his throat. "You did tell me that."

"But Brandy, while you're using all your wiles to talk him into reuniting, don't ever forget, he's now my friend. I take friendships seriously. I will always have the back of one of my friends. You hurt one of them, and I'll hurt you."

There was applause. Had the act of Luna sticking up for him converted the town's people to her side? God, he hoped so, because now she'd made a great enemy out of Brandy. A woman he'd never known to let an insult go unpunished.

Brandy's smug expression faltered. "Mitchell, let's get out of here."

26

Mitch hurried back to the booth. He ignored the locals standing in pods, heads together, no doubt analyzing his latest embarrassment.

"Where's your girlfriend?" Luna asked the moment he stepped behind their table. Her tone screamed blameless indignation. And her glare dared him to utter even one word of reprimand.

He blinked. He'd expected her to give him the benefit of the doubt and ask for a clarification of what had happened. To trust him. Wasn't that what they had promised one another? "She's not my girlfriend." Taking a moment to calm his own careening emotions, he busied himself with reorganizing his brownies, all the while trying to dissolve the stress in his stomach with some deep breaths.

He picked up a cockeyed package, intent on straightening it, and realization struck him in the gut. It was a package that belonged on her side. Fuck. A customer must have picked it up and dropped it back in the wrong place. He should have never left the table. His brownies were his responsibility.

Luna tapped him on the shoulder. "How could you tell Brandy I forced you into taking me out?"

He turned to Luna. "Because if she thought we weren't a real thing, she wouldn't feel the need to turn people against you. Why couldn't you have just trusted me and gone with the story? I told you I'd always have your back in public."

She reached out and shoved him.

Shocked, he stumbled a step back. "What in the hell has gotten into you? I just explained why I did what I did."

"That was your idea of having my back?" She moved forward and tried to shove him again, but this time he grabbed her hands and held them.

"If you'd stop emoting all over the place and look at this logically, you'll see that I'm right."

"Are you kidding me?" she said. "Your cover story humiliated me. Our calling it a contractual obligation was an inside joke."

"Not really." Sure, they'd laughed about it later, but it had been a contractual date. "When I asked you out, I told you I was contractually obligated to do so. It announced to the world that we are friends."

"You are so fucking unbelievable." She yanked her hands out of his grip.

"How? Everything I've done was with your best interest at heart." Even inviting her to join his table despite knowing how angry that would make the mayor. It had been his silent way of making sure the mayor knew he was serious about a contract. No contract, no deal.

"Carrying her down the street like a princess whose prince has just swept her off her pedicured feet was in my best interest? Have you stopped to think for one moment how humiliating that scene was for me?"

"The only reason my carrying her down the street should bother you would be if we were a couple. We're not. We're friends. I'm sorry for what she said about the contract, that's why I rushed back here to be by your side. That should be enough for you. That should tell anyone who knows me that I care about you."

His words slightly softened the mutinous set of her lips.

He took advantage of the reprieve and turned his attention back to the table. He spotted another of Luna's brownies on his side of the ribbon. He moved it to where it belonged.

"All it tells them is you have a hard-on to sell your pot brownies," she muttered.

He grappled for calm. He didn't want to fight with Luna. "You can't really believe she's who I want after what we did the other day."

A soft growl came from somewhere deep inside Luna's throat. "What we did the other day, you called a blunder. So, yeah, I was well within my rights to believe otherwise."

"*You* called it a blunder. I just didn't disagree. And the only reason I was carrying her was because she twisted her ankle. And the only reason I didn't set her words straight is because she can be vindictive, and I didn't want her venom spewing your way."

She blinked. "Is that true?"

"Of course it's true."

"Oh." A flicker of what looked like relief registered in Luna's eyes. "For future reference, I'd rather face her vindictiveness than be made a fool of in front of the whole town."

He had not made a fool of her, but he'd argue that point later. "Are we good?" He braced for her to come at him with another item that they should fight over. It was his experience women never easily got over being mad. Even when faced with a sincere apology.

She rolled her eyes at him. "I'm still plenty mad, but I'll eventually burn through it. Emphasis on eventually. So, don't do anything stupid like step in front of me when I'm behind the wheel of a moving car any time soon."

He semi-relaxed. He'd never had *knows how to fight fair* on his list of things he'd like to have in the woman he gave his heart to, but he should have. The trait was as attractive as fuck. He tugged at his ear. "Now that we have that settled, let's talk about the brownie situation."

She stilled. "What brownie situation?"

He glanced at her side of the table. "Two of your brownies were on my side of the ribbon and"—he reached over and plucked a package from her side—"fuck. One of mine is on yours." He paused for a beat and took a breath. "Did we have a customer who couldn't make up their mind? Were you about to move everything back to its place?" He waited for her to say yes. That he had nothing to be upset about.

Red spots raced up her neck and flooded her cheeks. "I knew something was off. I just knew it."

He broke out in a sweat and panic welled up inside of him. "What's off? What's wrong?"

"How do you know whose are whose?" she squeaked.

Was she for real? "Mine have a pot warning sticker on the back." Not to mention his were wrapped ten-times neater.

Her mouth dropped open. "And you're just now mentioning this?"

"Why is that shocking, Luna? It's the law. You must know that. My product has to be labeled."

She covered her face with her hands. "Oh. God. Yes. Of course. I'm so sorry. I wasn't thinking." She shuffled through the brownies on her platter and came up with several that belonged on his side. "Oh fuck, oh fuck, oh fuck."

His gut fisted. Whatever she was *oh fucking* about, it wasn't good. "Just spit it out. What is going on?"

She moved more brownies around and then heaved out a breath. "Earlier today, Ms. Houdini got antsy and needed a restroom break."

The panic building inside of him spiraled. He grabbed the table for support. "Please don't tell me you left the table unattended to see to the needs of that damn goat of yours?" Of all the asinine—

"Of course I didn't leave it unattended," she bit out between clenched teeth. "But the mayor showed up and offered to watch the table while I took Ms. Houdini behind a building."

Mitch frowned. Why would he do that? Unless he was trying to set Mitch up for further blackmail. Punishment for sharing a table with Luna. "Are you saying the mayor messed with our brownies?"

"I don't know. Maybe. I didn't actually see him do it. I—" Her words cut off and she lost all color.

"What?"

"Fuck. Fuck. Fuck," she said, wringing her hands.

"Stop saying that and just tell me," he whispered again.

Luna's eyes widened to the size of dinner plates. "I sold six brownies," she croaked. "To a church lady. What if some of them were yours?" She motioned toward the spot she'd opened when scooting brownies around.

He looked. Pot warning labels unattached to brownie packages. He snatched them up. "Chu...chur..." Words snagged on his faulty windpipe. This went beyond the mayor gathering blackmail material. Mitch could go to jail. He could become a felon like Mom. "Where is she? Do you see her in the crowd?"

Bad Luck Luna scrambled onto a chair and wildly glanced around. Her head practically going in circles. "I can't see her." She glanced at him. "What if they've already left to go home?"

He pinched the bridge of his nose. "They?"

Luna nodded. "She was here with a group of ladies from her church. She bought brownies for each of them. She was very nice. Gave me a tip and everything."

He stood on his chair. "What did she have on?"

"White blouse. Nice jeans. I failed to notice her shoes."

The crowd was full of people wearing white shirts. "What church were they with? Maybe we can call it, and they can let us know how to contact one of them?"

"I don't know. She didn't say. I gave her my card. She didn't give me hers."

"Of all the—"

Luna held up a hand, stop-sign style, and jumped off her chair. "Save the lecture and hold down the fort."

Lecture? He had much harder words pressing for release than the ones one would use in a lecture. "Where are you going?"

"To search for her, of course."

He watched her scurry off and shook his head. Bad Luck Luna had struck again.

27

“I didn't find her,” Luna said to Mitch when she made it back to their booth. Right now, more than anything, she needed a hug. Today had been hard. So hard. And there wasn't a single person she could turn to for comfort. Especially not Mitch. Not right now, anyway.

“How hard did you look? It's not that big of a venue. She must be around here somewhere,” he said, pacing back and forth.

Couldn't he tell by the sweat running down her cheeks how hard she'd looked? “Trust me when I say, she's not here. Our church lady has disappeared like a fuzzy-wine dream you wake up from on a Monday morning," she rambled. "Or a pending orgasm interrupted by the shrill of a telephone. Or—"

"For Christ's sake, stop yapping," Mitch snapped. "This is all the fault of your damn goat."

She fisted her hands. How dare he! "You are a first-class wanker blaming Ms. Houdini. "I'll have you—"

Loud laughing caused them both to jerk around. Several locals quickly turned away and pretended to be busy. Several others just continued to stare.

"Now see what you've done?" Mitch turned his back to the crowd.

"What I've done?" This day was careening downhill faster than a sale at Macy's on Black Friday. "You're the one who told Brandy our date was contractual!" Why in the hell had she gone there? Brandy had nothing to do with pot brownies possibly being sold to church ladies. "I'm—"

"I should have known you weren't really going to let that go with an apology."

"Whoa, Fuckhead, I think it's time you took a breather," Johnny said, appearing out of nowhere with Amahle. The couple stepped between them.

"Hi, doll." Amahle laid a hand on Luna's shoulder. "You okay? I wanted to stick around and check on you after Mitch's monumental dickhead move but couldn't."

Luna gave her a tight smile but didn't answer.

Mitch took a step away from Johnny and glared at Amahle. "It was not a dick—"

"Fuckhead, it was," Johnny said. "Trust me on this."

Amahle beamed at her husband. Then turned her attention back to Luna. "Johnny and I will take care of your booth. Why don't the two of you take your argument somewhere private? Like one of your houses so you can enjoy makeup sex when it's over."

Luna snorted. "Makeup sex? This guy has probably never had makeup sex in his life."

"Mitch, is that true?" Amahle stepped out from between them and snuggled into the crook of Johnny's arm. "If it is, let me be the first to highly recommend it."

"That's not happening." Mitch grabbed a box and loaded it up with his brownies. "I believe Luna and I have spent enough time in each other's company for one day." He nodded sharply at his friends, not at Luna, turned, and stomped away toward his home.

Luna released a low growl of frustration, and then took a deep breath and released it. "Thanks for trying," she said to Amahle and Johnny. She leaned down and unhooked Ms. Houdini from the table. "Come on, girl. Let's get out of here."

"Luna, don't give up on him," Amahle said. "Underneath his starchy personality is a really sweet guy who just wants to be loved no matter how much he might screw up."

Luna gave her a puzzled look. "Loved? Trust me, I'm the last person Captain SOS wants to love him."

She hooked Ms. Houdini up to the wagon, tossed her product inside it, and walked away. There would be no recovering from today. Not with Mitch. Not with the town. She wasn't even sure Luna 2.0 would recover. At least she'd been spared the embarrassment of angry tears while yelling at him.

"SOS? What do you suppose that stands for?" someone said.

"Probably shit on a shingle," another answered.

"Maybe sex on a stick. He is hunky. Even if he did treat her like crap today."

Luna steps faltered. Gah. Had someone just stuck up for her? Someone who wasn't Amahle or Johnny?

28

Monday morning, Luna stifled a yawn. Leading a group through Almost Sunrise Yoga while sleep deprived required reinforced toothpicks to prop open the eyes and massive amounts of black coffee. So far, she'd lost two nights of sleep fretting about the brownie incident.

Mitch had surprised her by calling later in the evening Saturday night to see if the church lady had called to complain. She hadn't. After hearing her answer, he'd mumbled something about the mayor and had cut off the call. She'd responded by drinking too much wine while contemplating the idea of moving. Going somewhere else to get a fresh start. By the end of the bottle, she'd convinced herself it was her only option.

"I'm here. Sorry, I'm late." Amahle rounded the corner of the house and came into view.

Luna's eyes chucked the toothpicks. "What a nice surprise. We're just about to start."

"In my defense, I have an excellent reason for being late," Amahle added in a cheerful tone.

"I'm sure you do," Luna said. One of the nicest things out of Saturday's catastrophe had been Amahle publicly supporting her.

"I probably shouldn't share," Amahle continued, "but since I'm sure we're all going to be the best of friends in no time at all, I'm late because the boss insisted on receiving a blowjob before he'd give me time off for a yoga class."

Luna chuckled. She could learn something from Amahle and her apparent disregard for what others thought.

"Your boss gets blowjobs for giving you time off?" Speedo asked.

Amahle's gaze swept toward Speedo and then crashed all the way down past his potbelly to what lie underneath. "Holy guacamole, that's a tiny speedo."

Speedo preened. "My partner tells me it makes my eyes look bigger."

Amahle gave him the once-over. "That's not all it makes look bigger."

Luna sniffed to keep from snickering. "Everyone, this is Amahle. Her boss is also her husband. No need to feel outraged on her behalf."

"Oh...did I forget to mention that?" Amahle squeezed between the rows and set up on a mat in the third row, behind Abby and Speedo.

"Well…damn. That's not worthy of tongue-wagging," Speedo said to Amahle. "If it's all the same to you, I think I'll repeat it without Luna's buzzkill caveat."

"I wouldn't have it any other way," Amahle replied.

The class laughed, said hi to Amahle, and then faced forward.

"Let's bow in," Luna said, placing her hands in prayer position.

Luna took them through several warm-up poses. Had Amahle come this morning to further show solidarity? "Let's move into downward dog."

"Speedo, what the frack'n fuck," Amahle yelled, startling the calm out of everyone.

Luna straightened so she could see what the problem was.

"On the back row," Amahle ordered him. "Go."

"But—"

"Butts aren't the problem," Amahle pointed at his crotch. "I don't mind seeing Paris and France, but I draw the line when you're about to flash the Lances."

Speedo rested his hands on his potbelly. "Honey, this is a no-judgment zone. Go ahead, Luna, tell her."

Luna gave Speedo an apologetic smile and then made eye-contact with Amahle. "We have a no criticism, or envy, policy."

Amahle pursed her lips. "I'm not being critical. I'm purely stating a fact. You've got way too much going on down there to have it all packed away in a speedo. Take the compliment and get thy ass to the back row."

Speedo looked like he didn't know if he should huff or puff. In the end, he did a little of both as he grabbed his towel and swept regally to the back row.

"Where are the goats?" Amahle asked as if she hadn't just caused a scene.

"Let's transition into a triangle," Luna said to the class. In that position, she answered, "The goats were having a hard time waking up this morning." She sneaked a peek at the barn where they were still cuddled up on their new beds. She was pretty sure they'd been out honkytonking on Main Street while she'd tossed and turned.

"I've missed Ms. Houdini," Abby said. "Actually, I've missed all of you."

"We're happy to see you back in your spot this morning," Luna replied. "Your energy has been missed."

"I've missed the energy this class gives me." Abby sounded sincere. "Life just isn't the same when you don't start it with yoga and friends."

"Where have you been?" Amahle asked.

"From here, let's move into warrior pose," Luna said. They all straightened, pivoted right, bent their left knee, and raised their hands above their heads, looking skyward as they did. She should probably shut down the conversation but didn't.

"Let's just say Brandy wasn't thrilled that I like Luna," Abby answered. "And it took us a while to hash out what it means to be a friend."

Luna ordered herself not to ask what definition they'd landed upon. Then again, if she knew, perhaps it would help her be more successful with friendship. Possibly her and Amahle's. Obviously, she and Mitch hadn't succeeded using their model. "Is your definition sharable or would that be breaking a trust?"

"It's complicated, but basically, we don't have to like or dislike the same people. We're free to choose. It helped that she's made a few new friends that have her distracted from me."

"Twist to face the sun and let's sink down in an extended angle pose," Luna instructed.

"Free to choose what?" a newbie asked. College Freshman had brought her.

"As long as you haven't done something to me personally," Abby replied, "it's okay for me to enjoy your company. Brandy and I fight our own battles. Not each other's."

"That's a refreshingly grown-up view of life," Amahle said. "I think I'll suggest to my boss that we adopt your motto."

Luna led them through another downward dog, a pigeon pose, and a camel pose.

"Have you had any more dates with Cinnamon Roll?" College Freshman asked.

"I heard it was a contractual date," Abby said. "Is that true?"

Gasps erupted from the listeners.

Luna winced. "Let's move into a forward sitting bend." She waited until everyone was there before she replied. "He asked me out. I said yes. As such, one could reason we had a date based upon a verbal contract." She'd come up with this canned response and had practiced it so it would roll believably off her tongue.

"He gave Brandy the impression you forced him to ask you out," Abby pushed.

Luna laughed. Or at least she tried to laugh. "What sort of leverage would I have to force a guy like Mitch to take me on a date?"

"I know Mitch," Amahle said, "and I can assure you he enjoyed his date with Luna. He told me as much."

"Abby, I don't think I like this friend of yours," College Freshman said.

"Brandy's not bad," Abby said. "She's mostly very nice. Unless you get in the way of what she wants. Then she can be a bit unpredictable."

"Move into cow face pose," Luna instructed.

Abby contorted her body into the pose. "Luna, you should probably watch your back where Brandy's concerned."

"Is she dangerous?" College Freshman asked. "Should Luna buy a gun? Or hire a bodyguard?"

"She's not dangerous from a physical standpoint. But she's damn good at dishing out subtle payback. The kind you don't see coming. But when it hits you, trust me, you'll be left looking like the person in the wrong."

Luna released her clasped hands. "Thank you for the counsel." She'd grown up surrounded by women like Brandy. Hell. Mother was a Brandy. And Luna 1.0 hadn't fallen far from the apple tree. Mean girls didn't worry Luna. Not that Luna could tell her class this without explaining her background.

"Are you going out with Cinnamon Roll again?" College Freshman asked, sounding truly concerned for Luna.

The concern felt good. Better than good. It was like the gentle hug she'd been craving.

"I'm not suggesting you should, but, if you don't," Abby said, "everyone will assume it's because you forced the first date upon Mitch by dubious methods."

"Trust me, I've already done the leg work to put that belief to bed," Amahle said. "Everyone in town knows Luna is a good sort and Brandy just had a moment of blind jealousy which led her to say things that weren't true and Mitch—big teddy bear that he is—was too confused by the moment to offer a legit rebuttal on Luna's behalf."

Luna glanced away as she blinked back tears. She really did have a new friend. Maybe she wouldn't sell her house and move away after all.

29

Mitch didn't spend the weekend waiting for the police to arrive and arrest him for selling unmarked dope product to an unsuspecting consumer. Instead, he took charge of his fate and canvased the town and social media for images or videos of Saturday's fair. Anything to prove Regis had purposefully messed with his product. The guy was out of control.

Now, standing in the mayor's office, Mitch's pulse raced. As of this morning, he'd found no hard evidence.

"Son, I'm going to get straight to the point," the mayor said. "I received a disturbing call Saturday evening from the pastor of Second Baptist over in Hurly. One of his parishioners had confided in him she unknowingly consumed cannabis."

"Fuck." Yes, Mitch had expected this, but hearing it took his breath.

"Fuck indeed," the mayor said.

Mitch glanced at the closed door. Was law enforcement on the other side?

"As it is, the pastor and I go way back. I was able to smooth things over and no charges will be filed."

Mitch stilled. "Thank you." Was Regis telling the truth? Or had the church lady been a plant? Was she someone he'd blackmailed into helping him pull off his diabolical stunt and everything else was fabricated?

"I wish I could say you're welcome, but it's obvious by your actions of inviting Luna to the fair you never had any intention of upholding your end of our bargain, and to be honest I'm feeling disrespected."

Mitch placed his hands on the back of the chair in front of him to prevent himself from reaching across the desk and grabbing the mayor by his neck. "That's not true. I had every intention. When you failed to keep your end in a timely manner, I invited Luna because it was the neighborly thing to do." And because sometime over the weekend, it had hit Mitch what a hypocrite he had been to consider doing the mayor's slimy work all to save his own reputation or that of his friends. He'd spoken to Johnny and Amahle, and they weren't at all worried about the mayor's threats toward them. And they'd agreed, the mere act of doing the mayor's bidding would have been what would have earned Mitch a bad name. Even if he'd gone about it with honesty, his character would have been trashed. He would still have been the guy who hadn't stood up for the underdog.

Regis pounded a fist on the desk. "You not only defied me, but you did so after I told you how important it was the fair be without flaw."

"Luna did nothing to cause you problems with your backer," Mitch bit out.

"She made a scene with Brandy," the mayor said. "My financial backer was appalled."

Luna had done that, so Mitch said nothing. Ever since the fair, he'd been so busy trying to unravel the brownie situation he'd not taken the time to revisit his complicated feelings toward his friend.

Regis stood and pointed a finger at him. "Don't just stand there like you're afraid to speak up. What do you have to say for yourself?"

Common sense said now was a time to mollify not antagonize. But Mitch had made a commitment to Luna to stand up for her in public settings. Even if she wasn't here to see him do so, it was what friends did for one another. It's what he'd want her to do for him. He walked around the chair and dropped his hands on the desk and leaned forward. "If there was a scene caused, it was Brandy's fault for poking at Luna with half-truths."

Brandy had had the nerve to email him after the fair to tell him how wrong Luna was for him. And that Luna was the sort of woman who would always make a spectacle of herself. And he'd be smart to stay away from her because Brandy knew how much he valued a calm life. This coming from the woman who had left him at the altar in front of a full church.

It was like a two-dollar blunt calling an edible a cheap high.

The mayor's lips went white.

Mitch stiffened and prepared for the threat that would no doubt follow.

The mayor surprised him by smiling. "There is a more important issue we need to discuss. Please sit."

Mitch reluctantly did. "I'm listening."

Regis took a seat and thrummed his fingers on the mahogany top. "Son, when you received a license for a dispensary in this town and I, in turn, helped you financially by renting you a house at a price significantly below market value, we had the same vision for Rocky Mountain Springs."

Mitch placed his foot on his knee and leaned back. "My vision—"

"Doesn't match mine or that of my backer. Which, as it turns out, is just as well."

The words came at Mitch fast and slimy. He tugged at his ear. "What do you mean by just as well?"

A sly grin slid onto the mayor's face as he pushed back from his desk, stood, and walked to his large picture window and stared out. "First, I am officially withdrawing my offer to sell you your home."

"Which is just as well since I'm no longer willing to do your dirty work. And I'm officially putting you on notice that I will make your life miserable should you try and sully my name or that of my friends or run Luna out of town."

The mayor turned, his face red. "The Luna matter will take care of itself."

"What does that mean?" Mitch asked.

"As it turns out, the Chamber of Commerce has an important agenda item coming up for vote at its next meeting." He walked back to his desk, removed his tie, and gently placed it in a drawer. "That is the matter of which I spoke when I invited you to come see me. Everything that happened after, unfortunately for you, cemented my decision."

"What vote?" Mitch stood and shoved his hands in his pockets so the mayor couldn't see them tighten into fists.

"I shouldn't tell you this, but the vote revolves around a chance for the town to pursue a lucrative investment." He pushed his chair back and propped his feet on his desk.

"And?" Mitch prompted.

The mayor pulled a cigar out of his pocket. "What I'm about to tell you, I do so because I truly care about you. Almost as if you were my son."

Mitch shook his head. God, he just couldn't get a break in the parent department.

"We often have entrepreneurs approach us asking for permission to open a business on Main Street. In one week, we are scheduled to vote on one such proposal."

Mitch relaxed. On more than one occasion since moving to Rocky Mountain Springs, the mayor had told him about such an upcoming meeting. Regis reveled in making a big deal about the possibility of new businesses coming to town. The last one had been Molly Henson's request to open a bakery. The big deal was that Molly was the estranged daughter of the owner of the Henson's Fruit and Flower Farm.

"There aren't any empty buildings for new companies."

The mayor studied his cigar as if it were a bar of gold. "For now. That can change. Did I mention the latest proposal came from Mr. Princeton, Brandy's father?"

A startled laugh erupted from Mitch. He placed his palms on the mayor's desk and leaned forward. "Are you sure that offer's still on the table? Have you checked with him since the fair?"

"We spoke just this morning. He would set the business up, and Brandy would oversee its operation."

Mitch straightened and paced. That would be something Mr. Princeton would do for his only daughter. Had the idea materialized before or after Mitch had told her he wasn't interested in rekindling old flames? Wasn't interested in her father buying his house for them to live in?

He stopped pacing in front of the mayor's desk. "What kind of business? Brandy's degree is in Antiquities. I don't see a museum in Rocky Mountain Springs succeeding." Could he and Brandy coexist in the same town? Could Luna and Brandy coexist?

"Not a museum." The mayor smirked. "A big box dispensary. Daddy Dearest plans to buy her a Galaxy Dope franchise for her upcoming birthday."

The blood rushed out of Mitch's head, and he dropped down in the nearest chair.

Galaxy Dope was a massive chain of techno-weed dispensary stores. A franchise described by media as: *Sold-out-concert meets New-York-City meets rave of the weed world.* All their stores were state of the art tourist attractions the moment they opened. Music. Flashing lights. And a treasure cove of cannabis products for medical and recreational use.

The blood rushed back in his head and pounded there like Class VI rapids in his ears. "One of those in town will put me out of business as well as the dispensaries in our neighboring counties."

"You scorned his daughter," the mayor said in a tone of reprimand. "I'm sure he's been waiting for a chance to avenge her honor. As would any self-respecting father."

Mitch had to unclench his jaws to get words out. "I didn't scorn her. She asked me to go to work for her father, I told her no, she got pissed, and walked out of the church."

"The bottom line, if we don't welcome him and Brandy into our community, he said he'd open the franchise in Peculiar." The mayor chewed on the end of the cigar. "If that happens, the whole town loses business—not just you. Instead of people traveling to Rocky Mountain Springs for vacation and conferences, they'll head to Peculiar."

Mitch groaned. Peculiar was a small town that Rocky Mountain Springs competed with for tourists. If a big box dispensary went in there, it would hurt more than him, it would drive away tourism dollars. "Our town is built on the concept of mom-and-pop shops," Mitch argued. "Not large box stores. That chain will ruin the whole vibe of Rocky Mountain Springs."

"They have plans in place to address that."

"Oh."

"The fiduciary thing for our town to do is to join them. It's what's best for everyone...but you. Which is a shame. But as a leader, I must do what's best for the majority."

"Don't you think the town should vote on this? That franchise has a hand in the sale of more than just weed. I don't care what you say, it will affect everyone's business."

The mayor's smirk was back. "Actually, it will only affect you...and a couple others whose leases have expired and whose space we'll need. It's up to the Chamber of Commerce to vote it in or vote it out. Anyway, if it makes you feel better, Mr. Princeton promised to build a scaled down one that focuses on cannabis and a world class spa for the first five years."

Cannabis and a spa. That's what the mayor meant by it would work itself out. Brandy's father planned to put both Luna and Mitch out of business. "You're being shortsighted if you believe it won't affect the other businesses. Brandy's father is greedy. He's not going to leave profit on the table for someone else to take."

"You should let me worry about that," the mayor said.

"I won't sit idly by and allow this to happen. I plan on fighting the proposal."

An amused tilt lifted the mayor's jowls. "You? Must I remind you what is at stake for you should you decide to get in my way?"

Anger ripped through Mitch. The kind of anger he had to work to confine. When he thought he had it under control, he spoke succinctly. "If you go after me, I will go after you. I will report you for your illegal background searches and for tampering with my product at the fair. I have a witness who saw you moving brownies from one side to the other."

The mayor's face went red. "What witness?"

"They prefer to remain anonymous...for now."

"You're lying," the mayor said.

"Test me."

"Now. Now. Let's not get carried away," the mayor blustered. "I'll tell you what, son. Here's what I'm going to do for you. I'll sit back and allow you to present the Commerce with an alternative option. One that can compete with Galaxy Dope. If you think you can do that, I'll happily put you on the agenda for the evening of the vote. As I mentioned before, this isn't personal."

Mitch fought back the bile rising in his throat. How in the hell was he supposed to come up with an exciting alternative in that short amount of time? His brain had been called a lot of things but never creative. Then again, what choice did he have? He fixed Regis with a stony stare. "Consider it done."

The mayor held out a hand. "May the best man win."

Mitch ignored the proffered hand and left without a goodbye. Once on Main Street, he broke out in a sweat, and his breathing grew labored. He stumbled to a bench and dropped down on its seat right as a panic attack took over his vision and hearing. He gripped the wooden planks on either side of his legs for balance, closed his eyes, and waited for the terrifying loss of control to subside.

Once his senses were back to normal, he pulled out his phone and made a call. To Luna. His friend. The one person he knew who could think outside the box better than anyone. Right now, he needed her creativity to help him fight Brandy and her father's plans for the town. But more than that, he needed her.

It rang once. Twice. The line went dead.

30

Luna blew out a breath and stared moodily at her parents, who'd once again shown up unannounced and uninvited almost immediately after her Monday morning yoga class had ended.

She glared at her father. "You can bully and bluster all you want, but just like I told you the last time you blew into town with your demands, I'm not bending to your will. I'm not coming back home."

To even have to say those words bordered on asinine. The mere idea someone, anyone, thought they could, in this day and age, force their grown-ass child to live where they dictated should be grounds for having them locked up in an establishment for the delusional.

"We will just see about that." Her father spoke in a tone of certainty. One that held no hint of insanity.

Luna shivered. "Father, get this through your thick head. I'm not moving back home. I'm not living in the penthouse you bought me as a bribe. And, again, because it bears repeating, I'm not giving up my dream to run a successful goat yoga establishment to go to work for you in some position with some title you totally invented to make your only child look successful. Just so you and Mother can then brag about me to your *friends*."

"The position I'm offering you is a far superior career option than this damn stupid dream of yours to stretch for a living while goats step all over you."

"And yet, it's my dream. Sending my friends here to talk me into coming home didn't work. Having them trash me in their reviews didn't work." Well, that had sort of worked. She'd yet to get another group booking. "And your pathetic attempt to control me by taking away my trust fund sure as hell didn't work."

This shook him out of his calm. So much so his nostrils actually flared. "Young lady, I did not raise you to be disrespectful."

Hello. He'd done very little parenting. That's what boarding schools and nannies had been for. "Instead, you raised me to be the fall guy for your and Mother's illegal activities."

Mother gasped.

"Grow up. Your mother and I did one thing, and it was for you. And it wasn't that illegal. Everyone does it. Plenty of our friends did it. They just didn't get caught. You don't really think London and Paris got into the University of Columbia because they were bright?"

Their parents had bribed their way in as well? That explained so much. Luna had often wondered how the twins had pulled off getting into the university. They'd always been much more into partying than studying.

"It was simply bad luck how it all went down," Mother added, as if that made it all better.

Luna laughed manically. It had all gone down by *their daughter* getting arrested because the funds had come from *their daughter*'s bank account. Luna had been in the dark about it all. The prosecutor on the case had thought her parents would immediately admit to the crime to keep Luna from being charged with a felony, and he'd have the feather of their convictions going into the primaries. It had all quickly backfired on everyone.

"People who commit crimes always believe they'll never get caught. You two should have known better. You've made a living off criminals who got caught. And to make it worse, you set it all up so I unknowingly committed the crime for you."

"Don't compare what we did to what real criminals do," Father said. "We simply tweaked a rule in order to help our daughter get an excellent education." His voice had lost its steady volume, one of the few signs he ever showed of uncertainty.

"It was a victimless crime," Mother said. "And you excelled. Had they allowed you to graduate, you were to do so with honors. It's not like you didn't belong there. Their entrance rules are biased against rich children. Children with so many more things to juggle in their lives than poor children who only have studying to keep them occupied when school is out. Any child should be allowed to attend any university they want to attend. If colleges have more students than they have room for, they simply need to raise their tuition to balance out quantity and demand."

Luna made a buzzer noise. "Wrong. I'm the victim of your crime, and I have the lovely felony record to prove it."

Father's face lost its color. "There is plenty of blame to go around. If you would have studied harder," he continued, "your mother and I wouldn't have been forced into bribing your way into a college worthy of our only child."

"For the love of sex, I had a 3.8 high school GPA."

Mother clutched her diamonds. "Vulgarity is not attractive on a lady of stature."

What had she said that was vulgar? "You know what, guys? I'm not arguing this any further. I now live in Colorado. My legal name is Luna Parker. And I am pursuing a career as a small business owner. End of story."

Father gave her a smile. The same one she'd seen him use countless times on trial witnesses he was about to bury. "Don't force my hand. You're our only child. I will not stand for you throwing it away living in a nobody town making a living with barn animals as your props. It's unseemly for an Alexander."

"First of all, I'm no longer an Alexander. Second, why do you care so much? I would think it would be easier on you and Mother not to have your child—the one with a felony record—around to embarrass you. After all, the two of you failed to pull off what other parents were able to do without a hitch. My presence would constantly remind them of the time they outshined you. Which would lead them to talk about you. Is that what you truly want?"

"Your felony doesn't concern us in the least. Do you have any idea how embarrassing it is for us to know our friends believe you didn't have the backbone to stick around when a little negative attention came your way? And you compounded your cowardice by changing your name. Which of course, you did incompetently, and so it was quickly discovered. And while their children are moving up in corporate jobs, you're living in Colorado, wearing off-the-rack clothes and serving awful food to your guests on chipped, mismatched dishes."

Luna swallowed. "My name change was discovered because you told everybody." Only one of them would win this battle. The fact she'd won their last skirmish by not following his lead when she'd been arrested for their misdeeds didn't mean she'd triumph now. In fact, it meant quite the opposite. Father would double down and draw upon every weapon in his arsenal to come out the winner. Mother would stand back and watch it happened.

"Of course we told your friends. We thought they would be able to talk some sense into you," Mother said. "Plus, if you must know, it was our little way of helping you financially. I can't bear the thought of you going hungry."

That made absolutely no sense. "I may not have disappeared this time in an efficient manner, but if you push too hard, I bet next time I'll get it right. And your private investigator won't find me."

Mother clutched her chest.

Father's posture softened. "Maria, come home. We miss you."

"It's Luna now." Maria Luna Parker Alexander no longer legally existed. Just Luna Parker.

Father flattened his lips. "*Luna*, come home with us. In return, we'll give you back your credit cards, and tomorrow you can shop all day on Fifth Avenue. Just think how much damage you could do with my credit card in a day's time."

"Then stay and have dinner with us," Mother added. "I'll have the cook whip up your favorites."

"If, after you've listened to what we have to say," Father said, "you're still not interested in moving back to Manhattan, then I'll see that the jet is at your disposal to bring you and all your purchases back to Colorado. Hell, in a day's time, you could buy all new furnishings for your home here...or the one we bought you in Manhattan."

On the surface, the proposal reeked of big-heartedness. Luna didn't bite the bait. Once she got back home, the jet would not be at her disposal. They would say she'd misunderstood. And there would be other roadblocks thrown up ensuring she didn't return to Colorado. "I don't need your money. And I don't need your approval of my lifestyle. You and Mother may come back when and only when you're ready to have a relationship with your independent daughter, who lives in Colorado, and whose life you have no say over. And bring the goats a treat."

They both huffed.

"This isn't over," Father announced.

"Oh, but it is," Luna countered.

He stood stiff and straight and peered down his nose like a king at an unruly subject. "What comes next, Maria Luna Parker Alexander, won't be pretty. And when it happens, you remember my next words, and you remember them clearly. It is your fault, and yours alone, that I had to play my ace card."

With that cryptic statement, he and Mother turned and walked out of her front door.

31

Monday evening, Mitch stood unshaven in front of Luna's door and knocked. Probably harder than he needed, but it helped release the tension in his body. When no one answered, he knocked again. He would not leave until he and Luna talked. She might be able to ignore his calls, but surely she couldn't ignore his physical presence on her property.

"I'm coming," he heard Luna say.

The door swung open to reveal her standing in front of him in a vintage Superman T-shirt, one like his own, and form-fitting sweats. The shirt had blotches of red on it. "That's not blood, is it?"

"I should have known it was you and not my soul's twinsie," she replied stone-cold serious.

He fought an urge to reach out and pull her into a hug. If he did, he might never let her go. "What in the hell is a soul's twinsie?" That was not one of his decided upon subjects for this meeting.

"Your soul's twinsie is the one your own soul yearns to spend time with for eternity." She pulled her hair up off her neck and secured it with a pink band she had on her wrist. "Lore has it, the Universe will send your soul's twinsie to your front door on a Tuesday. So if you're single, you should always answer if some-one knocks on that particular day of the week."

"I'm sorry to have disappointed you. I'm definitely not your soul's twinsie." Why had he said that? It might not be true. Where Luna was concerned, he didn't know how he felt, but he sure as hell felt more than friendship.

As if suddenly remembering she was mad at him, Luna scowled. "What do you want? It's not like we're friends anymore."

Her words gave him heartburn. "Friends don't stop being friends just because they fight. I refuse to let you out of our friendship ceremony promises."

A look of something like relief softened her scowl. "Fine. We can still be friends."

Her words gave him the first bit of joy he'd felt in days. He stabbed his fingers through his hair and ex-haled a calming sigh. "Now that we have that cleared up, I need someone who knows how to think rich. Someone who's lived a life of excess."

She wrapped her arms under her chest and tapped a bare foot on the wooden floor. "Why do you need someone who knows how to think rich?"

"Because when you were raised in poverty, you think like a fucking poor person." The words came out rawer and angrier than he wanted.

She motioned for him to come inside. "Tell me what's going on." She walked into the living room and took a seat at an old piano bench. There was no piano in the room to go with it.

He considered his options on where to sit and decided to straddle the bench simply because it placed him close enough to Luna to inhale her scent. "The mayor is going to ruin us."

A small sound of dismay parted her lips. She turned and laid a hand on his arm. "Does this have something to do with him being mad you invited me to the fair? Has anything come of the brownie incident? Or are we in the clear?"

"The brownie incident has been handled."

"Handled? That sounds fierce." She studied him. "Handled how?"

"That doesn't matter. Not right now. What matters is Brandy didn't take it well when she discovered I wasn't interested in giving our nuptials another chance."

Luna stood and walked to the fireplace, so he stood and walked to the window. All three goats were lying under the tree in the front yard.

"What does the fact Brandy is a spoiled rotten socialite have to do with the mayor wanting to ruin us?" Luna asked.

He turned to look at her. "Brandy convinced her father to defend her honor by stripping each of us of the one thing that means the most to us."

"That bitch dumped you and tried to humiliate me. If her honor's bad, that's on her. Not us."

"Agreed, but after I told her on Saturday I wasn't interested in trying again, her father approached the mayor with the idea of opening a Galaxy Dope."

Luna grimaced. "Truthfully, it's not an unreasonable step for her father to take."

"Not unreasonable? In what world?"

"Let me qualify that. It's not unreasonable if you're wealthy and like to go after those who dare stand up to you in any way. I mean, honestly, it's exactly like something my father would do. In fact, if there was a goat yoga equivalent to Galaxy Dope, my father would probably put one of those in Rocky Mountain Springs as a way to force me back home. Wait. Does Galaxy Dope come with a spa?"

He nodded.

"Fuck. That's what he meant when he threaten me that *what happens next* will be my fault for not coming home. He somehow knew."

"I don't know. That sounds dubious. I'm sure he loves you too much to destroy your dream."

"I'm not so sure about that, but I hope you're right."

Mitch took a seat. "I'm sure I am."

She came and sat next to him. "What are we going to do to fight this? That is why you're here, right? You want my help in fighting it?"

He nodded. "The mayor has agreed to put me on the agenda so I can present a counter proposal to the Chamber of Commerce."

Luna took her time mulling over his words. "Excellent. What's your plan?"

"You."

"Me?"

He stabbed his hand through his hair. "Beating Brandy and her father isn't going to be solved with the normal thinking of an average guy. It's going to take something abnormal. You've proven you can think abnormally. And you have the experience of knowing how the rich think."

Her eyes lit up. "Have you mentioned any of this to Johnny and Amahle? Or any other business owners in town?"

"I wanted to speak to you first."

Luna popped up and hurried to a cabinet. She grabbed a yellow legal pad and a pen out of a drawer. "Follow me." She led him into the kitchen where she took a seat at her table. "What does your company offer that this big box dispensary can't?"

He sat down across from her. "Nothing."

She rolled her eyes. "Nothing? Hello. You grow your own stuff. You're knowledgeable and approachable. You're a hands-on small business owner." She wrote as she spoke. "Those are just off the top of my head."

Did she really find him approachable? Most women found him closed off. "These dispensaries are a huge hit wherever they lay roots. So apparently consumers are more concerned with other things when deciding where to purchase their weed or get their spa fix."

"You mean to tell me Galaxy Dope comes in and crushes the little guy and the locals are okay with that?"

"It appears that away."

"Then we need to keep them out of Rocky Mountain Springs. When does the vote take place?"

"Next Monday."

"Lucky for you, I'm excellent at planning hijinks."

He frowned. "I didn't agree to hijinks. The matter is of a serious nature. It will not be resolved by your doing something flakey like yoga in the nude. Or voodoo in the moonlight."

"Captain SOS," she said with a cheeky grin, "we don't have time to play fair. If we want to win, hijinks are of an utmost necessity."

He locked his jaw and considered his response. He had no wiggle room to do anything that could smear his reputation. "I've told you, in my line of business, I have to play by the rules. One misstep, and I can lose my license to sell cannabis. I was damn lucky to be chosen out of the hundreds of applicants who applied. The losing applicants are waiting like thieves in the shadows for me to stumble so they can steal my license away. That's why I got so upset about the brownies."

Worry flickered across her face. "Oh."

"But it won't do me any good to have the license if I can't sell enough of my product to pay the bills. So I ask that you keep my situation in mind as you plan your shenanigans."

"Deal." She picked up an ink pen. "Let's start by making a list of the business owners in town that you trust."

"The only ones I know for sure who are not in debt to the mayor are Amahle and Johnny, Molly Henson, Jimmy the butcher, Tina from the bar, and Pearl Simpson from Pearl's Beads. There are probably others. I'm just not in the know about everyone's finances." The mayor was the landlord to so many in town.

"Let's bring the ones you know of for sure in on our planning. The more thoughts and ideas, the better."

"Shouldn't we at least have an idea before we involve others?"

"The idea is the minor part of what we need to do. Rallying the troops—that is where the magic happens."

Her not-quite-a-plan made him uneasy. "I'm not doubting your ability to pull off a miracle, but I'd prefer to have an idea, any idea, before we include others. I don't want to set my friends up to be targets for revenge unless we know we have a winning idea."

She leaned back in her chair and crossed her arms. "Fine. If you insist."

"I do."

She stared him in the eyes and thrummed her fingers against her lips. Like she was brainstorming. Then she startled him by jumping up.

"So it shall be."

"So what shall be?" he queried.

Instead of responding, she walked out the back door, across the yard, straight to the barn.

He hurried to catch up.

She didn't stop until she reached the loft ladder.

"What are you doing?"

"Going to my thinking spot."

He turned and headed toward the picnic table. There he leaned a hip against it. "This is my thinking spot," he said loud enough for her to hear. He had no intention of scrambling up that ladder and working ten feet off the ground.

"Truly?" She cocked her head out the barn door and gave him a what-the-fuck look. "Can't you try and get over your fear and climb the stairs? I'll even let you go first, and I'll stay at the bottom, where I promise to break your fall with my own body should you tumble."

"I truly can't." Maybe that made him weak in her eyes, but it couldn't be helped. On one of those nights long ago when he and Mom had had to jump out of a window to escape a gun-wielding man she'd owed rent to, he had broken his leg. Ever since, he'd suffered from the fear of heights. Hell, living in Colorado on top of a mountain had been something he'd had to work through. "What's so special about being up there?"

She twisted her lips to the right and then to the left. Then sighed loudly. "It's where Ms. Murphy did her best thinking. Chances are her spirit is up there, rubbing its hands together in anticipation of helping us with our plotting."

He laughed. Of course that was something Luna would believe. "What makes you so sure that's where she did her thinking?"

"Because I found her journals up there. She wouldn't have written them down here and then carried them up there. Not with the awesome seating area and everything."

"You go to your thinking spot. I'll sit here. We'll Facetime."

Luna wrinkled her nose. "I have a secret. One I planned on telling you over dinner after the fair, but then you ruined my plans. Now if you want to know what it is, you have to climb the stairs."

He rubbed the back of his neck. Here it was. The why of her changing her name. "Luna, I've had one too many or-else demands placed on me lately. I can't handle another. Please allow me to sit here and hear your secret."

32

The set of Mitch's chin told Luna his fine ass wasn't going up those stairs today. And his admission told her it wasn't a good day to bring up her felony story. It would make her feel better to know she'd told him, but it wouldn't make him feel better. He had enough on his plate.

Why was it every time she planned to tell him her history, something happened to make it not a good time? Was that the Universe telling her to keep it to herself? Or maybe Nanny Nonna? Anyway, if she wasn't telling him her felony secret, she had to tell him another

since she'd mentioned having one. "Remember my super-secret project?"

"You've never mentioned a super-secret project." He stretched his legs out in front of him and leaned back.

Of course she hadn't. "That's because it was a secret. And I'm a really good secret keeper. Anyway, it may be just the thing to yank the rug out from under Brandy's diabolical stilettos." And to help her with her bad reviews situation.

Mitch laced his fingers behind his head. "I'm listening."

"My plan, once I'm making money from my yoga studio, is to take the profits and turn the barn into a mercantile that sells products made from goat milk."

"Seems logical. But why wait? Don't you have money in the bank?"

How did he know she had money? Had she told him about her insurance money? "Where's the fun in succeeding that way?" Plus, she had a fear Father would discover the insurance windfall and find a way to have it revoked, and then she'd have to pay it all back to Nanny Nonna's trust.

Was that what his threat had been about when he'd left yesterday? Not Galaxy Dope? Had he already discovered the windfall? Was he going to try and have the policy repealed?

Mitch chuckled and the tension left his face. "That's very Luna of you."

"What does that mean?" No way would she share a secret project with a man who even in the face of adversity felt the need to ridicule her.

Ms. Houdini came up to the picnic table and nudged Mitch's leg with her head. Mitch straightened and petted the goat between the ears. "It means you're unique.

I like unique. It's one of the things I've place on my pro list where you're concerned. Tell me more."

He'd made a pro list with her as the header? She should do a pro list of what she liked about him. "I've been playing around with recipes"—she motioned to the stains on her shirt—"and have several that are ready to market. Some were a complete flop and unfortunately have been mentioned in reviews but that's a story for another day. Anyway, I planned on rolling them out one item at a time as I find product suppliers. But if the community were to partner with me, it could become a reality much sooner."

"This is going to sound really selfish, but I don't see how this applies to the problem at hand. What do goat milk and weed have to do with one another?"

She walked to the table and sat next to him. Ms. Tinker and Mr. JJ wandered over to their beds, which were currently laying under Mildred, and plopped down. "In your business, the goat milk will be used in the creation of your edibles. That gives you another uniqueness that millennials will get behind and support."

"Why would you involve the whole town and not just use this marketing idea for yourself? Won't it be diluted if everyone has it?"

Ms. Houdini left Mitch's side and trotted over to Luna where she sat and waited for more ear rubs.

"If I market goat milk products, then I'm just another small store selling to tourists," Luna said, adjusting Ms. Houdini's bow, which had slipped sideways on her head. "But if the locals get involved to save the town from a scorned woman and a shifty mayor, then it's a town that has a story. The kind of story you can market the hell out of online. The kind of story that will save Rocky Mountain Springs."

He sat up straight. "That's not bad. Not bad at all. It's like on *The Voice* when the contestants tell their stories. Then the voters aren't just voting for their voice, they're also voting for their stories."

"Exactly." Luna would have never pegged Mitch as a fan of *The Voice*. "Or on *Shark Tank*. When the contestants tell the story behind the product they're hoping to get financial backing for. America loves a story with a heart. We'll sell a story of a town overcoming the odds to win against a corporate giant and a devious mayor."

"What kind of products do you make from goat milk?"

"Soap. Shampoo. Ice Cream. Body Lotion. Yogurt. Butter. Muffins. Dope brownies. Hell, dope lots of things. I mean the list is long. I thought we'd start with lavender-infused goat-milk products."

"Why lavender?"

"Because lavender anything is big at the moment."

"Where would you get the lavender? We don't have a lavender farm around here."

She held up a finger. This was something she'd already considered. "We don't have one yet. Amahle mentioned at yoga this morning that the mayor is threatening to repossess Mr. Henson's produce and flower farm. I understand he's behind on his mortgage. Anyway, this got me thinking. And my thought was to help him get his mortgage up to date and then see if he'd be willing to turn his land into a lavender farm. I understand he used to raise and sell the best produce in the state."

Mitch scratched his chin. "You heard right. Unfortunately, when his wife got sick and died, he lost his will to continue gardening."

"Do you think he'd be interested in my idea?"

"I do. Cultivating a lavender farm will create a whole new purpose in Mr. Henson's life while being a different set of experiences for him. Experiences that don't have painful memories connected to them. Who else would be involved?"

"How about his daughter?" Luna had spoken to her a few times since moving to town and would love to know the story behind her and her father's falling out. "Any chance she'd join us in something her father's a part of? Or does their feud go too deep?"

"I bet we can get her on board."

"Great, then she's the baker we need in our scenario. We'll need at least one other chef to open a café. Of course, a weed dispensary."

"I get the impression this isn't the first time you considered turning your super-secret project into a community one."

She grinned and stood. "When I realized the whole town was upset because I got this place, I started thinking of ways I could win them over. This was one of my many ideas. Plus, I'll be super honest with you, right now I'm struggling because of bad reviews from my first event. I'm hoping that this will give that part of my operation new life."

"Let's say we can get enough people on board with your project. How would it all kick off?"

"Small at first. We'd make and sell all kinds of products with the common ingredient—goat milk. And then expand. Ooh. We can even make my goats our mascots. And sell products with their picture on them. Like planners. And washi tape. And—"

"Washi what?"

"Doesn't matter. What matters is"—she walked circles around Mildred as she talked—"by uniting under one umbrella, we market ourselves as something special, not just another small town with tourist-trap shops." Ideas flowed through her head faster than she could spit them out. If they marketed the goats right on social media, it could lead to tourists choosing their favorites. They could market T-shirts featuring each goat's photos and sayings above them like *Team Ms. Houdini. Team Mr. JJ. Team Ms. Tinker.* "And this idea really embraces the hippie vibe of Rocky Mountain Springs. The vibe that drew me to this town when I decided to relocate my life."

He stood and held out his hands to her. "Stop pacing. You're making me dizzy."

She went to him and placed her hands in his. Looking up at him, she said, "I'm telling you, this idea can work."

"I think it can be good for a large portion of the town's merchants, and no matter what happens with Galaxy Dope, you should pursue it. But I don't think it will fix my problem. Just because I'm selling products made with goat milk is not going to be a strong enough calling card to steal away Galaxy Dope's customers. And Rocky Mountain High must be able to compete for the Chamber of Commerce to turn down the opportunity to bring a Galaxy Dope to town."

"Oh, but I have a plan." A smile she had no desire to control lifted her lips. "You see, your shop will have exclusive selling rights of one weed product with my secret ingredient. And trust me, that edible will have a huge demand. Like people will get on a plane and travel to Rocky Mountain Springs just to get their hands on your product."

He scratched his head. "You really think it will result in a cult-like following?"

She nodded. "It will fly off the shelf."

He laughed. "I guess, we could call it the Ms. Houdini, since she seems to be my weed's biggest fan."

"Excellent idea."

He frowned. "There's one problem. I can't afford to buy the rights off you for your secret recipe. Not right now, anyway."

"How about instead of buying the rights, we co-own the rights and split the profits? After all, part of its specialty will be your prize weed."

"It sounds intriguing, but I have a hard time believing it's any more potent than any of the other supposed aphrodisiacs on the market."

She wiggled her eyebrows at him. "According to Nanny Nonna's warning on her recipe card, individuals shouldn't eat one without a sex partner handy or a willingness to masturbate."

His right ear turned red. "That sounds as farfetched as Superman wearing kryptonite boxers."

"We could, and by *could* I mean *should*, whip up a batch, try it out, and put this argument to bed."

"Or whip up a batch and allow Johnny and Amahle to try it out without telling them what the ingredient is supposed to do."

"That doesn't sound nearly as fun."

"It will be more scientific," he said. "And truthfully, I don't believe it's possible for me to be any more aroused by you than I already am."

She smiled at his honesty. "Same." She blew out a breath. "Moving on. From what I gather, Galaxy Dope hypes big and shiny."

"You've gathered correctly."

"We'll hype green and friendly."

"Not bad. I actually like that."

"Our tag can be *Hashtag - No Small Businesses Were Hurt in the Making of Our Products*."

"Were you a marketing major?"

"No. Goat yoga."

He groaned. "That is not a major. Is it? Please tell me that's not a major."

"If you must know, I majored in art history," she said.

"That is barely better than goat yoga." He pulled her into a hug.

With her cheek pressed into his chest, she said, "In all seriousness, thank you for choosing me. I'm not normally the one people turn to when they're in a bind. It feels good you trusted me enough to do so. I consider it a win for Luna 2.0."

"Have I told you lately how much I like Luna 2.0?"

"That makes two of us. I think she's a keeper. Now, tell me, Mitch Johnson, what else is on your list of pros and cons where I'm concerned?"

"Great kisser. Best friend. The list is a long one." He kissed the top of her head. "I'll tell you what, when this is all over, no matter the outcome, we can go out to dinner. Not as friends, but as two people who have a connection, both physical and otherwise that they'd be stupid not to explore."

She wiggled her nose to keep from getting all teary eyed at the admission. "I'd like that. I mean, you did knock on my door on a Tuesday and everything. We should at the very least explore the possibility the Universe sent you."

"There is that."

"And when we go out on this date, there's something I've been wanting to tell you and the timing never quite seems right, so no matter what, on that night, I pledge to tell you."

33

Wednesday night, Mitch closed shop early per usual and met Amahle and Johnny at the bar. He quickly filled them in on everything that was going on. Then they spread the word to those they thought could be trusted. There would be a meeting at Luna's house after closing time.

Now Mitch, Tina, Amahle and Johnny, Molly the baker, Song Li the bar owner, Jimmy, the town's eccentric butcher, and Mr. Henson all sat around Luna's firepit while she stood in front of them and laid out her plan to turn the small town of Rocky Mountain Springs into a destination location based around products made from goat milk and great marketing.

Mitch watched as she explained how she'd gotten her idea from a similar business located in New York—Beakman 1802. A company that specialized in skincare products made from goat milk. She'd even set up a screen and a projector so they could watch the Beakman company's story and have a better feel for what Luna proposed.

"Your idea sounds wonderful for a few companies, but I'm not sure how it will support an entire town," Amahle said. "And the only way this will work is if we can convince the town that they will make more money with your idea than with Brandy's father's plan."

Mitch nodded and waited for Luna to respond.

"As you heard, Beekman has a hundred and eighty employees. That's more than are currently employed in Rocky Mountain Springs. You and Johnny will raise goats on your land and be paid as an employee of the corporation."

"But what about my bar? It has nothing to do with goat milk. I don't see there being a place for me in your idea," Song Li said.

Mitch stiffened. That was a good question.

"And I don't hear anything that's going to help me sell dog beds," Mr. Henson said.

Luna glanced at all of them and twisted her lips as if deep in thought. Then she shrugged. "I'm going to be honest. I don't have a full-fledged business plan in place. I know the possibilities are limitless, and I'm convinced if we put our heads together, we'll find a way to fit all your current businesses into this project for our town."

"Our town? Missy, you're still wet behind the ears as a member. I don't think any of us need to take advice from you on what's best for the rest of us," Mr. Henson said.

"True." Luna smiled softly at the town's curmudgeon. "And I'm happy to take a step down and let any of you talk about how you would do this differently."

"Just as I suspected. You're all blow and no go," Mr. Henson snapped. "The moment someone gives you a little flak, you run. That's not what we need in someone who's going to run this town the way it used to be run. Before Regis was elected mayor."

"How did is used to be run?" Luna asked. She'd truly like to know.

"Like a family. All for one and one for Rocky Mountain Springs."

"That's what my vision is, as well," Luna said. "I guess I didn't do a great job of getting that across."

"Who is funding this startup?" Johnny asked.

"A while back, I inherited some money," Luna replied. "Money that I'm willing to use to finance our venture."

"You got enough to pay off my mortgage?" Mr. Henson asked. "Because if you don't, it goes back to the mayor, and we won't have my land for your damn flower farm."

"I believe I have enough. Oh, I just had an idea for your bar," Luna said to Ms. Li. "On certain nights of the week, you can have the goats in your business as a calling card to get tourists in to have their picture taken with our famous goats. Of course, you'll charge for the honor. They will be an Instagram hot item."

"That might work," the bar owner said. "And I could serve drinks named after the goats."

"Mr. Henson," Luna said, "what if you sold dog biscuits made from goat milk to go with your dog beds?"

Mr. Henson harrumphed. "That might work. I do have my late wife's recipe that she used to make dog biscuits for our dogs. It could be tweaked to use goat milk." A smile lifted his lips and made it to his eyes.

"See, all of our brains put together can conquer this plan," Luna enthused. "Together, we can make my idea work."

"But how do we sell it to the rest of the population?" Johnny asked. "We don't have statistics to back up what we're saying."

"We can use Beekman's statistics," Luna answered. "I've Googled their business plan. They started as we're starting."

Mitch was in awe at how fast Luna thought on her feet.

"Won't they be pissed if we're stealing their idea?" Tina asked.

"It's possible. But if I present it to them correctly, I think I can talk them into partnering with us on some shared advertising."

"That's mighty pie-in-the-sky thinking," Mr. Henson replied, once again wearing a frown.

Everyone grew quiet.

"It is," Luna admitted.

"I like it," he said after several seconds of dead air. "I like your spunk and even your damn goats. Any plan to overturn Regis has to be bold. No balls no glory is what my wife and I always said. By God, I'm in."

"I don't mean to be a kink in the plan, but what if the Chamber of Commerce votes to let both ideas fly?" Johnny asked. "I can see them doing that. If that happens, Mitch may not survive."

Luna held up a hand. "We present our plan as an either-or option. We won't be on board with them choosing both. They can't have their cake and eat it too. They have to decide which is best for Rocky Mountain Springs. I strongly believe it's ours. Of course, we need everyone to be at the meeting Monday afternoon to back us when we're presenting. This means some of you may have to close your businesses for a few hours. Which is no doubt why the mayor moved the time for the meeting to the middle of the afternoon. He figured there'd be less turnout."

Mitch took a breath that didn't have to struggle to get to his lungs. Bad Luck Luna was no longer bad luck. She'd suddenly become his lucky charm. Hell, she'd become the whole town's lucky charm.

A cacophony of phones dinging filled the air. As if someone had sent out a group message. They all retrieved their phones to check.

"I don't have anything," Luna said.

"Neither do we," Amahle and Johnny added.

"Me either," Mitch said, waiting for someone to tell them what the message was.

Tina cleared her throat. "It's a message from Mr. Princeton. He's offering a significant financial incentive to anyone who signs a petition supporting his proposal."

34

Luna couldn't believe how fast the week had flown by. Ready or not, it was time for the do-or-die meeting. She'd be a little more ready if Mitch wasn't MIA. How could he be late to such an important event?

She once again stepped up on a metal chair and surveyed the jam-packed meeting room to see if he'd slipped inside in the last two minutes. Her action triggered a decrease in the rambunctious chattering as the foes among them gave her side-eyed looks. "Do you see them yet?" she asked Amahle. They'd sent Johnny in search of Mitch.

Amahle didn't respond.

Luna glanced over her shoulder to see if there was a problem. After the fair, Luna had begun to think of Amahle as a friend. A person she could talk to about things women talk to women about. Like men.

Amahle mumbled under her breath as she pointed one-by-one at individuals.

Luna took several mindful inhales while she waited for Amahle to finish whatever it was she was doing.

Amahle stopped pointing and looked at Luna. "If my calculations are right, we have thirty friendlies. But the resistance has thirty-three. And there are seven Switzerlands."

"How do you know where the uncommitted are sitting?"

Besides offering a financial incentive to sign his petition, Brandy's father had issued another financial incentive to the locals if they showed up and supported Galaxy Dope. As a result, a few Luna and Mitch had thought would be on their side, ones who hadn't signed the petition, were currently undecided.

"They're all gathered in the back of the room in chairs that sat apart from the delineated sides."

"Do you think they're holding out in hopes of a bigger payday? Or are truly undecided?"

"It's anyone's guess. When the boys show up, we'll have thirty-two," Amahle said. "Not that it will matter, if the Commerce has already made up their mind. This whole hearing could be nothing more than a formality."

From this position in the room, Luna could see everyone except the members of the Chamber of Commerce. They sat behind her at a horseshoe-shaped table located in the front of the room. "What do you think is keeping the guys?"

"Chances are there's a rush at Mitch's shop, and he's having trouble closing."

"I wouldn't put it past the mayor to send a bunch of last-minute shoppers to keep our spokesperson from showing up to make our case."

Amahle checked her phone. She sighed. "Still no text messages from Johnny."

Luna tried calling Mitch. She got voicemail. She sent a text. *Call me.*

"It's time to start today's meeting," Mayor Regis thundered. "Jimmy, please lock the door," he said to the town's butcher who stood in the back of the room.

"This isn't good," Amahle whispered as she stepped off her chair.

Jimmy, bless his heart, didn't immediately twist the lock. Instead, he checked his nails as if contemplating their cleanliness.

"Why are you requesting the door to be locked?" Luna stepped off her chair. She didn't trust the mayor any further than she could throw a Bounce dryer sheet in a windstorm. "You know very well Mitch and Johnny aren't here."

"It's a standard procedure." He adjusted his royal blue bowtie. "Once our meetings start, they are closed to latecomers."

Luna glanced at Amahle. "Is that really a thing?"

"Sounds like a bunch of river trash to me." Amahle didn't bother to whisper.

The friendlies laughed.

"I demand respect, or you must leave," the mayor ordered.

Amahle opened her mouth to respond but then shut it. Which spurred Luna into speaking up, because, you know, someone had to keep the stalling going. "I respectfully request, ass..."—about to say asshole, she smartly sucked that hole back in and instead spat out—"toot...astute...leader of our town, that you wait a few minutes to start the meeting."

The mayor's jowls plumped out and pinkened. They reminded Luna of a night-clubber's butt cheeks bound in magenta spandex. The image made her giggle.

"I most certainly will not—"

The squeak of a door opening dithered the mayor's spew.

Luna did a one-eighty spin. *Please let it be Mitch.* Instead of seeing Mitch, she saw spots. The slant of the sun now blinded her view. Ugh. "Who is it?"

No one responded.

Luna shielded her eyes and squinted. *Please let it be Mitch.* The town needed Mitch. Hell, she needed him. He was her honesty in a world of counterfeits.

The hand shield yielded her no better view of who'd come inside. She settled in to wait for the door to close and block out the sun so she could see.

And, of course, the door meandered endlessly on its journey to latch.

Please let it be Mitch.

Without Mitch as the walking, talking poster boy behind their proposal, the members of the Chamber of Commerce probably wouldn't even blink before voting for the opposition.

A gazillion heartbeats later, the figure of the fashionably late guest magically materialized.

Luna's hope kerplunked to her feet. Feet painfully pinched into a pair of black pointed-toe Valentino's. Her power heels, not donned since moving to Colorado. The one and only pair she'd brought with her, mainly because she'd been wearing them on the day of her departure. How had she ever weathered these on a daily basis?

"What is she doing here?" Luna asked no one in particular but at the same time everyone. This couldn't be good.

"Who is she?" Amahle whispered.

Luna couldn't take her gaze off the newcomer. Her high hopes for today's outcome circled the drain. The interloper's appearance had changed. Better dressed. Different hair style. No friendly smile. But there was no mistaking her identity. "The Church Lady."

"Who—"

The sharp sound of the gavel coming down on the podium caused Luna to jump out of her chilling skin. *Calgon take me away. No really...take me.*

Calgon, the fickle bath product, did not take her.

Luna swallowed a lump of dread.

"The meeting is now in session," the mayor proclaimed. "Please, take a seat."

Like a ragdoll, Luna slumped into her chair. Was this Karma's way of righting a wrong from Luna 1.0's past? Had the visitor come to tattletale? Or worse, announce a lawsuit against the town for selling dope brownies to unsuspecting customers?

Fuck. Fuck. Fuck. Fuck. That would be a legit lawsuit. Not one a good lawyer could easily have dismissed.

Or worse. What could be worse? *Mitch could lose his license. Or go to jail.*

"We'll start with our visitor. Ms. Habbernabby. I'm glad we were able to accommodate your request to speak before the town." The mayor glanced at the crowd. "Ms. Habbernabby is one of the fine citizens who lives in our sister town, Peculiar. Let's give her a warm Rocky Mountain Springs welcome."

Luna pressed her knuckles over her mouth. Holy Batman. The Church Lady was here to tell the town she was going to sue them. The Switzerlands would for sure turn against Luna's idea and maybe the others currently on her side.

Hell, this was even worse than Luna's own personal worst moment in life. And that had been humiliating at best...

Ms. Habbernabby, wearing what could only be described as a poker face, walked up to the microphone. She glanced around the room, specifically made eye-contact with Luna, and then smiled.

Luna lowered her hands. Goosebumps evaporated. Only the devil would smile at a person they were about to devour.

Then again, it would be just like the devil to masquerade as a church lady.

"Before I say anything, let me just start with how impressed I am by how many of you have shown up for a town hall meeting. I understand the Chamber of Commerce has a lot of exciting items on tonight's agenda, so this won't take but a delightful moment."

Delightful? Delightful wasn't awful.

Luna's insides went from nervous nausea to hushed anticipation.

"Back to the why of my showing up tonight. A little over a week ago, a rumor surfaced that I was poisoned by bad brownies I purchased from Luna's Goat Yoga. A rumor I became aware of when my pastor dropped by my house to do a wellness check. An act prompted by your mayor who had called him with concerns I'd been unknowingly sold pot brownies," Ms. Habbernabby said. "I am happy to say, that rumor is absolutely false."

"What?" the mayor said. "That's not—"

"When I personally dropped by to thank Regis for sending my pastor to check on me, and to let your fine mayor know his concerns were unfounded, he pressured me to show up here and say otherwise or else—"

"I never—"

She gave the mayor a pursed-lip stare that had him snapping his mouth shut. "I apologize, Regis, for misleading you into thinking I would do your dirty bidding." She paused and clutched the pearls at her neck. "But you see, the Lord laid it upon my heart to be truthful and to trust he'd take care of your threats."

"Did you know anything about that rumor?" Amahle asked Luna.

"Not that one," Luna answered.

The church lady glanced at Luna. "The brownies I bought from Luna's Goat Yoga were wickedly delicious. So delicious, I didn't share any of them."

Luna gave her a wide grin.

With that high praise, Ms. Habbernabby stepped off the stage and click-clacked to the back door, which Jimmy rushed to open.

"Have a good evening, ma'am." He dipped into a perfect bow. One that went deep and weirdly lasted forever. His reason for doing so became apparent when Mitch and Johnny swept inside.

As soon as they cleared the door, Jimmy popped out of his bow.

"Stop right there," the mayor roared into the microphone, causing it to screech like a mother whose child was about to run into the street. "You must leave. Our rules clearly—"

"Regis, let them stay," a man said.

Luna glanced at the man who'd spoken. She'd noticed him earlier. He stood next to Brandy, so she could only assume he was her father. Mr. Princeton. Which would explain why he felt like he could tell the mayor what to do and not to do.

"Are you sure?" Mayor Regis asked.

The guy tugged on his cuffs, showing off shiny gold links. "I'd hate for Mitch not to hear first-hand what I have to say." Smugness ran down his face like Luna's new cheap mascara when she got caught out in the rain.

She shivered. Brandy had a strong proponent in her camp. This guy looked like he could do battle with her own father and come out the victor. For the first time, she worried their proposal might not win.

"Next up on tonight's agenda," the mayor said, his voice not quite on board with his words, "we'll discuss the two dueling business plans that have been proposed for Rocky Mountain Springs. Having had the honor of reading them, I can tell you, they're top-notch and the Chamber of Commerce will have a hard time choosing between them. I can only hope our speakers will give us strong arguments on why their plan is the best plan for Rocky Mountain Springs. We will start with opening remarks by both parties. Starting with Mr. Theodore Princeton. When the proceedings are over, the Chamber of Commerce will conduct a private vote."

Mr. Princeton walked to the microphone. The way he carried himself reminded Luna of the ever so snooty maître d' of La Grenouille. A man who had allegedly once served tea to the Queen of England. *Broadway's Queen of England.*

"It's an honor to speak with the warm, generous citizens of this wonderful town," he said. "My name is Theodore Princeton. But most of you know me simply as Brandy's father."

The mayor straightened his tie and took a seat.

"I've made no secret—with all of you who lowered your resistance long enough to listen—I want to bring Galaxy Dope to your town. As a Fortune 500 businessman, I have no doubt the numbers I've prepared and given you ahead of time are accurate."

"Ugh," Luna whispered to Amahle.

"For those of you whom I've not had a chance to chat with, let me just tell you, what I propose will put profit in everyone's pockets. And because Brandy is fond of all of you, she is the one who will run the franchise." He glanced dotingly at his daughter. "I'm willing to put my money where my mouth is. By that I mean, if at any time over the next three years, your business fails to exceed what you made on average over the past three years, I will personally make up the difference in your bank account. Thank you."

Loud hoots and hollers erupted. Brandy turned and smiled at her crowd of followers and waved like a proper bitch princess.

The mayor walked back to the microphone. "Mitch, you're up."

Luna clapped.

"Enough," the mayor said, staring death holes through her forehead.

Like a robot whose battery had fallen out, Luna's hands stalled mid-clap. She gave the mayor her best WTF look.

He bristled. "If we take time to applaud after each speech, we'll be here all night."

She finished her last clap and primly folded her hands in her lap.

Wearing khakis, a white button-down shirt, and a sweater vest, Mitch made his way to the stage.

Thank God he'd shown. Why had he been late?

As if reading her mind, he said, "Let me begin by apologizing for my tardiness. I had an influx of last-minute customers, and one of them had trouble with their payment method." His hand fluttered to his pant pocket.

Luna cocked her head and stared at his pocket. What was in there? Or was the pocket-pat nothing more than a nervous habit?

"As all of you know," Mitch said, "the proposal on the table is the brainchild of Luna Parker." He gave her a grin that slipped inside her chest and snuggled with her heart.

She slid her gaze to his ears. Red. Both of them. Interesting. Both ears red meant he had sex on the brain. She glanced back at his pocket. Slightly bulging. Could it be possible that it was stuffed full of condoms? Even as he stood there about to fight for an excellent cause, was Mitch also thinking about their date later tonight? The thought made her smile smugly. She bet he had a rule about thinking about sex while addressing the town, and yet there he was...doing just that. He was as mystified by her as she with him.

Mitch cleared his throat. "The proposal also includes the names of several other business owners in town." He slowly glanced around the room. "What we're proposing is for all of us—even those of you who are currently leaning toward Galaxy Dope—to unite, brand ourselves with a unique element that ties us together and become a destination town. Not a tourist trap town, but a town with a heart-tugging story, and a passion, and quality products that can't be found one or two towns over, or even six states over. A proposal that allows us to stay true to our reputation of being a green community."

The mayor made a buzzing noise. "Time."

Mitch glanced back at the mayor. "I didn't realize there was a time limit on our presentations."

"It was in the information I sent you. As it was in the information you either had to be here on time or forfeit your right to participate." The mayor walked to the mic and nudged Mitch aside. "Best you not complain lest I decide to enforce that rule. You do know what rules are, don't you?"

35

Bullshit. Mitch didn't give the mayor the satisfaction of a response. Instead, he strode to his chair. He'd read what the mayor had sent him. All of it. There'd been nothing about time limits. He plopped down next to Luna, who reached over gave his knee a squeeze.

"You did fabulous," she whispered.

Heat filled him. The sweet kind. The kind that turns a man to a blob of sugar incapable of thought. He moved her hand so he could think. There'd be time, later tonight, for touching. Over dinner, he intended to admit just how hard he'd fallen for his friend.

"Theodore, you're up," Regis said.

Mitch observed a look between the mayor and Theodore. A look that reminded him of two members of a street gang about to pounce on an unsuspecting target. What were they up to?

Brandy's supporters broke out in applause.

Luna huffed out a breath next to him. "Why do they get to clap, and we don't?"

If the mayor heard her, he didn't show it. He waited several seconds before holding up his hand to stop their noise.

"Asshole," Luna whispered.

Mitch tried not to smile. After all, he shouldn't encourage her tendency to speak her mind without first thinking of the fallout. Then again, wasn't a variation of that one of the qualities he'd moved to his pro list where she was concerned? *The hell with it.* Thinking was an overrated attribute. Mitch reached over and twined his fingers with Luna. They both squeezed at the same time. Like their hearts were in sync.

"Citizens of Rocky Mountain Springs," Theodore said, "it brings me no pleasure to present to you the next piece of my argument as to why my plan for your town is the only smart one you have at your disposal."

"Here it comes," Luna whispered. "The bullshit fact I told you he'd offer. It's a lawyer tactic."

What bullshit fact did Mr. Princeton possess that caused him to ooze so much certainty?

"While Mitch, other than not showing up for his own wedding on time—or even showing up here to fight for those of you who are on his side on time—is a satisfactory man..." He paused and made eye-contact with Mitch.

Mitch narrowed his eyes. Was this his ace-in-the-hole? Insults disguised as compliments?

"His partner-in-crime however, isn't a fine person."

Luna squeaked.

"I beg your pardon!" Mitch yanked his hand out of Luna's and fisted his fingers. How dare this man slander his girl?

"Your eagerness to defend her is charming." Brandy's father smirked. "Unfortunately, it's going to come back to haunt you. But I'll let the audience be the judge of my claim she's not a fine person." He glanced at the crowd. "Luna Parker is an actual criminal. As in a convicted felon."

Mitch jumped up, but Luna grabbed his arm and prevented him from lunging at Theodore.

"What are you doing?" He glanced at her from over his shoulder. "Didn't you hear him?"

"Sit," she said.

Mitch sat and shifted to fully see Luna. She'd turned ashy white and fat beads of sweat were causing one of the freckles on her nose to run. He peered closer. She had a fake freckle. Were they all bogus?

He pulled at his collar. Freckles were not the issue. False claims were. Theodore's accusation couldn't be true. The mayor had put him up to it as a way of rattling Mitch. "What's he talking about?" he quietly asked.

Luna just sat there.

"Mitch, by the look on your face," Brandy's father said. "Am I correct in assuming you didn't know?"

Mitch kept his gaze on Luna while anger built inside of him. It had been a while since he'd been in a fight, but if ever there was a time to revisit that particular skill from his past, it was now. "He's lying... Tell me he's lying so I can kick his ass," he whispered for her ears only.

Luna shook her head, and her bottom lip trembled.

"He's not lying?" Mitch asked. No, that was wrong. She would have told him if she was a felon. In her daze, she must have misunderstood his question. "Luna, tell everyone Theordore's lying."

More tears fell, taking more freckles with them, but Luna said nothing. What was wrong with her?

"That in itself," Theodore said, now addressing the audience, "tells me, and the fine citizens of Rocky Mountain Springs, you're not suited for being one half of the brains behind such a huge endeavor."

"This is a load of crap." Mitch jumped up. "Whatever Luna did or did not do in her past, does not reflect on who she is today, nor my ability to be a leader. Fuck you for insinuating otherwise." She had to have a logical explanation. She was just shell-shocked and that's why she wasn't defending herself.

To believe anything else was to destroy his heart.

This Amahle grabbed his wrist and tugged him back toward his chair until he gave in and sat.

"I disagree," Brandy's father said. "You see, to be a successful businessman, you must be aware at all times. Trust no one. Suspect everyone. Even women who have designs on your last name."

"When you say 'women who have designs on my last name,' are your referring to your daughter?" Mitch asked. "The woman you sent to seduce me into coming to work for you after I turned down your headhunters?"

"Daddy, who told him?" Brandy wailed. "You said no one—"

"Hush," Theodore said to his daughter. "Your imagination, Mitch, would be humorous if you weren't trashing my daughter with your theories. Tread quite carefully."

"You're the one who needs to tread carefully." Mitch would not back down.

"Luna," Johnny said, "put a stop to this bullshit and tell us what this fucker is yapping about."

"Yes, please do," Amahle said. "It's okay. We're your friends."

Luna came out of her stupor and stood, knocking her chair over in the process. She took a jerky step toward the microphone. And another. And another. Until she stood at the bottom of the stairs that led to the stage.

"Luna, you don't currently have the floor," Theodore said in a patronizing tone, "but if you'd like to come up and explain, I'll be happy to yield the remainder of my time to listening to you tell the outstanding citizens of this town about your felony."

Luna climbed the stairs like they led to a guillotine. Once at the microphone, she turned and looked out at the audience.

"You've got this," Amahle said encouragingly.

Luna opened her mouth, but no words emerged. Instead, another tear dropped off her lashes and splashed onto the microphone causing a hissing noise.

"Oh, for crying out loud, stop with the theatrics." The mayor rushed to the microphone and shouldered her to the side. "What Luna is too much of a coward to admit to is she bribed her way into her college of choice. She comes from one of those elitist families who believes rules do not apply to them."

Mitch's carefully constructed adult world wobbled.

"Which makes her a felon," the mayor continued. "She didn't even bother to deny the charges, which is probably why she didn't have to do time. As soon as she finished her paltry community service, she used the vast amount of income at her disposal and disappeared. Reappeared here, under an assumed name. With a large bank account. Who knows what devious plans she had for all of us? You can bet they weren't pure."

Luna grabbed the microphone from him. "Mitch, I'm so sorry. I was going to tell you. Remember, I told you I had something to tell you tonight."

She had said that. He struggled to ward off the panic attack brewing.

"Having a felony shouldn't matter in our plan for Rocky Mountain Springs," Luna continued.

Felony. The woman I love is a felon. Mitch's vision blurred as a day-terror elbowed in on his panic attack. Growing up, he'd often had night-terrors but only occasionally did he have wide-awake day terrors. His day terrors were why Mom had told everyone his brain didn't work. A demon lived inside his day terrors. Mitch rubbed his hands on his pant legs in an attempt to stay grounded in reality. In the event he couldn't, he needed to get out of here before things got ugly. Before *he* got ugly.

Only he couldn't leave. His community needed him.

Still rubbing his pant legs, he focused on Luna. Her mouth was moving, but he couldn't hear her words. How could he? The thunderous noise of a train barreling down the tracks straight at him made hearing anything else impossible. The rhythmic song of its wailing horn hypnotized him to the spot with its one-word song. *Felon.* Mom was a felon. He cocked his head. Was that Mom he heard?

He put a hand behind his ear and tried harder to listen. Was she telling him to jump? To get off the tracks? No, not jump. Run.

Run or they'll give you to the monsters?

Mitch glanced wildly around for an exit, an escape route. There was none. No hiding spots. He was stuck on a train track. He struggled to get air in his lungs. And the train was so close he could see the engineer.

The fucking mayor was driving the train, and he was hanging out the window pointing at Mitch. Right before the train plowed over Mitch, he heard the mayor say, "Gotcha."

Then the impact of the train sliced open Mitch. Despite the pain, he desperately tried to put his pieces back together before all of Rocky Mountain Springs saw the demon that lived inside of him. Only he couldn't because he couldn't find his fingers. They were gone. Mom was gone. *Run.*

Anger spewed from the demon as it emerged. Mitch fought for reality. Fought for his voice. He had to explain. *Run.* "NO!" His exclamation gave him a moment of reprieve, and everything went quiet. Quiet enough he heard those in the room.

"Mitch, I promise you, my criminal record doesn't matter," Luna shouted. Why was she shouting?

"On the contrary," Theodore was saying, "locally, the reputation of the owners of dispensaries must be above reproach. The mere fact Mitch is friends with you could be probable grounds for him to lose his license to operate in our town and probably all of Colorado. And if you were to, say, *get married*, then there's no way he'd keep his license."

Mitch grappled to find his voice amidst all the panic still churning his insides. "My reputation is just fine. I've done nothing wrong."

"Your naivete is tiresome." Theodore didn't bother to hide the smile on his face. "You'll need to take your defense up with the authorities who govern those who have dispensary licenses. You see, I've turned the situation over to them."

Authorities. An icy sensation rushed through Mitch.

Run. They'll give you to the monsters.

He fought for calming breaths. Calm would free him of the terror. But all he could manage were shallow breaths. Breaths that didn't fill his lungs.

"Please, Mr. Princeton," he heard Luna say, "don't do that to Mitch." Then she clasped her hands in prayer position.

Mitch laughed. Prayers were no defense against the monsters. Had her mother taught her nothing?

"It's too late," Theodore said. "The deed is done."

"But Mitch is right," Luna said. "He shouldn't be punished for my felony."

"I'm pleased you see it that away, Ms. Parker. Or should I say, Ms. Maria Luna Parker Alexander? And as such, I have a proposal for you."

Hearing Luna's name jerked Mitch out of his hell, and he slumped.

Luna, who still stood on the stage, lowered her hands. "I'm listening," she said to Mr. Princeton.

"Sell your land to me and move away. In return, I'll withdraw my complaint against Mitch and, because"—he gave Mitch a sly look—"I'm not a monster, I'll offer him a management position at Galaxy Dope. Of course, Brandy will be his boss."

Monster.

Hearing the word, dragged him right back into the terror. Once again, he fought and clawed, this time succeeding enough to hear Luna. Something about her voice kept him grounded.

"Why are you doing this to us?" Luna asked. "He doesn't even love your daughter."

"It's okay, Luna," Mitch croaked.

Theodore turned his attention to Mitch. "Mitch, you're not looking well. Is everything okay?"

"Fuck...off," he rasped.

"I see they're not. Are you having a terror? Does the town know about your brain that doesn't quite work?"

"Leave him alone," Luna said, then she was there in front of Mitch. Down on her knees holding his hands in hers.

Mitch tried to reply but his voice wasn't there.

"Brandy shared with me your stories about terrors," Theodore continued. "How certain words would trigger you when you were a child. I do hope I haven't triggered one tonight. I'd hate for you to remember what it was like to be homeless and jobless. To be at the mercy of others for food."

Mitch moaned and jerked. He told Brandy his secrets because that's what you do when you're in love, and she'd told her father how to use them against him.

"He will never be homeless again," Luna yelled. "He can live with me and work with me. Stop trying to scare him."

"Go to hell," Mitch shouted at Theodore. He jerked his hands out of Luna's. "I can't love another felon." He jumped up, spun around, and spotted an exit. While his brain allowed him, he made a mad dash for solitude.

36

Luna watched Mitch leave. Was it that easy? Could you just decide who to love and not love?

Not that she blamed him for not wanting to love her. It had been her secret that had sent him into a panic attack from hell. A panic attack viewed by all his friends. He'd hate that and never forgive her.

She stood and squared off with Theodore. "You're an evil man."

"Just ruthless."

She snarled. "Who even gave you this information?"

"You poor ignorant child," Theodore said. "Have you not figured it out by now? It was your father."

She'd known that. It made sense. But hearing it still hurt.

"And your friends. Did they tell you we met?" Brandy said. "They're really not very good at keeping secrets."

The mayor cleared his throat. "As entertaining as this little scene tonight has been, Luna, it's time for your decision. Will you sell your land to Theodore to protect Mitch from losing his license?"

"No." Luna swirled and looked out at the crowd. No one would make eye contact. "Those of you who want our business proposal to win, you can still push for it. I will sell my house to Mitch, and I'll leave Rocky Mountain Springs altogether so Mitch is not guilty of cavorting with a criminal, and when the investigation into Mitch's reputation happens, there will be nothing there for them to rule against him."

As if suddenly given permission to breathe, the room erupted into a gazillion conversations.

"Are you sure you want to do that?" Amahle asked. "I don't think it will fix things with him."

"I know," she replied. "But with me gone, the town can still rebrand as a united community with all the businesses having a common theme and a story to tell about being the underdog who won against the giants of industry. And why wouldn't you do that?"

"Yeah, why wouldn't we do that?" Tina asked.

Several more voiced their agreement.

"Nothing personal, Luna," Tina said. "It's just business. I think you're grand and don't give two cents about your past mistakes."

"I'm glad you're all in agreement," Luna said, even though having them choose Mitch over her hurt. Even though common sense said that's what they should do. "Truly, I am. Because the alternative is to go into business with someone like Theodore. And I don't care what he says about wanting to help you all get rich—this guy only wants revenge for his daughter for an action that was her own damn fault. And if it means taking down an entire town in the process, he's not going to lose any sleep over the fallout."

"My fault?" Brandy shouted. "He showed up late to our wedding because he couldn't be bothered with setting aside a comic book."

Luna rolled her eyes. "That's not why he showed up late, and you damn well know it. He simply kept quiet because it was the gentlemanly thing to do to take the blame for a runaway bride."

Brandy stomped her foot. "Daddy, turn him into the authorities. Let them strip him of all his hopes. Don't give him an out. I don't want him working with me at Galaxy Dope."

"Pumpkin—"

Luna gave her full attention to the residents. "I'm sorry."

The mayor slammed his gavel on the podium.

"The Chamber of Commerce and I will now convene to my office to take a vote on the two proposals—"

"Not so fast," Mr. Princeton said.

Luna watched Brandy and her father whisper. Whatever it was they were talking about, their body language painted a clear picture of disagreement.

"Well?" Regis tugged at his bow tie, which sat on his neck at an awkward angle.

Mr. Princeton stood. "Considering tonight's rather satisfying turn of events, I'm withdrawing my offer to bring a Galaxy Dope to Rocky Mountain Springs. Brandy and I will submit the proposal to Peculiar tomorrow morning. There are too many painful memories here for her to be happy."

"But I thought we had a... You simply can't withdraw your proposal. We'll sue. We've put a lot of time into—"

Brandy grabbed her father's arm. "Daddy, let's get out of here. This place is giving me hives."

She and her father walked stiffly out of the room.

As soon as they were gone, the mayor stepped up to the microphone. "I hope you're all happy."

"I, for one, am very happy," Amahle said. "Now the Chamber of Commerce has nothing to vote on. There's only one offer still on the table. We're going to bring Luna's vision to our town."

"I say we table the vote for a week," Johnny said. He glanced at Luna. "Give Luna here some time to consider her options. While she did screw up by not telling Mitch her shit, she's also had some pretty big turds dropped on her tonight. Her father ratted her out to the enemy, and the guy she's in love with can't love her back if he wants to stay in the cannabis business."

"I second that motion," someone in the back said.

"What are you waiting for?" Amahle said. "Go find him. See where you stand."

"Wait just one cotton-pickin'-minute," Mr. Henson said from the back of the room. He slowly made his way to wear Luna stood and pointed at her. "You can't go around rushing an apology. Take it from an old fool who knows. You've got to take your time, come up with a plan, and get it right. Trust me, you say the wrong thing, and it won't matter that you're sorry, it will all go to hell, and he won't pick you—he'll pick Rocky Mountain High."

"But isn't that what's best for him?" Luna asked.

37

Luna stood on the sidewalk and read a text just sent from her father. *I'm sending the plane to pick you up.*

She screamed inside of her heart and then fired off a reply. *How could you do this to your own daughter?*

Her phone vibrated. She glanced at it. Two messages.

One from Amahle. *I'm still your friend. Text me if you want company.*

The other, a reply from her father. *A day will come when you have a child of your own, and then you'll understand. Besides, you can do much better than a cannabis store clerk who suffers from mental illness.*

He hadn't even said he was sorry.

It was time to plan revenge. Against her parents. Keeping their secret when it had only affected her pride was one thing. But keeping it when it affected her heart? That was a line they shouldn't have crossed.

She stopped walking and angrily read the next incoming text.

If you come home, I won't make you come to work for me. I'll help you open a yoga studio in Tribeca. And because I'm not a monster, I'll foot the bill to make sure Mitch doesn't lose his license as a result of being associated with you.

Unbelievable. She texted back. *I'm not coming home.*

Twenty minutes later, she sat in the barn loft with a fully loaded brownie, a bottle of wine, and her planner. After sending Mitch a text telling him she wanted to sell him her home—she had left her phone on her kitchen table with three unread messages. Dad could send her as many get-on-the-damn-plane texts as he wanted. It didn't mean she'd do it.

The wine and brownie were sitting on Ms. Murphy's planning table. Untouched.

Indulging in mind-numbing substances would have to wait until after she had a plan for revenge.

Her gaze fell on Ms. Murphy's dusty journal. Luna picked it up and thumbed through the pages. Now was as good a time as any to check for a list of numbers which would lead to the combination of the padlock. Before getting the hell out of this town, she wanted to know what was inside the damn thing.

Finding no numbers, she went back to page one, snuggled up in the chair with the view of the mountain, and prepared to read a journal written by a woman she'd never met.

Today I fell in love.

Luna glanced out at the mountain. When exactly had she fallen in love with Mitch? Could she narrow it down to the day? An hour? A moment?

Had the auction been the beginning of her heart's demise? One look at his vintage tee and it had signed its death warrant? Maybe. Stranger things had been known to happen.

She'd been so looking forward to masterminding a community that spread joy and success. Why had she handed it over so easily? Because she'd given her heart to a damn guy? Not just any damn guy. A damn guy who didn't want to love another felon. Luna was the stuff of his worst nightmare.

She turned the page in Ms. Murphy's diary.

I fell in love with a swindler.

The guy's no good.

Pompous as piss.

Nevertheless, I gave him my heart. Probably because he also hails from New Orleans. So he gets me and my mystical ways.

Luna paused. Interesting. What were the odds Nanny Nonna and Ms. Murphy were both from New Orleans? Was that why they'd teamed up in death? They'd bonded over their magical recipes? Ms. Murphy being from New Orleans helped explain the frozen flowers from Mildred. Luna went back to reading.

Fortunately, he has no idea I love him.

I may be a drunk, but I'm not stupid.

Well, hell. Luna should have read this sooner. She'd given her heart to Mitch and all of Rocky Mountain Springs knew it. Which, according to Ms. Murphy, made her stupid.

Then again, Mitch wasn't a swindler. He was quite decent. And he'd given her his heart as well, if only temporarily.

Sure, he had a boring rule-following side, but his sweet-ass side showed up ninety-nine percent of the time.

Pompous? Maybe. Mitch did believe he was always right.

Damn it. Why was she sitting here trying to make him out to be the bad guy? She'd kept a truth, a truth that, when announced, sent him into a spiral he couldn't escape. When he recovered, fully recovered, he'd double hate her. One for the lie. Two for the humiliation. And she couldn't blame him.

She wandered over to the safe, ate the brownie, swigged some wine, and tried a series of random combinations. Her birthday. Mitch's birthday. Ms. Houdini's birthday. Her broken heart day.

Halfway through, an idea fuzzily tickled her brain.

She picked up the journal and glanced at the date Ms. Murphy had fallen in love.

Carefully, Luna entered those numbers in as the combination. She held her breath and tugged on the lock. Nothing.

She did them backward.

Nada.

Damn.

She sat down in front of the safe and stared at the door. Maybe if she did it hard enough, she'd develop X-ray vision and see inside the thing.

Five minutes later, she gave up, took a swig of the wine and tried to lean against one of the table legs, but she missed and fell flat on her back. Laying there, looking up at the underside of the table, she saw an envelope taped in place. She reached for it, tugged it free, scooted out from under the table, opened the envelope, and pulled out a sheet of paper. It was titled: The Power of Numbers 3, 7 & 9. The article was on why the numbers three, seven, and nine were so powerful according to folklore.

Luna glanced at the lock. Could it be? She grabbed it and twisted the tumbler to the right to the number three, then going left, she went past the number seven and stopped on it the second time around, and then back to the right to the number nine. Holding her breath, she yanked, and the lock opened.

38

Mitch escaped the meeting via the back exit and made it to his back porch where he collapsed. With the cool night air on him, emotions rolled through him like the smoke of a thousand joints being inhaled at one time. Only when he exhaled, he wasn't left with the normal don't-give-a-shit-because-you're-high calm.

Instead, a mixture of negative feelings swirled inside him. Leading the emotion pack was fear.

Fear he'd never be able to fix things with Luna.

Fear he'd lost his friends.

Fear the mayor would evict him and he'd lose his license and he'd have to start from scratch rebuilding his life. A life he'd worked hard to make normal.

His phone rang. It was Amahle. Was she calling to end their friendship? "Hello."

"Are you okay?" she asked. "Do you want us to come over?"

It took him a moment to comprehend the message behind her words. "We're still friends?" Was that possible?

"Fuckhead, of course, we're friends," he heard Johnny say. "Don't make me come over there and kick your ass."

Mitch pinched the bridge of his nose in an attempt to minimize the magnitude of gratitude sweeping through him. One of his fears had been unfounded.

"Have you spoken to Luna?" Amahle asked.

Was that a trick question? "Why would have done that? There's nothing to say."

"How about you tell her what you're feeling?" Amahle snapped.

Mitch grimaced. "My feelings are irrelevant. No woman wants a broken man." Luna had witnessed him at his worst. If she hadn't already, she would soon realize he was nothing but a junkyard boyfriend. A guy made from the broken and battered parts one finds in the garbage lot of life. "Things can't be fixed between us."

"Of course you can fix things," Amahle said in a no nonsense tone. "But it's going to take a conversation."

"There is no *of course* when it comes to me and women," Mitch said. "You better than most know I suck at communicating with them. Especially one who is a felon." A fucking felony! That part made him mad. Had he known ahead of time, he could have been mentally prepared. His public melt down could have been avoided.

"Damn it, Mitch. Dig deep and figure this shit out." Amahle heaved a heavy sigh as if he was trampling her last nerve. "You can't let the mayor and Brandy destroy what you have with Luna. That being said, after all the things I—and the rest of the town—heard you say to her, she will be well within her rights if she throws a firebomb or two at you before she settles down and allows you to speak."

His grip tightened on the phone. Fuck. "What all did I say?"

"You don't remember?"

"I wouldn't have asked if I did."

Amahle was slow to respond. "Let's just say you spewed stupid shit about choosing your career over her. And there was an emphatic *fuck you* thrown in for good measure."

He tried to remember the conversation for himself but couldn't. "Choosing my career over her isn't that stupid. There are rules. I could lose everything if I reconcile with her." Hell, not all his fears could be debunked. His career and Luna were an either or situation. He could have one but not both.

"If it comes down to your license or Luna, which one will keep you warm at night?"

"Damnit, Amahle. Stop giving me heartburn. Maybe I should just let sleeping dogs lie. If I stay away from her, my reputation isn't brought into question, and I can keep my license. And you and the whole town now know she deserves a hell of a better man that I can ever be."

"Fuck that last piece, and what I know is Princeton is quite capable of bribing those in power to find a reason to rescind your license. One that has nothing to do with Luna.

She was right about Theodore. It could happen. The rich could do things the poor couldn't. But even so… "I'm a little mad she didn't tell me."

"I don't blame you. In fact, considering how her secret turned you inside out, it's okay if you're a lot mad. But Luna is still Luna," Amahle said softly. "The fact she chose not to share her most painful moment with any of us doesn't change who she is at the core."

Now that he could think straight, he knew that. "You're right, she is. But I stand by my belief she deserves better."

"Mitch, go and talk to Luna. None of this is her doing. She met a guy. She liked a guy. She thought the guy liked her back. She tried to help the guy and his whole fucking town."

Luna had tried to help all of them. "What would I say?" He dropped down on the porch step.

"Think about all of this from Luna's viewpoint. If you do that, you'll know the answer."

Before Mitch could respond, she'd disconnected. He lit up a joint and tried to think like a man who deserved Luna Parker.

He needed to come up with an epic way to apologize. He patted his pant pocket and remembered what was there. The seed of an idea formed.

39

At seven o'clock, Monday evening—mere hours after yet another monumental moment in her life—Luna's suitcases sat messily packed next to her couch. She was leaving Rocky Mountain Springs.

Mr. Henson, bless his heart, had made the decision easier when he'd dropped by to check on her. He'd graciously agreed to take the goats to his farm for a sleepover. One that would last until Luna sent for them.

The only problem was, she had no idea where to go.

She certainly didn't want to stay in Rocky Mountain Springs and be a rusty kink in Mitch's ability to run a dispensary.

Why hadn't it crossed her mind that her being a felon could seriously place his livelihood at risk? Then again, why would it have entered her brain? It wasn't like her felony was the result of some horrible crime. She hadn't been found guilty of murder or drug trafficking or wearing summer-white past Labor Day weekend. Surely the licensing board would take that into account if it went that far. Especially if she was no longer in the picture.

Then again, the only thing certain in life was that it was uncertain. Oh…and that some people in authority could be bought. There were bad apples at all socio-economic levels in every career.

She kicked her largest suitcase. There was one thing she was certain about. If the licensing board decided to revoke his license, she would have no choice but to out her parents for the felons they were. She'd take them to court and prove it was them, not her, who had bribed the college admissions guru to admit her into their esteemed university. She hadn't even wanted to attend school there.

It was one thing for Mother and Father to ruin her life, but when their actions hurt the man she loved, she wouldn't sit by and do nothing. Of course, they'd have to admit on the record they'd done it because she had zero admissible proof. This detail they'd made a point of drilling into her brain the day they had had her bailed out of county jail. But that detail wouldn't stop her from trying. Not now.

Even if it meant being back in the limelight of journalists who loved any opportunity to write a story about the children of rich socialites getting caught being bad. And then there were the haters. Those social media gurus who entertained their followers with lists of people they should haze with insults. Those holier-than-thou influencers who took every opportunity to trash the poor little rich girl for bribing her way into college instead of earning the opportunity.

Luna might not have fought for her own right to getting the truth told, because pissing off her parents had seemed more important at the time, but she would fight for Mitch. She'd done a lot of growing up over the past several months.

Boom.

The thunderous knock on her door rattled her out of her thoughts. She glanced at the clock. 7:15 p.m. Could it be Mitch? Had he come to talk?

Hope blossomed. Stupid hope because of course he wouldn't forgive her. But hope, nonetheless. She ran her hands over her hair smoothing any strands that might be sticking out, took a deep breath, and hurried to the front door.

Boom.

She jumped again and hope disappeared. Whoever it was, their knock didn't say, "I'm in love, and have come to grovel for breaking your heart." Sure, she understood his response had come from trauma, but that didn't stop the pain.

She swung open the door.

Holy Batman. Not Mitch. How in the hell had they gotten here so quickly? Had they been on their way before any of this had gone down?

"Mother. Father."

"May we come in?" Mother said, not sounding like her normal ice-queen self.

Luna stepped back and motioned them inside. "If you're here to pressure me to come home, that's not happening. If it's to make sure I don't out you as horrible parents, that option is still very much on the table." Damn it. She wished she had her phone on her, she could record them admitting to what they'd done. She walked into the living room. They followed.

"Maria, your father has something to say."

Luna glanced around. Where in the hell was her phone? "I'm listening."

Her father didn't speak, so she put her attention back on him.

"Fred, we didn't come all this way for you just to stubbornly stand there."

Father puffed out his chest. "Maria—"

"It's Luna." Luna corrected.

"I'm not good at being defied. So of course I had to join forces with Theodore Princeton and reveal your past to him."

What the ever loving… "There is no *of course*. I'm your daughter. A daughter you've already damaged."

He bristled. "Do not use that—"

Mother punched him in the arm. "Fred—"

Luna watched as her parents had a staring contest. Father blinked first.

He turned his attention back to Luna. "What I did, while callous, was for your own good."

"How in the hell did you come up with that conclusion?"

"Theodore said the man you were interested in is known to be a player and a user and suffers from mental illnesses."

Luna opened her mouth to tell Father exactly what he could do with his opinion when she spotted her phone. She casually retrieved it and opened the record function. "Did you check Theodore's facts or just blindly believe?"

"He said he knew for certain this man was only with you because he believed you had money. Funds he needed to buy his house and business."

"And you believed that to be true because you don't believe any man can simply love me for me?"

"Not a poor man," Father said in a tone suggesting she'd lost her mind for even asking.

"What?" She couldn't even process that statement. "Why can't a poor man fall in love with a rich woman for no other reason than he loves her personality?"

He took a seat on her couch. Mother sat primly beside him.

Luna dropped down across from them.

"We've accepted the fact you're not going to make money in your ridiculous choice of careers," Father said.

Luna's nostrils flared, and her blood pressure went up.

"Fred," Mother admonished.

"It's our job to make sure you find a husband that can keep you in the standards to which we made you accustomed," Father said. "No matter what ludicrous career path you careen down. That's why we need you to come home, so we can introduce you to men who would be worthy of your hand."

"You believe it's your job to find me a husband?" The rest of what she wanted to say had to be put on hold. To say anything else might unleash the dam holding back her messy emotions. The ones Father abhorred.

Father nodded solemnly. "You've proven not to be able to see beyond your emotional tantrums. We would be negligent parents if we didn't take matters in our own hands."

Despite her best efforts, the dam broke. "Really? Really!" she yelled. "You've possibly destroyed a man's livelihood because you didn't think I could take care of myself? Of all the stupid—"

"Not think. Know. At the rate you're going, you'll be on a budget the rest of your life. That is not acceptable for a child of ours."

"Did you ever stop to think that maybe I'm okay with budgets? That maybe I took a look at my life and decided I wanted something different than what you gave me? That I wanted to raise my own children differently?"

In unison, Father and Mother shuddered.

"And did you ever stop to think that your decisions reflect badly upon us?" Father asked.

She raised her hands and made a motion of wanting to strangle something. Strangle them. "You did not just say that!"

He raised an eyebrow. "Don't be so emotive. We gave you everything."

"You gave me four nannies and a felony record."

"I'll have you know, young lady—"

"Fred."

Father huffed out a breath. "Don't blame your felony on us. It's your fault you didn't take advantage of the plan we had built in to get the charges dismissed should they ever arise."

"I am a felon because of you," she persisted, wanting to get their agreement on the record.

"On the contrary. You're a felon because of you. Had you simply followed our instructions instead of behaving irrationally, your charges would have been dropped. We clearly told you of the loophole in the law."

Luna glanced at Mother to see if she agreed. She had her hand to her mouth as if determined not to say a word. "News flash, Father. I didn't commit the felony. You and Mother did."

Mother made a noise.

Luna glanced at her. "Did you want to say something?" Neither of them had admitted to it yet.

"I had nothing to do with any of this," she blurted. "It was all your father's idea."

"An idea you knew about and condoned," Luna pushed.

"Fred."

Father laid a hand on Mother's leg. "Your mother is not always privy to the decisions I make."

Luna jerked. "You really didn't know?" She stared intently at Mother. "Why didn't you tell me? Why did you let me be mad at you all this time?"

Mother gave her a puzzled smile. "Maria, when you're in love, you support one another in public and in front of your children. Even when the other is wrong."

Was that true? Was that the true measure of someone's love for you?

"Maria," Father said, "you need to listen carefully to what I have to say."

"I'm all ears." Sarcasm dripped from her pores.

"If I come forth and admit I bribed the committee," Father said, "no judge will believe me. Especially now."

"Please, do elaborate."

"Brandy's father will accuse me of taking the fall for my daughter so she can be with the man of her heart. He'll say it's something any loving father would do for their child."

"Why would he care?"

"Mitch hurt his daughter and embarrassed the family name. Theodore will not stop going after Mitch until he's stripped him of everything. He doesn't care if innocent bystanders are hurt in the process. Trust me on this."

"Trust you? Trust works both ways, yet you didn't trust me enough to tell me you bribed my way into college. Or even that the authorities were coming to arrest me."

"I meant to tell you about the bribe. I didn't know of the arrest prior to it happening."

"What stopped you from telling me about the bribe?"

"I guess it just never came up."

"You should have made it come up." Just as she should have made her felony come up with Mitch. Sure, she'd tried, but not hard enough. Hard enough would have resulted in succeeding. "Why are you here?" she asked her parents.

Father crossed his arms. "We've been over this. You need to come back home so we can introduce you to some other viable marital options now that Darren has backed out of our deal."

Mother hit him with the back of her hand. "Fred! That is not why we're here."

"We're also here to apologize," Father said.

Luna laughed. It was a little late for an apology. "I'm listening."

"I'm remorseful," Father said. "I need for you to forgive me. I know what I did wasn't justified. I forget that I can't go after you the way I go after those I'm up against in the court of law."

She swallowed. "Do you mean that? Or is this an act?"

"I can count on one hand the number of times I've apologized in my life. If I say I'm sorry, you can be certain it's not an act."

Damn it. She believed him. But that didn't mean she was ready to forgive. He'd hurt her. Cost her everything. "You didn't just hurt me. You also hurt the man I love. I can't forgive that."

"Are you certain you're in love with him?"

"Head over heels." She should go to him, apologize for triggering his intense panic attack, and trust everything would work itself out.

Another noise came from Mother, who once again had her hand over her mouth.

"Did you want to add something?" Father asked her.

Mother slapped his arm again. "I'm happy for you. I truly am. I am so sorry we've been bad parents. You deserved so much more love than we ever got around to giving you. If this Mitch guy makes you happy, then I am happy for you. Fred, tell her what you're going to do."

"Not that I approve, but if you insist Mitch is your only path to happiness, I can, of course, fix the trouble I've caused Mitch. I always have a plan."

Hope was back. "How?"

Three hours later, after Luna had heard her parents' plan, they left. Without her. As soon as their rental car was out of sight, she slipped on the new dress she'd purchased for tonight's cancelled date, grabbed a bread tie out of the junk drawer, and headed to Mitch's. She was on a mission, and nothing would get in her way.

She found him sitting on his deck, Ms. Houdini snuggled up next to him chewing on something leafy and green. "Are you sober?" She couldn't say what she wanted to say if he was drunk or stoned.

"What are you doing here?" he groused. "The rules say—"

"Fuck the rules." She looked into his eyes. They were clear. "Do you love me?" What if he said no?

"You can't just fuck the rules, and why does it matter if I love you? I don't—"

"It just does." She took a seat in a chair across from him.

"Of course, I love you. Despite the bad luck and chaos you bring to my life, I'm at my happiest when I'm around you. But that doesn't change anything. You deserve a man who has his shit together and can provide for you."

The tightness around her chest eased. "Luckily, your heart is all I need. With it, I'm the richest girl in the world. Without it, I'm impoverished."

He rubbed a hand down his jaw. "You saw me. I'm broken. I'm a junkyard..."

Luna went down on one knee, took the bread tie, which she'd fashioned into a ring, out of her pocket, and held it out to him. "Mitch Johnson, I know I hurt you, and I'm so sorry. I was an idiot. There's no excuse great enough for why I didn't insist you learn of my secret. And sure, there are some things we need to talk through, some things you need to work through, but they can wait. I came here tonight to ask: Will you marry me?"

He grabbed her hands and tried to yank her up, but she stayed on one knee. "What are you doing? You can't ask me to marry you. You're fucking right, I have things I need to work through. Until I do, I have nothing to offer. And I won't marry under those circumstances."

"Your heart is all I'm asking you to offer me."

He groaned. "Luna, of course, you have my heart. That's not what this is about."

"Then what is it about?"

"For one thing, it's not okay for you to go around asking a man to marry you."

She blinked and twisted her hands out of his grasp. "Why the hell not?"

"Because it's against the rules. When a marriage proposal is in order, the man asks the woman."

She rolled her eyes. "I don't like rules. Especially your sexist rules. Let's make new ones."

He stood and paced. "Rules are important. They create calm in storms. I need for you to respect rules."

She stood and paced next to him. "Rules keep you from challenging the status quo. Rules keep you from embracing the storm. Some storms are worth riding out." She stepped in front of him so he couldn't pace and went back down on one knee. "Will you marry me?" She wanted to add more to what she told him, but she needed for him to say yes without knowing there was a solution to his license issue.

She needed him to love a felon one more time.

Mitch's heartbeat raced so fast he could hardly think. Of course, Bad Luck Luna would break the rules of a marriage proposal. He didn't have to look in a mirror to know his ears were red.

"Well?" she said, back down on one knee holding a ridiculous bread-tie ring as if it were a square-cut one-carat diamond. Her damn goat was kneeling beside her, one of his plants hanging from her lips.

He ignored the goat and stared into the eyes of the woman who made all the mixed-up parts of his personality feel good enough. Not just good enough, but perfect. Like all the ball-twisting life events of his life had happened for a reason. For a perfect reason. They had happened to create a man Luna Parker could fall in love with.

How lucky was he to have turned out to be the man of her dreams?

He glanced away. How unlucky was he to have to say no...for now. The man of Luna Parker's dreams had to stay true to the guy she'd fallen in love with. Otherwise, he wasn't the guy she loved. And a big part of that guy was that he followed rules. One of the rules of marriage is that you don't ask, or in this case say yes, if you can't support your spouse.

"I can see that you're struggling," she said, drawing his gaze back to hers. "But all it takes is a simple yes."

He shook his head. "Luna, we live in a world that has rules." The words were a paraphrase of a famous line spoken by Jack Nicholson's character, Colonel Jessup, in *A Few Good Men*. "And those rules have to be followed by men with backbones." He continued to give his own twist to the famous monologue. "You scoff at those rules and mock what they stand for. You have that indulgence. You have the luxury of never experiencing what I know." Poverty was what he knew. He had no desire to introduce her to that.

She shifted to her other knee. "For the love of sex, I'm dying here, get to the answer already and stop quoting some old movie star."

He ignored her interruption. "Rules, while stodgy, save relationships. And my championing of them, while nerdy and inconvenient for you, makes us a stronger couple. Right now, you don't want my rules because they deny you a chance to play in a thunderstorm. But rules are the backbone on which a man hangs his love. Rules keep you from being hit by lightning."

Luna rolled her eyes. Something he realized she did often to him. But not out of ridicule. Out of friendship that allows you to tease with one another. Like Johnny calling him a fuckhead.

"So, is that a maybe?" she asked him.

40

Mitch groaned. This woman tested his will. And obliterated his common sense. And, in typical Luna 2.0 fashion, had just made it abundantly clear—as if it hadn't been clear enough earlier—how lucky he was to have her in his life. She was here, not because she was wrong—because she wasn't—but because she loved him enough to forgive him for being a dick.

God, he didn't deserve her. And more importantly, he hadn't been wrong when he told Amahle that Luna deserved someone so much better than him.

"Luna, I fucked up. Not you. It's I who should do all the groveling. You should have stayed home and stipulated

I come to you. You should have demanded diamonds, and chocolate, and foot massages. And when I delivered all those things, you should have laughed and told me to go away and come back the next day and try again. And thrown a couple firebombs at me."

She rolled her eyes. "Whatever."

"I'm serious. You deserve so much better than me." He groaned. "I was cold and hateful. You should be livid toward me, not forgiving. God, I don't deserve easy forgiveness. Hell, I don't deserve forgiveness at all."

She wrinkled her nose, and he counted five and a half freckles.

"I'm not going to lie," she said. "You hurt my heart. And for a little while I hated you. And, truthfully, I know there will be moments in the future when I think about tonight, and you're going to have to hold me and make it all better again. But part of loving someone is sometimes fixing something you didn't break. This time I'm the glue that puts us back together. The next time—and we both know there will be next times—you can be the one who glues us back together. Deal?"

Was this how love really worked? How healthy relationships worked? "My darling, I am in awe of you." He was the luckiest man in the universe.

She giggled. "Well, of course you are. I'm pretty awesome."

He took a plastic egg out of his pocket and went down on one knee.

After running an errand this afternoon, he'd stopped for gas. Inside the gas station had been one of those toy machines, where you put in a quarter, turned the knob, and got a cheap toy. The sight had reminded him of begging Mom for a quarter, and she'd told him they were too poor for such nonsense.

Today, he'd spent a quarter to get a trinket. Inside the egg had been a plastic ring with a fake blue square gem. Instead of tossing it, he'd stuck it in his pocket to remind himself that he deserved love.

"Luna Parker, I walked into town hall this afternoon loving you. Then the meeting happened, and you saw what a broken man I am. What I went through as a kid complicates and destroys things in my life. Things that are important. And it never does it neatly or quietly. It does it loudly and messily and amidst much pandemonium. You deserve a man so much better than my dumb ass. I'm so sorry I bankrupted your heart for even a second, let alone for hours. Knowing all of that, witnessing all of that, if you'll have me, I want to spend the rest of my life making it up to you. What I'm trying to say, in the most awkward way ever is—Luna Parker, will you marry me?"

She scowled. "I asked first."

"Rules," he said sternly. This woman would probably be the death of him, but at least he'd die a happy man.

"How about we count to three and say yes at the same time? Will that satisfy your silly rules of engagement?"

His heart thumped hard against his chest, trying to escape and comingle with hers. "I can live with that compromise."

She grinned. "Those are words I never thought I'd hear you say."

"One." Mitch started the count down.

"Two."

"Yes," Mitch answered.

Luna blinked. "Wait. What?"

He shrugged. "Some rules beg to be broken." He held out his ring finger.

She slid her homemade ring onto his finger. "I love you, Mitch Johnson. Will you marry me?"

He nodded. "So, this is what happiness feels like." A sense of wonder filled his heart. He opened the container that held her ring and pulled it out. "Thank you for being all the things I didn't think I needed but did. Will *you* marry *me*?"

Her eyes popped wide as she stared at the gaudy bauble of a ring. "Oh. My. You shouldn't have."

He chuckled. "Go big or go home. Right?" He wasn't sure how the future would work. He'd obviously have to change careers. They'd probably have to move. The thought didn't terrify him. Well, it did, but he was willing to work through it.

"Absolutely, but first, before you put that most-perfect ring on my finger, you should know, your license is safe. No one is going to take it from you because of my arrest record."

He stilled. "Maybe. Maybe not."

"And they can't take it from you just because we get married."

"Explain."

"My father looked into it. Being the legal savant that he is, he has found a loophole."

"There's a loophole that allows me to be married to a felon and still run a dispensary? I'm afraid I'm going to have to call bullshit."

She shrugged. "That's what I've been told." She held out her hand and wiggled her ring finger.

"If I say no to utilizing a loophole to get around a rule that others have to follow, are you going to change your mind about wanting to marry me?"

She wiggled her finger again. "I fell in love with you because you are a calm in my storm. Together, we'll find our way forward."

He slid the ring on her finger. "I love you so fucking much."

She squealed and wrapped her arms around his neck. "I love you more."

Ms. Houdini bleated and licked at Mitch's pant pockets.

41

Two hours later, coming down from the afterglow of makeup sex, Mitch and Luna lay on their backs in a double sleeping bag in her backyard, looking up at the stars while a fire crackled in the fire pit. "This is nice." He probably should have said something much more romantic, but his brain was currently mush.

"I told you sex in a sleeping bag would work." Luna stretched languidly and rubbed the left side of her slick body against his right side in a manner that relit all his passions.

"I'll never doubt you again," he managed to say. Their feet tangled and they played footsie.

Several seconds later, her foot stilled. "We should probably talk now."

As much as he wanted to say no, to just enjoy this night that had gotten off to such a rocky start and ended here with this woman beside him, he knew she was right. "What's on your mind?"

She laced her fingers in his. "You should know, my parents are the ones who committed the crime. I had no idea they had bribed my way into the university. I thought me and my A- average got in because my essay and interview swayed the committee. Egotistical me."

He shifted, leaned up on an elbow, and gave her his full attention. "If that is the case, why in the hell were you the one convicted?"

"The bribe money came out of my personal bank account."

He laid back down and stared back up at the sky. Fuck. At eighteen, he hadn't had a penny to his name, let alone enough money in a bank to bribe his way into a college. "You didn't notice the withdrawal?"

She rolled over and curled into his side. Her palm splayed over his stomach, causing his muscles to tense. "Some of the money that was in that account, my parents had given to me specifically for my education after high school. When I noticed the funds gone, I just assumed my parents had accessed it to pay my tuition."

"How could they withdraw money from your account?"

"They had my passwords and were signers on my account." She propped herself up on an elbow. "They'd set the account up when I was born. Anyway, when I got arrested, and they didn't immediately say they did it, I was hurt and angry."

He could tell by her voice she was trying to simply speak the facts and not give away how much saying the words hurt. "That's understandable."

"Instead of owning up to what they did, they wanted me to take one for the good of the family and allow a slick attorney to get the charges dropped via a loophole. In all my rash wisdom, I thought if I lashed out at them by telling the judge I was guilty of the crime, it would be a way of getting even. I thought the idea of their little girl possibly doing time, would devastate them. And I guess a part of me thought if I pled guilty, they would then certainly step inside the judge's chambers and take responsibility for their actions. Prove their love for me. They didn't."

Her impassioned speech tugged at all his protect-the-damsel-in-distress buttons. He leaned up on his elbow. Shadows danced over her, making it hard to read her eyes. "Your parents are not my favorite people." That was the kindest way he could put what he wanted to say.

She snorted and ran a hand down the side of his face. "Mine either." Laying back, she continued, "Believe it or not, I've slowly come to realize they meant well."

He dropped a kiss on her forehead.

"I tell you this because I do have my father on record admitting to the crime. I can turn it over and take legal action to have my felony dismissed."

"And your father would then be charged and possibly face prison time?" It's what her father deserved. But he knew from experience it was hard to turn a bad parent in to the authorities. How many times had he lied for Mom to keep her out of jail because he'd believed the story about the monster who raised children who were taken from their parents?

Luna exhaled softly. "Yes. That's what it would mean."

He laid back. "If that's what you need to do in order to heal, then I will back you all the fucking way."

Several minutes of silence ensued.

"I've given it a lot of thought," she finally said, "and it wouldn't help me heal."

He turned his head toward her. "Then don't do it. I support your decision."

She stared into his eyes. "Can I tell you about the loopholes?"

He found her hand, pried open her fist, and clasped her hand with his and squeezed. "Sure."

"According to my father, Colorado doesn't care who a dispensary owner fraternizes with as long as they're not your business partner or your spouse. Therefore, there are two loopholes we can take advantage of which allows us to be together and your pot career not be in jeopardy. One is, for now, we live together, as an engaged couple, without getting married." She sat up. The moonlight highlighting her beauty made it hard for him to think.

He closed his eyes and turned that loophole over in his brain. He quickly discarded it and sat up next to her. "I want to marry you. I want to watch you walk down the aisle, hear you say I *do*, take you on a honeymoon…"

She nodded as if he'd given the right answer. "The other loophole is we get married. A big ass wedding that my parents have to pay for. But we fail to file the marriage certificate for three years. If it's not filed, we're not legally married."

He stiffened. That one sounded an awful lot like fraud. "Why three years?"

"In three years, I'll be eligible to have my record sealed."

He sat up. "You're saying neither loophole is illegal? Neither could be considered fraud?"

"They are perfectly legal. Did you know it's an actual thing between couples to choose to have a wedding ceremony but never file the license?"

His rule-following self urged him to dismiss both ideas. Yet, he didn't. If he and Luna were to work, and they *would* work, he had to work at not being so rigid with rules. "Do you have a preference on which one of those we'd choose if I stay in the pot business?"

"The big wedding, of course." She gave him a huge smile. The smile of a woman who appeared to have spent plenty of time thinking about her wedding day.

How could he deny her a ceremony just because he wasn't comfortable living his life in loopholes? "Hmmm. I'm not saying no to your loopholes. But I'm not saying yes, either. I need some time to look into other options for us. Do you trust me to do that?"

She wrinkled her nose. "Will your options include a marriage? It would be a shame for our lovely rings to not be shown off to the world?"

He laughed. "It most certainly will include marriage. But I have every intention of buying you a finer engagement ring."

"You most certainly will not. Tell me more about the other options rattling around in that smart brain of yours."

"Like, I get out of the pot business. There are other things I can do with my degree." Somehow, saying the words didn't result in him having a panic attack.

"You would do that for me?" she whispered, sounding as if the mere thought left her awestruck.

"I'm sorry that's a question you even have to ask. I should have never put anything before our love. I'm so fucking sorry I chose weed over you. It was the dumbest thing I've ever done in my life. It will never happen again."

Her bottom lip trembled. "Thank you. I know a lot of what you said was the result of your panic attack, but I still needed that apology. I forgive you." She sniffed and then gave him a smile "Now, there's one more thing for you to consider." She leaned down and quickly kissed him on the lips.

When she went to pull back, he held her in place and gave her a much more thorough kiss before releasing her and saying, "And that is?"

Her fingers fluttered to her lips. "I need to tell Captain SOS what I found in the safe in the barn loft."

He startled. "There's also a safe in the barn loft? Not just a freezer?"

"There is, and I found the combination." She rubbed her hands together in glee.

He chuckled, loving her enthusiasm. "What was inside?"

She slipped out of the sleeping bag and, in all her glorious nakedness, held out her hand. "Come see for yourself."

His body reacted to the vision in a way that made the idea of leaving the sleeping bag quite awkward. "As if I could say no to anything you ask when you're naked." He climbed out, hard as a brick, and started toward the house. Intent on getting her flat on her back in her bed.

"It's not in the house. It's still in the loft," she said from behind him.

He turned. "But..."

"Holy Batman, that's one fine boner you're sporting."

He grinned like a man deep in the aftermath of a good high. "Shall we take it inside and put it to use?"

"Good try, but I will not be swayed from my mission."

"Remind me again of the mission?"

"The loft." She plopped her hands on her hips and raised an eyebrow. "And before you say no, please recall, you said you would do anything I asked as long as I was naked."

"I did. Didn't I?" He stabbed his hand through his hair. Luna Parker quite likely would be the death of him. But oh, what a way to go.

She came and looped her hands around his elbow. "I promise not to let anything happen to you if you climb those stairs."

"Why does it matter to you so much for me to go up there?" he grumbled.

"Because I can't heal you of all the things that happened to you when you were young, but if I can help you get over your fear of heights, then I feel like I've made a difference in your life."

She was most definitely the best thing that had ever happened to him. "Parker, the fact that I'm standing outside in the nude should tell you you've made a difference in my life."

"Please."

It took several attempts to get Mitch to take the first step up the ladder, but now he stood in the loft of Luna's barn, holding the papers she'd found inside Ms. Murphy's safe.

Not waiting for him to read through them, she said, "The flowers from Mildred are what made her pot taste so much better than what you could grow in your soil—not the essential oils. She would grind them up and mix them into the dirt before planting her cannabis seeds. That's why she has a freezer full of Mildred's spring flowers." Come to find out, according to Ms. Murphy's notes, the flowers from a Thundercloud Plum Tree had many uses. Many, many, many uses. Most of them marketable. She and Nanny Nonna would have made the grandest of friends.

Mitch walked to the freezer and glanced inside. "You weren't kidding. Why in the hell didn't she just tell me that when we were running our tests?"

Luna shrugged. "It's my guess she liked the company of having you around. She was probably afraid if you figured out the secret, you might not spend as much time with her."

"That's not true. She was great company." He turned and leaned against the freezer.

"If you read through her journals, you'll see she was also a keeper of the town's secrets. I haven't read those yet. I've been debating with myself if Luna 2.0 would do that. So far, the jury is still out. But Ms. Murphy also has formulas for different concoctions. Those I read. There's even a recipe for a drunk-no-more potion. Do you know anything about that?"

"She talked about it, but said she never got it right."

"Maybe we can tweak her recipe and figure it out. We could sell the rights and use the money toward our new adventure with the town. Nanny Nonna taught me a little about the art of creatively mixing ingredients."

"You still want to allow the town to benefit from your plan? Even—"

"LUNA. MITCH. COME OUT, COME OUT WHEREVER YOU ARE."

Luna and Mitch froze.

It sounded like all of Rocky Mountain Springs was in Luna's backyard. They tiptoed to the loft door and peaked out a crack in the wood.

"Fuck," Mitch said. "What are we going to do? Our clothes are down there."

Luna laughed. "Embrace our nudity. It's all we can do."

He chuckled. "I told you someday the whole town would come around the corner of your house and catch you in the nude. I just never dreamt I'd be there naked beside you."

She slapped at his arm. "Don't be such a fuddy-duddy." She sashayed to the freezer and pulled out a stuffed trash bag. She tossed it his way. "Here. Hold this over your lower half and go see what they want."

"Me?"

"Do you want me to go down there naked?"

He stomped to the top of the stairs and called out. "Close your damn eyes, I'm naked and I'm coming down the stairs."

Luna bit her lip to keep from laughing and waited until he disappeared from sight before emptying another trash bag and fashioning a dress out of it. She slipped it over her head, and then made her way down the stairs.

"Fuckhead, save our eyes and get some clothes on." Johnny tossed him his pants.

Mitch caught them, turned, and saw Luna.

The crowd hooted and hollered.

"Nice ass," Tina from the bar shouted.

"I knew you had ink but not that much." Amahle said. "Why in the hell haven't you shown it off by now? I might have left Johnny for you years ago."

Johnny growled.

"She's not wrong," Luna said. "But, just an idea, you might want to cover your backside with your bag of flowers."

Mitch quickly did. "I thought you were staying up there," he said in a stern voice.

She shrugged and openly ogled his package. Even at rest, it was a mighty fine package. "And let you have all the fun? No way."

"Anytime now," Johnny said.

Mitch's right ear turned red. "You're bound to be the undoing of my sanity," he said to Luna, before slipping behind the barn door.

"Just think how much fun you'll have losing it," she whispered loudly to him. Then, she turned and stared at her company. She couldn't imagine why they'd all showed up at her place. Had they discovered Mitch gone and come to drag him out of the arms of a felon? Or had Mr. Henson told them of her plan to leave town, and they'd come to make sure she didn't change her mind?

Mitch stepped out wearing jeans that rode low on his hips. The look scrambled her brains and re-revved her sexual desires.

Mitch cleared his throat. "What brings you all to Luna's?"

Amahle stepped forward. "Luna, we came to apologize for being lousy neighbors."

Luna blinked. "Amahle, you've been a friend. You don't owe me an apology."

Amahle came up to Luna and hugged her. "I could have done more to turn the town around. You didn't deserve the silent treatment."

One by one, the town's people walked by Luna, shook her hand, and apologized.

After each one, Luna said, "Apology accepted."

Mitch cleared his throat. "Now that you have all absolved your guilty conscience, it's time for you to leave. Luna and I have more celebrating to do."

"Joke's on you, Fuckhead," Johnny said. "We're not going anywhere."

"What?" Luna and Mitch said simultaneously.

"I told everyone to bring their sleeping bags," Amahle said. "Just in case you forgave us. We're here for a do-over on your under-the-stars sleepover invitation. Is that okay with you, Luna?"

Luna placed a hand on her chest and bit her lip to keep it from trembling from all the emotions swarming her heart. This was the best moment of her life. A magnificently, marvelous momentous moment. It was the moment Luna Parker discovered the love of a found family. She nodded at the crowd and then turn her face into Mitch's chest.

"What is it?" he whispered.

She looked up at him and grinned. "Mitch Johnson, I'm so glad I never got around to punching you in the nose."

Two Months Later:

FOR IMMEDIATE RELEASE

Rocky Mountain Springs Has a New Mayor and a New Motto.

ROCKY MOUNTAIN SPRINGS, CO—According to newly sworn in mayor, Mitch Johnson, Rocky Mountain Springs had a new motto. Kindness. With this new motto, the town is rebranding their community under the theme of a common ingredient. Goat milk.

"We will build our new brand awareness neighbor by neighbor," Johnson said. "A community that works together is happier, healthier, and stronger together."

"The residents of Rocky Mountain Springs are one big functional family," said Mr. Henson, owner of Henson's Lavender Farm. "This was most evident at a recent town hall meeting where we unanimously voted Mitch Johnson to be our new mayor after our old mayor was arrested for property fraud."

The newest member of the community, Luna Parker of Luna's Goat Yoga, says, "Living in Rocky Mountain Springs is like waking up every morning at a sleepover under the stars with your best friends."

Tourist activity has started to pick up due to Instagram goats, and a new edible sold at the town's dispensary, owned by the town's mayor, that enhances one's libido. The town's official launch of their community-wide effort to increase tourist opportunities and make RMS a desired getaway location is scheduled for late spring.

Rocky Mountain Springs was founded in 1803. To support their new commerce contact lisawells@gmail.com.

Thank you for reading Rocky Mountain High-Jinx. Your honest review will help future readers decide to take a chance on a new-to-them author.

Looking for your next read? Try: VOGUEish
You know what they say about fake fairy godmothers, it's all sunshine and stilettos, until they take it upon themselves to find you a spouse. (VOGUEish)

Enjoy this sneak-peek into:
VOGUEISH

PROLOGUE
Nine years + seven months earlier

Chased by cruel laughter, Isabella P. Chance blindly darted toward the exit.

"Hey, don't forget to send us that dick-pic," the ringleader of the popular girls said. "That is if you still want to be a part of our group."

Just as Isabella hit the hallway, she smacked into a pillar. *Really. Who erects a pillar right outside the doors of a ballroom? Do people not know they are used for fast exits...emphasis on fast?*

She shoved her hair out of her eyes and came eye-to-tie with the pillar. Only it wasn't a pillar, it was a chest—a chest that belonged to a face with a pair of startled blue eyes.

"We'd love for this year's prom queen to be one of us." This came from the ringleader's sidekick from somewhere inside the ballroom.

"Bathroom?" Isabella pleaded with the pillar.

"That way." He pointed, not taking his gaze off hers. "May I get somebody for you? Or, you know, pummel someone's face?" He held up his fists, grinned, and winked.

She tried to say something pithy like *I could really use an impressive dick-pic. Do you have one of those?* But when she opened her mouth, a sob poured out.

The mean girls must have heard her cries and decided they weren't through abusing her because laughter and the sudden clacking of stilettos on tile drew closer.

The thought of continued taunts was more than Isabella could handle. She yanked up the hem of her gown and made a mad dash for safety, not slowing until she was inside the stark bright restroom. She stumbled toward the back stall.

Please let it be empty.

Inside the double-wide, she slid to the floor, and allowed her precious prom gown—the one she'd saved and saved and saved to buy from a couture consignment shop—to crumble around her along with all her ridiculous dreams of how tonight would play out. She should have known it would be a catastrophe when her best friend couldn't attend. That had been the Universe telling her to stay home. And she would have, except one of the most popular girls in the whole school had made a point of telling Isabella that she really hoped to see her at the dance. And Miss. Popular's dreamy boyfriend had stood behind her, nodding his enthusiastic agreement.

All a con. Premeditated bullying.

Now what?

Recover your dignity?

Like that could happen while sitting on a dirty bathroom floor sobbing and snotting. Gross.

Was she a bad person? Did she deserve this? Had she done something awful to any of her classmates without realizing it? Other than having the audacity to attend a private school on a scholarship, no. Did being poor warrant such meanness?

She wearily removed her glasses and used the tail of the sash she wore to rub the tears out of her eyes. Remembering what the sash had written on its backside, she yanked it off and shoved it in the trash bin. "Stupid, stupid—"

"I don't mean to intrude," a guy said in a loud whisper.

Isabella peeked from under the stall to see who had followed her. The entry door to the bathroom stood slightly ajar, and a pair of shiny black dress shoes greeted her view. Was he one of her haters? "Go away."

"Certainly, but first is there someone I could call or get for you?"

She grabbed a wad of toilet paper and blew her nose. "Who are you?"

"The guy who pointed you here."

"Oh." Someone who didn't even know her had checked on her. "There's no one at the dance, and I can never let my parents know about this." *My classmates are right, I am a loser.*

"I'm sure your parents would want to know you're hurting," he said soothingly.

"My mom is fragile. This would undo her." Gah. Why had she told him that? Could she be any more pathetic?

"I'm sorry."

His kindness caused a fresh sob to escape her throat. She slapped her hand over her mouth.

"In a perfect world," he said. "I'd have a silk handkerchief to offer the damsel in distress. Unfortunately, it's in the pocket of my jacket that I ditched right after giving my best man speech."

"I learned a long time ago we don't live in a perfect world." She'd learned that particular lesson the first time Mom tried to end her life.

"I'm going to be honest with you...women in pain are not my strength."

"It's okay. You can leave." She watched his foot, waiting for it to move. "It was nice of you to check on me."

"I saw you were wearing a tiara. Does that mean you were crowned Prom Queen? Was your date not crowned king? Is that what the tears are about?"

She reached up and ripped the tiara off her head and did her best to snap it in half...only it wouldn't break. A drop of blood drawn from one of its pointy tips formed on her index finger and splashed onto her silk gown. *Fuck.* Now she wouldn't be able to resell it. "Please go away. I just want to be alone."

"It would stress me greatly to abandon a woman in tears. Not to mention, Nonna would set my hair on fire if she ever discovered I did such a thing."

Isabella leaned against the wall and picked at one of the pink floret flowers embroidered on her black, floor-length gown. "That would be harsh."

"Not that this is any of my business, but I couldn't help but hear someone mocking you over a picture request. Want to tell me what that was about?"

Heat flooded her cheeks. "If I won prom queen, I was supposed to send a dick pick to the popular girls' text group. It was to be my final initiation to become one of them. First, prom queen. Second, turn in a prom night dick-pic by midnight—you know, because everyone sleeps with someone on prom night. Third, become overnight popular."

He sighed loudly. "At the risk of sounding stodgy, I don't recommend doing that. It could go wrong in so many ways. Legal ways."

Her classmates would scoff if she used that as an excuse not to send them one. It would be enough to justify their continued bullying. "I've never even had a boyfriend." *And there it was...one more pathetic thing I could and did say that would help him understand the level of loser he had happened upon.* "So, unless you want to give me a dick-pic out of the kindness of your heart, you don't have to worry about me breaking any laws tonight." Not quite true. She had acquired one—via the web—before arriving at the dance. This because she'd received an anonymous tip that if she were to win, one would be required. Granted hers was courtesy of an underwear ad and thus clothed.

"Listen, before I came to check on you, I texted my Nonna, and she's—"

A commotion occurred cutting off his words.

Isabella tensed. Was it her haters? Had they found her hiding spot? Would he allow them—

"Thank God you hadn't already left," her Pillar said to someone.

Isabella relaxed. Not her haters.

"I owe you. Big time," her Pillar said.

"That, you do. Now, you stay right here and don't allow anyone to enter." The command was spoken in a strong female voice. Not a young voice, but an elderly one.

Isabella unlocked the stall door and pushed it open prepared to tell the intruder to go away. The demand died on her lips as she stared instead in fashion-awe at a woman wearing a to-die-for formal gown that she'd paired with this season's crystal-covered Jimmy Choo pumps.

She glided toward Isabella and held out her arms. "Come here, my child."

About to cave and comply, Isabella's phone dinged twice. One was a text wanting to know if that had been Isabella's supposed date, aka her cousin, that she'd left with. The other taunted her yet again to not forget the dick-pic. Pressure built in her chest. They were relentless. How would she ever be able to face them come Monday? She couldn't. Unless...

She pushed every ounce of common sense she had ever possessed away and opened the popular girl group chat. The one she'd been given access to just this evening when the rumor circulated Isabella might win prom queen. Not giving herself a chance to overthink her decision, she uploaded her make-do dick pick and added a message.

Yes, that was my guy at the door, and he's much too classy to want a dick-pic being passed around to a group of minors. This is as good as you're going to get. - Isabella

She hit send before she could change her mind and then opened the stall door and gave the woman her attention. "I'm not the huggy type."

Total lie. She absolutely wanted to be wrapped up in a hug that smelled like expensive perfume, but she didn't know this woman.

The woman gave a deep sigh. "Fine, but do me a favor, and get up off that disgusting floor. And then I'll explain everything."

"Nonna, I'm needed back at the reception for another toast," Pillar said, still standing in the hallway and speaking through the cracked-open door.

"Go. I've got this," Nonna replied.

"Um. Runaway Prom Queen," Pillar said. "You're now in good hands."

Runaway Prom Queen made it sound like she was living out a romcom. This wasn't that. "I don't need good hands. What I need is a time machine." One that took her back before that moment she had gullibly believed someone like her could be legitimately voted prom queen.

"Trust me. You will want to hear her out," Pillar said.

Isabella twisted her lips in a jeer. "Trust is how I ended up here. Trust should be a four-letter word like *hope*. Hope is a four-letter word, forget that at your own risk. That's what life's taught me."

"I get that." With the vague reply hanging in the air, he silently exited Isabella's life and left her with his Nonna.

"Darling, what is your name?" Nonna wore the prettiest pink ballgown Isabella had ever seen. And she had the prettiest silver hair. And she did not look like a person who would take no for an answer.

"Isabella."

"Isabella, I know you won't believe me, but this moment right here is what they call in the movies your fairytale moment."

Isabella wrinkled her nose. "Only if the fairy tale is actually a scary tale." Perhaps this was all a bad dream. Isabella pinched herself and grimaced from the pain. Gah. It wasn't a dream. She hated when that happened.

The woman gathered several paper towels from the dispenser, carefully arranged them on the floor, and then perched next to Isabella. "Tell me what happened and don't leave out any of the sordid details."

After a deep inhale and drawn-out exhale, Isabella spilled her woeful tale. A recounting that took less than five minutes. One would think an event in which she'd experienced utter humiliation would require more time. Not true.

When Isabella trailed off, Nonna leaned forward and cupped Isabella's cheek with a soft hand. "Thank you for sharing that horrid story. It is my hope that by saying it out loud, it will have taken the power of the horrible event and flushed it down that toilet you insist on sitting beside."

Another round of tears formed in Isabella's eyes. "Nope. Still hurts."

Nonna nodded. "Then let's move on. Without giving it a whole lot of thought, I want you to tell me what you want your comeback moment to look like."

Isabella choked on a gasp. "Comeback? Are you kidding!" Her heart pounded painfully against her ribs. This woman couldn't make her go back...could she? "It would take a navy seal team and their badass mommas to drag me back to that dance."

Nonna chuckled softly. "You misunderstood. You're not going back into that den of evil. But there will be a time when you will face your tormentors as a victor, not as a victim."

Was this woman drunk? "I don't know what you're saying. Do you know what you're saying?"

Nonna chuckled and nodded. "I do. Now, what I want you to tell me are the circumstances of your spectacular comeback moment. The moment you, like a beautiful phoenix rising from the ashes, will appear in front of the nasties, and they will all realize how stupid they were tonight." She used her hands to emphasize her words.

"That's not possible."

"Sure it is. You know in *Gone with the Wind* when Rhett Butler told Scarlett, 'Frankly my dear, I don't give a damn?' That was his comeback moment. The moment he rose from the ashes of loving someone who hadn't loved him back and won. And the mean girl, his wife, lost."

"I've never seen that movie." Isabella tried to imagine anything she could do that would cause her tormentors to regret what they'd done to her. "But I get the essence of what you're saying."

"Excellent. I want you to dream big. Really big. Make it a movie-worthy moment." Nonna pulled a bag of makeup wipes out of her satchel. She held a towelette out to Isabella. "Clean your face while you envision."

Isabella took the wipe and scrubbed it over her cheeks. "Who are you besides Nonna to the man who may or not have been my hero tonight?"

"You may call me Ms. Birdie, and I am the President of the Fairy Godmother Project." She handed Isabella another wipe. "And you are?"

"Isabella Chance. I've never heard of the Fairy Godmother Project. Is it a charity of some type?" She used the clean wipe to remove her mascara.

"It's a group of women who don't have wands or fairy dust, but they do have connections. Connections they use to help young people, like you, to keep moving forward in life. So, tell me. What will your comeback moment look like?"

Isabella slumped against the wall. This all sounded much too bizarre to be true. And she'd already been stupidly gullible once tonight. Was she really going to let her defenses down twice? "I don't know. I need to think. And I'm too tired to think."

"Thinking isn't necessary," Ms. Birdie replied in a no-nonsense tone. "In fact, it's frowned upon. The best comeback story originates from your heart, not your brain. Just open your mouth and spew your deepest desires that will lead to your moment of triumph."

Isabella tossed the wipes in the toilet. "Okay." She closed her eyes and conjured up the moment. "At my ten-year class reunion, I see myself waltzing into the event with a gorgeous guy on my arm, a fabulous engagement ring on my finger, and the most interesting stories about what I've been up to since high school graduation."

Ms. Birdie smiled triumphantly. "Excellent. Tell me about those stories."

Isabella imagined herself facing her enemies. "My career will be such that it resulted in my traveling the world. Each exotic location a stepping stone toward the career of my heart. A career I will have begun before the night of reckoning." Travel wasn't an option for her family since her father worked two jobs to make ends meet.

"And what will that career of your heart be?"

Isabella stood and walked to the mirror. Her limp hair had fallen out of its simple updo, her teeth were crooked, and her skin blemished. To think when she'd left her house tonight, she'd convinced herself she was beautiful. "I'll be the new fashion editor at *Naked Runway*." Fashion editors were never ugly.

"I can work with that. Paint for me the rest of the picture. You've walked in with Prince Charming on your arm and a diamond on your finger. You have a great job and lots of fabulous stories to tell. What else?"

"My teeth will be white and straight. My hair perfectly styled. My clothing impeccable. But most importantly, I'll have power. Power that will impact those who placed into motion my humiliation. I will have come to my reunion to exact revenge in a tangible way. It won't be burning the place down with telekinetic powers like in *Carrie*, but it will be poetic and perfect. You know, like a secret diary that outs them all for the ass-wipes they were in high school."

As if not used to hearing vulgarity, Ms. Birdie grimaced. "And after that?"

Isabella shrugged. "I guess I go on to live my best life knowing I had the last laugh."

The woman placed her hands on Isabella's shoulders and looked her in the eyes. "How will it feel knowing you had the last laugh?"

Isabella closed her eyes and imagined the moment. "Good. Excellent. Avenged."

"And once the ten-year reunion has come and gone, what will motivate you to continue?" Ms. Birdie's hands dropped away, and she took a step back.

"I don't know." It was hard enough to imagine that moment, let alone beyond it.

Ms. Birdie's smile faded. "Before I can grant your wish, I need you to know how you will continue once you have proven that losing you as a potential friend was the biggest mistake of their lives. Chances are great they won't care, or they won't even remember. It would be irresponsible on my part to give you your wish if it leaves you worst off when it's over."

Isabella nodded. It was a good policy to have if you were in the Fairy Godmother business. They had to be careful not to create someone who then went forth and wielded their new self-esteem with ill-will. "How about, after the comeback—or even as part of the comeback, if there's a way—I make it a point to pay your kindness forward?"

"Can you give me an example of what that might look like?"

"At the very least, I could pledge to become a member of the Fairy Godmother Project and help the next young person in crisis."

Ms. Birdie nodded. "What I hear you saying is you are requesting a 13 *Going On* 30 package, meshed with a *Bridget Jones* experience, and sprinkled with the good-feel parts of *The Devil Wears Prada*. Topped with a billionaire Prince Charming ending." She pulled a card out of her pocket and handed it to Isabella. "Come to my office tomorrow, and we'll get the paperwork out of the way."

Isabella glanced at the card. On the front were the letters FGP embossed in gold, and on the back was an address. "Paperwork?"

Ms. Birdie pulled a tube of lipstick out of her purse and reapplied it. "You will have to sign a contract. If at any point you break the contract, then it's over. You will be on your own."

For the first time since the sash had been draped over her shoulders, Isabella smiled. "And if I don't break the contract, you have the power to make my comeback happen?"

Ms. Birdie dropped her lipstick in her purse and nodded. "It won't be me who is assigned to your case, but I promise to match you with the perfect Fairy Godmother to make your heart's desire come true."

Isabella grinned. "Thank you. And please tell Pillar, your grandson, I said thank you. What was his name?"

"He is my Godson, and I'm afraid I can't reveal to you his name. But I will tell him you said thank you. You know, you must have made an impression on him because this is the first time he's ever asked for my particular brand of help."

Dear Reader, I hope you enjoyed this excerpt from Vogueish and plan to purchase the book.

OTHER BOOKS BY LISA WELLS ROMANCE AUTHOR

CONTEMPORARY ROMANTIC COMEDY SERIES

<u>Manhattan Knitter's Club (Can be read out of order)</u> *The Manhattan Knitters' Club invites you to join them for Friday Night Knit Club. If approved, and that's a big IF, you agree to bring the following to each meeting: tiara, bottle of wine, and knitting supplies. Bonus points for dating hacks.*

Her Night In Shining Armani

<u>Naked Runway (Can be read out of order)</u> *Take one tipsy-turvy fashion magazine, add an eclectic group of employees, toss in a healthy dose of the lovebug, and you've got The Naked Runway Series.*

Vogueish

Rakeish (releases fall 2023)

<u>Rocky Mountain Springs (Can be read out of order)</u> *Settle into this small-town series and watch as one couple after another— despite their best efforts not to—fall in love. It must be something in the water.*

Rocky Mountain High-Jinx

ROMANTIC COMEDY – STAND ALONE BOOKS

Aggie the Horrible Vs. Max the Pompous Ass
The Impromptu Nanny Contract
The Seduction of Kinley Foster
The Attraction of Adeline

PARANORMAL ROMANTIC COMEDY

<u>Singles Town (Can be read out of order)</u> *Move into this cooky haunted town and watch as three semi-charming witches bring three determined bachelors to their knees all while trying and failing to stay off the radar of the local gossips.*
Hexes and O's
It's a Curse Thing
Cup of Spirits

PARANORMAL WOMEN'S FICTION

<u>Magical Midlife Moonlighting (Read in order - series completed)</u> *Molly Thorn used to be young and hip. Then she died. Now, she's back from the second veil as a hot-flashing, brain-glitching, middle-aged woman. What could possibly go wrong with her new lease on life?*
The Undead Life of Molly Thorn (Book 1)
The Magical Midlife of Molly Thorn (Book 2)
The Bewitched Life of Molly Thorn (Book 3)

NONFICTION

How To Add Humor To Your Novel: Learn To Write Funny Scenes
How To Add Unforgettable Dialogue To Your Novel (Winter 2023)

About Author

Lisa Wells writes contemporary and paranormal romantic comedy with enough steam to fog your eyeglasses, your brain, and sometimes your Kindle screen. She lives in Missouri with her husband and slightly-chunky rescue dog. Lisa loves dark chocolate, red wine, and those rare mornings when her skinny jeans fit. Which isn't often, considering the first two entries on her love-it list. Luckily, *mom* jeans are back in style.

To learn more about all of Lisa's books, visit:

Newsletter: https://bit.ly/LisaWellsRomanceAuthorNewsletter

Website: www.lisawellsauthor.com

Facebook: https://www.facebook.com/lisa.wells.737

Instagram: https://www.instagram.com/lisawellsauthor/

BookBub: https://www.bookbub.com/authors/lisa-wells

TikTok: https://www.tiktok.com/@lisawellsromanceauthor

Facebook Group: Lisa's Up all Night Readers: https://bit.ly/UpAllNightReaders

www.ingramcontent.com/pod-product-compliance
Lightning Source LLC
Chambersburg PA
CBHW031312210726
48287CB00005B/1514